Like A Pale Moon

Voices of the Dead: Book Three

Victoria Raschke

Like A Pale Moon - Voices of the Dead: Book Three

Copyright © 2019, 2020 by Victoria Raschke

For further information, please contact:

1000 Volt Press
info@1000voltpress.com

www.victoriaraschke.com

Cover design and book layout: keifel a. agostini.
Find him at keifelagostini.com.

The book is typeset in Brisio Pro. The font was chosen specifically for the shape of the letters and support of Slovene character sets.

Second Edition
ISBN: 978-1-7347422-2-0

for my sister and first friend, Lynne

ACKNOWLEDGEMENTS

There are many ways books come into the world, more so with the birth of self-publishing and print-on-demand publishing. I am very glad that this book and the others in the series happened to be ushered into the world by Eli Collier and Griffyn Ink Publishing. My fellow writers and friends there, A.J. Scudiere (a.k.a Savannah Kade), D.B. Sieders, Lulu M. Sylvian, and Steve Bradshaw, push me to be both a better writer and a better professional.

The physical copy in your hand is edited by Jennifer Goode Stevens, who wrangles my poor spelling and experimental grammar into something that can be more easily read and followed. And keifel a. agostini makes the pages flow and designs the covers. It may help that he can't fire me as a client, since we live together. I'm grateful for that and for him.

I owe huge thanks to a trio of Slovenian scholars: Dr. Mirjam Mencej, Dr. Monika Kropej, and Dr. Matevz Kosir. They were all generous with their time and expertise and incredibly helpful when I was looking for information largely unavailable in English. Anything you come across in the books that deviates from their research is fiction and not meant to comment on folkloric or historical scholarship. Thank you again to Irena Šumi and the Šenekar family for championing the books and being amazing hosts to me and my family when we are in Slovenia. I could not ask for better friends and only wish Slovenia wasn't quite so far away.

Having trusted early readers is such a gift, and I appreciate the insight and commentary from my colleagues at Griffyn Ink and from Su Fertall; it helped me get over a couple hurdles I'd written for myself.

And thank you, readers. I appreciate your reviews and messages and especially your excitement for new stories and your love of Jo and her family and friends.

A note on Slovenian pronunciation

Slovenian uses a few extra characters.
č is pronounced like the ch in church.
š is pronounced like the sh in shirt.
ž is pronounced like the second g in garage.
Familiar letters are pronounced differently.
e is most often pronounced like a in bay.
i is most often pronounced like the e in be.
j is pronounced like a y.
r without a paired vowel is pronounced like the ir in skirt.

CAST

Jo Wiley - a Voice of the Dead and co-owner of Renegade Tea

Jackie Wiley - Jo's aunt, another Voice

Mary Wiley - Jo's mother, another Voice

Rebecca Wiley - Jo's Civil-War-era great-grandmother

Rok Zorko - a Long-Lived, Jo's friend with benefits and a man of many names

Faron Črnigad Wiley - Jo's son and the white god, Belinus

Helena Belak - Jo's former lover and current spirit guide

Vesna Kos - Jo's best friend and business partner who can see auras and the future

Igor - an artist and Vesna's boyfriend

Leo Kos (formerly Brother Leo Kos) - Vesna's uncle, the Slovenian Witchfinder, and Jo's confidant, possibly more

Ivanka Novak - Faron's girlfriend and the oldest of the Novak witch sisters

Veronika Novak - Ivanka's sister and a powerful witch

Ana Novak - the youngest Novak sister, whose powers are still being revealed

Dušan Črnigad - Jo's ex, Faron's father and the Black God of Slavic myth

Goran Kralj - Jo and Vesna's neighbor and a witch who is teaching the Novak sisters

Gustaf Lichtenberg - Jo's Observer and neighbor

Bettine - A member of the Board and Gustaf's boss

"When it hurts we return to the banks of certain rivers."
Czeslaw Milosz, *"I Sleep a Lot"*

CHAPTER 1

Ana walked through the dark woods. Pine needles and twigs slid and crunched beneath her bare feet. The sounds of animals scurrying in the underbrush didn't bother her. She knew their names, and they knew she wasn't there to do harm. The clouds above the canopy parted, and silver shards of light sliced up the darkness in front of her. She was trying to get back to the place where she had seen her friend, but the forest was different in the moonlight.

He was tall, taller than her father had been, but not as tall as Mr. Kos. And he knew them. He knew her sisters and her teacher, Goran. He didn't tell her stories like Goran and her other friend, Breda, did. He wanted to listen to her instead. He asked her about school and visiting her sister at work at the teahouse. He said he liked the chocolate brownies Jo made the best, too. Her sister Ivanka's were okay, but they weren't the same. Jo had some kind of magic with brownies. Maybe it was an American thing.

Her friend had promised to meet her again, to bring her another treasure for her collection. When she had seen him last time, he had put the claw from a bear's paw in her hand.

It was dark, like an old shark tooth she'd found on the beach once. She stuck her hand in her pocket and ran her thumb over the smooth edge of the claw and down to the sharp point.

She called out hellos into the quiet places between the trees, but no one answered. It was darker than she had remembered, and she got lost after straying from the trail to the clearing where she usually met Breda and him. He hadn't given her his name yet.

There was another presence in the forest, but it wasn't one she was familiar with. It lurked along where the trees became too thick for light to filter in. It was a wrong thing, and it was hunting.

Ana followed the presence as best she could—it was more a mist than a solid—into the clearing and watched it from behind a tree. Mr. Kos stood in the circle of matted leaves and pine needles, looking out into the forest like he was searching for someone. He didn't see her, even when he turned in her direction. He didn't see the other presence, either, even when it rushed right at him. He looked around one more time, rubbed his arms like he was cold, and started back down toward the trail that would take him out of the woods.

Ana waited, watching the presence to see what it would do. It didn't follow Mr. Kos. When he disappeared, the presence turned in her direction. In the dim light, Ana couldn't see if it was a man or a woman, or even if it looked human. It moved like smoke, hovering and twisting like it was waiting. There was nothing to wait for. Mr. Kos had gone, and whatever the presence was, it was out-of-place enough to silence the woods around them. The smoke shot toward Ana's hiding place behind the tree and screeched at her.

"I'll take you instead."

Ana started awake, trapped in her twisted bedcovers and peeved that her friend hadn't found her, and that she'd had a bad dream. The sky had that rosy color it had in the morning before the sun is all the way up. School didn't interest her today, but she had to get through it before she could go back out into the woods with Goran and her sisters that afternoon. Other spirits sometimes came to her in other places, but this one, the tall one who told her stories, had only come to her in the woods. She had promised Goran she wouldn't sneak away again, but the spirits and the animals wouldn't come to her when other people were hovering over her.

The book she was supposed to be reading slid off the bed when she sat up. It thumped onto the floor and fell open to the chapter on supernatural beings and spirits. The beginning of the book hadn't interested her, with all its god and goddess names she couldn't keep straight, but the chapter on spirits and the wandering dead looked like it might be better. She picked up the book, tucked a candy wrapper between the pages, and put it back on her nightstand.

She thought her friend might be a ghost. He had definitely been alive at one point, but she didn't understand why he didn't go into the Next like her parents had. She had seen him in the woods near Škofja Loka, but he'd met her in her dreams before, too. She knew that wasn't something a regular person, or even most witches, could do.

Her foot itched, and she pulled it into her lap with her hand wrapped around her ankle. A long, dry pine needle was stuck to the sole; it left a faint pressure mark when she pulled it off. She added it to the candy wrapper in the book and bounced down the hall to wash her face and brush her teeth before Veronika got up and took over the bathroom for what always seemed like forever.

———

Jo Wiley scanned the short line of cars, checking each driver's face, but there was no sign of Michael. The Chattanooga airport offered almost nothing in the way of amenities, especially for those coming in on the last flight before they rolled up the carpets and shuttered for the night. After a day and a half of travel from one tiny airport and through two intercontinental hubs to another tiny airport, she wanted nothing more than a scalding shower and some sleep.

The waiting cars left with their collected travelers, and she stood alone in the flat, orange light of the arrivals area. An airport employee collected two traffic cones from the center line and waved to her before disappearing through the glass doors. Michael was usually punctual. He was the straight-and-narrow cousin, raised as a brother. What did that make her—the meandering, scattered near-orphan?

Despite the surrounding sea of concrete, the scent of a night-blooming flower found its way to her to punctuate her arrival home. Well, it had once been home. Coming back there always left her jet-lagged and culture-shocked. The roundhouse airport usually was the last liminal place where she could breathe before being engulfed in whatever whirlwind visit her aunt had planned. There would be no Hurricane Jackie to contend with this time, though, for she had been summoned for hospital visits and whispers in the hall, to keep vigil at her mother's bedside as she died.

The opening bars of "Whatever Lola Wants" wove their way into Jo's thoughts, announcing a different kind of arrival.

"I didn't think there were airports smaller than Ljubljana's." Helena, Jo's spirit guide, appeared at her side, dropping the ambient temperature a few degrees.

"Were you on the plane?"

"Yes and no. Physics was never my best subject." Helena looked out over the nearly empty lot, her dark bob shifting against the pale skin of her jaw with the turn of her head. "Are you the last one here?"

Jo nodded. She and Helena had made their peace, but Jo wasn't in a talkative mood. "I'm not sure high school physics apply to you."

"There are a lot of things that don't apply to me." Helena stepped in front of Jo. "You look exhausted, kiddo."

"Thanks?" Jo was tired, and her pent-up existential angst rivaled that of a teenaged goth.

"Exhausted and almost chic. No Slits T shirt this trip?" Helena smirked at her and pushed a stray lock of Jo's hair off her face before straightening the lapels of the jacket she didn't need in Tennessee's early summer heat.

The friend version of Helena took some getting used to. Helena's relationship to Jo had morphed rapidly from fuck buddy into spirit guide-slash-nemesis before they'd gotten themselves sorted into friends and allies. Sometimes those previous roles bubbled up when Jo least expected them, like when Helena touched her.

Headlights snaked around the drive with a shining hulk of black SUV in their wake.

"I think your chariot has arrived. I'll check in on you later after you've had a chance to wash off the airport funk." Helena leaned in for a peck on the cheek before disappearing.

Michael pulled up curbside and bounded from the car. "I am so sorry." He wrapped Jo in a hug, pinning her arms to her sides, before she could say hello. "I told Mom I'd get you, and then I fell asleep watching the news." He hadn't changed in years. With the beginning of a summer tan and the same close-cropped, sandy hair, her cousin was perpetually dressed for business-casual Friday in an open-collared pastel shirt under a sport coat.

"It's fine. Thanks for collecting me."

"Anytime. You know Mom, she doesn't like to drive in the dark anymore." Michael took her backpack and looked around for something else to carry. "Is this all?"

Jo nodded.

"You didn't learn to pack from anyone in our family." He swung her bag into the backseat and opened Jo's door for her.

She sank into the soft leather of the passenger seat. Michael had done well for himself and liked nice things, especially cars.

"You must be ready for bed." The dashboard lights came to life when he put the key in the ignition, and unfamiliar music blared through the impressive speakers. A dark whiskey voice asked if she had come there to get hurt. She was relieved when Michael scrambled for the knob and muted the sound before she had to come up with an answer to that question. She hadn't, hadn't come there to get hurt, but interacting with her mother almost guaranteed a new wound or a twinge from a badly healed scar.

"Actually, I'd like a beer and a fucking shower." Jo closed her eyes.

"Jolene Abigail Wiley, do you talk to God with that mouth?" He was teasing, but it reminded her to rein in her usual vocabulary. Jackie hated her "sailor mouth."

Jo smiled to herself. She had done way more than talk to a god with that mouth.

"If I know Mom, she's got your bed turned down, a stack of towels handy, and a six-pack of some new local beer in the fridge." He made the loop out of the airport and headed toward Shallowford Road.

"I'm hoping."

"Here I am jabbering at you, and you probably just want to fall asleep."

Her internal clock—set to Ljubljana time—was telling her it was early morning, but she hadn't slept on the trip. She hated flying, mostly because she stayed wide awake when she traveled, as if her vigilance was the only thing keeping the plane in the air. Her usual restlessness had been compounded by the reason for the visit.

"Jet lag. But it is good to see you. What's going on with you?"

"Same ol', same ol'. Working. Taking care of Mom's dogs when she's at the hospital."

Jo felt his eyes on her in the dark. He wasn't one for gently probing or emotional conversations, not that anything about this situation was subtle.

"How is she?"

"Aunt Mary or Mom?"

"Mary."

He looked out at the road, hesitating. "Not good. Mom said the doctor thinks she's been hanging on, waiting for you."

Jo's laughter startled her cousin. "Mother doesn't do anything for my benefit."

"Jo, that's not true."

Jo was right, and he knew it, but he would always be the person who put blood first, whether it earned that honor or not. In truth, she put family first, as well, but her mother hadn't been family for longer than Chattanooga had ceased being home.

———

As predicted, Jackie enveloped Jo in a hug and the scent of a perfume that hadn't been popular for twenty years. Jackie stepped back, put both her soft hands on either side of Jo's face, and looked deep into her eyes. Jo submitted herself to the checkup. This signature move had made Jo deeply uncomfortable as a teenager when she'd assumed Jackie was checking to see if she was high. In the years since, as their time together had shrunk to infrequent visits back and forth, Jo cherished those few moments Jackie took to really see someone.

"You look thin. And tired."

Jo smirked and tried to untangle herself from the two

corgis weaving between her ankles. "No one ever tells me I look thin except you."

"You look better with some meat on your bones."

That was where it was best to change the subject. Jo had fought hard to be at peace with her body. With her corn-fed build, it was occasionally difficult to keep that perspective in the land of the slender, athletic Slovenians. But she'd settled in a good place, and she wasn't about to let her nutrition-obsessed aunt convince her to try whatever new regimen she'd discovered. Nor would she spend her visit being force-fed cheesecake.

"Would you be horribly offended if I took a shower before we settle in for a chat?" Jo tried to stifle a yawn and hid it poorly behind her hand.

"Not at all. I was just staying up to meet you. It's been a long day."

Her aunt had always looked youthful for her age. The two of them were often mistaken for sisters, but fine lines of exhaustion dulled Jackie's usual glow. Guilt plucked at Jo's conscience. She'd come as soon as she could—well, as soon as she was mentally able—but it had been hard to leave Ljubljana. Her friends, Vesna and Gregor in particular, had finally threatened to chloroform her and dump her on a plane if she didn't get her shit together and buy a ticket after repeated calls from Jackie "to get her butt home."

"There are towels and a robe in the bathroom, and I put some water by the bed for you. Get some sleep. We can catch up over breakfast." Jackie kissed her on the cheek. "Goodnight, hon. I'm glad you're here."

Jo nodded and waited for Jackie to disappear down the hall, two wiggling dog butts in her wake, before she headed up the stairs to the guest room. Michael had insisted on carrying up her bag and had placed it on a luggage rack in the corner. Her cousin had come by his penchant for nice things honestly; Jackie's guest room beat the hell out of any four-star hotel. Funny that their tastes hadn't rubbed off on Jo. She preferred stark to luxe.

The French doors that lead to the balcony were open, and a breeze stirred the gauzy curtains into an invitation. Jo grabbed a bottle of the mineral water Jackie had left on the nightstand and curled up in one of the snug chairs angled into the corners where the wrought-iron railing met the cedar shingles of the house. The river moved, dark and silent, out beyond the railing. Its surface was interrupted here and there by lights twinkling from houses. Did Achelous have sway over the goings-on of this river, too?

As the thought slipped through her mind, the breeze kissed her with the heavy scent of orchids, the mark of Achelous' magic, and a milky green glow blinked in the depths near the island in the channel.

"All rivers run to the sea." Jo spoke the words into the quiet air like a prayer, unsure of who might be listening or what she should even pray for.

"And yet the sea is never full." Helena reappeared and sat in the chair opposite Jo as Sarah Vaughn whispered "Whatever Lola Wants" on the breeze. "You can take the girl out of Ljubljana, but you can't take Ljubljana out of the girl."

"Have ghosts, will travel?" Jo took a sip of water and screwed the metal lid back on to the bottle.

Helena gave her a sad little smile. "Something like that."

"I should be thinking of Jackie and my mother, but all I can think about is—"

"Your unfrocked priest or your immortal child?"

"Both. And ..." There were others who occupied her thoughts, but Leo and Faron absorbed the lion's share of her mental attention of late, for very different reasons. She was afraid of losing one and of getting closer to the other.

"They'll be there when you get back."

"It's not that." Jo pulled her knees up to her chin and looked out into the midnight-black trees that grew thick on Maclellan Island.

"They are grown men, Jo. You can't hold yourself responsible for them. I would have thought you had learned that lesson. Recently. And well."

She had. And though Helena was right about Leo and Faron, her father's shade wouldn't be in Ljubljana when she returned. She still didn't know how to get him back from the realm of nothingness he had disappeared into. Milo, another ex, wouldn't be there either. No one had figured out quite what had happened to his soul the night he had been killed.

The line she'd drawn for her life and the path she was on had taken marked leave of each other in the last year. Though she had come to believe she had a part in some grand plan, she could no longer pretend she had any idea what her role was, let alone anyone else's. If she wasn't able to help or protect the living and the dead she cared about, what was the point of all this?

CHAPTER 2

Ivanka snapped the book closed and rubbed her eyes. Did witches really need to know the correspondences of every tree, shrub, and weed? Wasn't the purpose of books not having to memorize all that stuff? Goran was a taskmaster of a teacher, and she was determined to not let her younger sisters outpace her. She opened the book again and smoothed down the page on alpine trees of southern Europe.

Faron appeared behind her. "May I?" His hand hovered over the edge of the book. She nodded. So much for willpower, but she'd have time to review again before their next lesson. She turned around in her chair and looked up at him.

His gaze raked the chaos of her desk. She'd crammed everything—desk, altar, worktable—into the corner of their bedroom. Their roommate was moving out soon, and she and Faron had agreed she should have the extra space for her "office." If she'd known how much real estate being a witch required, she would've thought about her answer to Goran's offer a little longer.

She still would have said yes. She was up to her neck in this now, and there was no going back. Jo had been honest with her, even after her sister Veronika had almost killed Jo and their younger sister. Well, technically, Veronika had killed Jo. Jo had said if Ivanka stayed with Faron, the weird shit would keep happening. And Ivanka had decided that if weird shit was going to keep happening, she needed to be able to protect herself and her family—which included keeping her sisters out of trouble. She'd made a promise to Goran and the local Observer, Gustaf Lichtenberg, that she would be responsible for Veronika. Despite dealing with Veronika's penchant for magical disasters, Ivanka was more worried about their baby sister, Ana.

Faron put his hand on Ivanka's shoulder. "You should get some sleep."

She yawned. "I should. Are you coming?" He was family now, too, as were his mother and everyone else in their accidental coven of sorts centered on Renegade Tea.

"I'll lay down with you until you fall asleep."

Faron slept less and less. Little by little the person she knew was being replaced by the person he would become. She had started tracking it, for her own purposes and to help Faron chart the changes as they occurred. She still hadn't been able to fully accept the idea that Faron would eventually be unchanging and immortal.

"I need a shower first. I smell like bakery and *scopolia*." Ivanka made a face and pinched the front of her shirt, pulling it away from her chest.

"*Scopolia*? Is that a plant or a spell?" He teased her, but he respected her work with Goran.

"A plant, false belladonna." She shrugged. "Goran burned

some this afternoon to see how I reacted to the smoke. We're experimenting, trying to figure out what works best, what kind of witches we are." The *scopolia* had been better than the fly agaric mushrooms. Those had given her scary-ass visions of rotting corpses and demons.

"There's more than good witch or bad witch?" Faron smiled, but it was half-hearted. They both knew what bad witches were capable of.

"News for me, too. Veronika is a natural witch—"

"Aren't you all natural witches? Isn't that what Dušan said?"

Ivanka bristled at the mention of Faron's father's name. Dušan was the latest catalyst for the many changes in her life. She shouldn't blame him more than the others, but she did because she felt he had been manipulative when he could have been direct about Faron's fate. "We are, but there are natural witches and then there are *natural* witches, according to Goran at least."

"Okay. And what kind of witch does Goran think you are?"

Ivanka hesitated, but they had agreed not to have secrets between them. "He thinks I might be an oracle."

"Like at Delphi?" Faron smiled a real, if lopsided, grin, the same one that had charmed her when she'd first met him after wandering into his mother's teahouse.

"More like the weird sisters in Macbeth."

———

Leo stood on the Shoemaker's Bridge and looked out over the Ljubljanica. Spring still showed in the pale green leaves of the plane trees and willows lining the banks. The season showed, too, in the brightly colored outfits of the tourists and locals walking the banks in couples and threes. He wished his mood matched the optimism of their clothing choices.

The incense of the church had followed him out into the city on his clothes. He still considered himself Catholic and still felt the need to go to confession, whether he was a brother of the Jesuits any longer or not. He had little to confess, little in deed, at least. He did not share his thoughts about Jo in the confessional. Separation from her was penance enough.

There had been so little time together between his official leaving of the order and her leaving to attend to her mother. A long, breathless kiss at the airport and the warmth it left came into sharp focus when he thought of her. It would have to sustain him until she returned and they could make their way gingerly through the thicket of their emotions. Neither of them was particularly adept at navigating relationships. He wasn't even certain "relationship" was the right word to describe what existed between them. Trying to decipher Jo's feelings was like trying to hold the Ljubljanica in a sieve.

Work would have to occupy his time, and would, he hoped, occupy his thoughts until she returned. Gustaf Lichtenberg, the Observer who lived in the same building with Jo and his niece, had been asked to convene a meeting of Bettine, Lichtenberg's superior on the Board that monitored those who lived behind the Veil, and the local Witchfinder, the title that had fallen to Leo with his brother's death. It was not a meeting Leo wanted to participate in or even allow to take place. The idea of Jo or her son becoming of keen interest to the Board left Leo with an icy sense of impending catastrophe. From his father's and brother's tales, he knew the Board to be ruthless in their dealings with errant Observers and persons or beings who were deemed a threat to the secrecy they all lived under.

Having Lichtenberg's minder in Ljubljana wasn't a good thing for any of them, even in the general sense. The Board didn't look kindly on large assemblies of supernatural beings and people with supernatural abilities either. They tended to attract attention to themselves, though Jo and Vesna's punk teahouse was good cover for the collective of strange characters they had formed. Jo, all by herself, seemed to be a magnet for the weird—good and bad. The bad manifested in especially unpleasant ways, but it had not deterred him from throwing his lot in with hers, to the extent she allowed space for another person.

This business with Bettine was yet another thing for Leo to worry over. He held Lichtenberg in little regard, but the man had a soft spot for Jo Leo couldn't explain beyond some fatherly sense of responsibility. Leo hoped Lichtenberg's affection for Jo could protect her and hadn't instead endangered her further.

Leo walked across the bridge and continued to *Zajčeva cesta* and Renegade Tea. He had promised his niece Vesna he would stop by while he was in town. Gregor, Vesna and Jo's silent partner in the teahouse and the owner of the building, had offered him one of the unoccupied flats above the storefronts, but Leo had chosen to stay in Škofja Loka. Jo needed her space, and, as it turned out, he needed his too.

Leo walked through the newly painted doors into the courtyard shared by the teahouse, Goran's antiques shop, the papered-over storefront next to Renegade Tea, and Dušan

Črnigad's gallery—the newest addition to the businesses on the ground floor. It was closed, but Črnigad was home. Leo could sense it.

Dušan Črnigad had moved into another of the empty flats in the building within a day or two of the events of Jo's birthday. Leo had been surprised Gregor had allowed it, but Jo had insisted it was better to keep her frenemies close. Leo had needed a brief explainer on the word "frenemy" but then agreed it was an accurate description of Jo's ex, the Black God of Slavic myth and her son's father. Leo had come to grips with his jealousy but still had little use for the man the god pretended to be.

The bells on the door to the teahouse clanged against the painted wood as he entered, and the scent of vanilla billowed out to greet him. A mournful voice singing of a love with neither rule nor reason wrapped Leo and the shop in a sense of loss.

Maybe he was projecting.

Vesna appeared, pink-faced, wiping her hands in her apron. "You're early."

"Not very. I took the bus in and walked the long way from the station. I didn't have much reason to linger anywhere when I can get tea here." He didn't share his time in confession with his niece. She had little thought for the church and its "antiquated ideas."

"Fred made a pot earlier that should still be warm, or I can make you something fresh." His niece hesitated at the counter and tucked her dark hair behind her ear.

"I think I'm up to a cup of Fred's special. How are you?"

Maybe he wasn't projecting after all. Vesna looked well, but a heaviness hung about her.

"I'm good. Worried about Jo and her mother and how all that will go, but things here are humming along." Vesna handed him the tea and waved him to the nearest table before poking her head back into the kitchen to check on Fred and Ivanka's progress.

Seated at the table with her own cup, his niece scrutinized his face before speaking. "And how are you?"

"I miss her. But this morning I have an additional concern." He looked down into his cup and back up at his niece. She could see the colors that swirled around him, revealing his true state of being. Hiding things from her was not an option, but he didn't wish to burden her with yet another concern. The daughter of a family of witchfinders, Vesna had tried to rid herself of her family's work. But her friends, Jo especially, had brought it back to her with little hope of reprieve.

Vesna spoke again before he figured out how to frame his concern. "It's the woman from the Board isn't it? Gustaf told me she wanted to visit."

It appeared Leo wasn't the only one who knew the uselessness of trying to keep Vesna in the dark.

"Yes." Leo took a sip of tea and continued. "Lichtenberg said she was interested in meeting with the local Witchfinder about the level of activity in Ljubljana and the unusual concentration of witches."

Vesna laughed. "Unusual concentration? Goran, Ivanka, and her sisters?" She set her cup down. "On balance with the deaths, we're only up by one from the previous count. The

Board doesn't count goths and nationalist posers, do they?"

"Not as far as I know. I suspect the sisters raised an eyebrow; a trio of witches doesn't bode well." Vesna knew the lore as well as he did, or almost.

"Goran's not really sure Ana is a witch, but I don't think he meant she doesn't have a gift. Just that something else is going on with her. So maybe not a trio of witch sisters after all?"

"She's, what, all of ten years old? She hasn't fully come into her power." He had never met Ana before the night Jo had almost died, but the girl he'd seen since then seemed unnervingly unaffected by what had happened.

"She's eleven, and I agree. I was trying to be optimistic."

"I admire your willingness to see the positives, but I think it's best if we dissuade Bettine from coming to Ljubljana at all. Even Lichtenberg seemed daunted by the prospect." Leo finished his tea and set the cup back on the saucer.

A fine line etched itself between Vesna's eyebrows. There was no love lost between his niece and the Board. For someone who prided herself on being organized and crossing all her Ts, she had almost no use for actual authority. It was something she and Jo had in common, at least the authority part.

Vesna shifted in her chair. "There's something else you should know. I mentioned the possibility of Bettine's visit to Goran. Did you know she was the Observer in Ljubljana before, when Goran was a kid? So, when you were a kid."

"I remember Father speaking of a woman Observer, with his usual distaste, but I didn't realize it was Bettine. She must be in her eighties by now."

"Gustaf didn't even mention it, and I don't remember Father ever using her name. I just remember how much he disliked the Observers' interference in his business. How bad is it if she comes?"

"I don't have the gift of sight." Nor did Leo want it.

"Do you need it? Surely Father and Grandfather had a thing or two to say to you about the Board." The line between her brows was now a furrow.

"They had a lot to say about the Board. As you said, they disliked the interference, especially Valter after the incident with Berta."

Vesna snorted. "Father completely missed the vampire connection. The Board should have interfered more then. Don't you think it's their fault Berta died in the first place?"

Those were memories Leo had no interest in returning to. "Many mistakes were made, by the Board, by Valter, and by me. Berta's blood is on my hands as much as theirs, but Gustaf was right about Valter's inattention to anything outside of his obsession with demons and witches after our father died. I'm sure there were many other derelictions of duty because of that." He had left things undone as well. Berta had been the only other woman he had ever loved, and he had never been back to her grave. He couldn't bring himself to face even her name chiseled into the stone.

His niece sighed heavily. "You are not your brother."

He nodded. "All of that aside, I don't trust the Board to see Jo and Faron as benign citizens of the Veil. In my understanding, the Board frowns on gods intermingling with humans. According to Lichtenberg, the Board believes Črnigad is an alchemist and a necromancer. If Bettine is at all sensitive—as most Observers are in their way, though they deny it—she will know Črnigad isn't just a photographer with strange hobbies. And she'll pick up on the change in Faron."

"What can the Board do? Jo and Faron have caused a bit of a stir, but Gustaf has managed to explain the events away in the public eye."

"I don't know for certain. The Board can demand the quarantine of anyone they wish."

"Quarantine? You mean imprisonment." Vesna leaned back in her chair and crossed her arms over her chest. The errant lock of hair she'd been trying to keep tucked back fell over her eye.

He shrugged.

She sat up and leaned across the table. "How can you be so calm?"

"Years of quiet contemplation."

Vesna snorted again and flopped back in her chair.

"I wasn't trying to be funny. My guts are twisted with worry. I'm more skilled at concealing my concern."

"Fair, and your aura at your crown is a stormy mess." She sat up again and took another sip of tea. "So, what are we going to do to keep Bettine from coming?"

"Anything we can."

CHAPTER 3

The cafeteria food at the hospital was mostly from scratch, if one didn't count the #10 cans of green beans cooked to mush for the patients. Jo poked at her meatloaf and nibbled on the dinner roll that was more like cake than bread. It reminded her of her grandmother's, though it wasn't nearly as good.

Every Sunday, Grandma Rose had started the rolls after breakfast. White Lily flour, yeast, salt, sugar, and milk. When the dough threatened to spill over the rim of the mixing bowl, her grandmother punched it down with her fist then rolled it out and wound it into a long snake on the scrubbed wooden countertop as she hummed hymns to herself.

She cut the snake into fat Tootsie Roll links and rolled those into balls. She dropped three balls into each cup of a greased muffin tin and let them rise again. No matter what was on the menu for Sunday supper, there'd be cloverleaf rolls, and Grandma would drop one into Jo's open hand as she left, a treat for her to eat in the car on the way home.

Grandmother. Jo was older now than her grandma had been during those Sunday dinners. She was only a couple years from being the same age her grandmother had been when she died. Such was the lineage in a family of teenaged mothers.

She looked down into her dinner where she had separated the soft roll into thirds and set the pieces off from one another on the edges of her plate. Her mother, her aunt, and herself. The last three Voices left in the world. She picked up the piece closest to herself and popped it into her mouth. Now there would be only two.

"There you are." Jackie rushed into the seat next to her at the laminate table that was trying its damnedest to be cheery.

"Where did you think I was?" Jo had said she was going to step out and get some food. She would have preferred to disappear somewhere into downtown Chattanooga. It wasn't far from the hospital to anything better than the lumps she had pushed around with her fork, but she didn't want to disappear for too long.

"I don't know. I figured you'd walk downtown."

"The thought crossed my mind."

"Well, I'm glad you didn't. Mary's awake, or at least she was when I left the room."

Jo stood and collected her wallet and the tray of plastic dishes and uneaten food.

"I'll take that. Go see your mom."

Jo heard the unspoken "you might not get another chance" as loudly as if Jackie had yelled it to everyone in the cafeteria.

The hallways of the hospital shouldn't have been confusing, but there were no real landmarks for Jo to find her way back to her mother's room. She turned the wrong way down a corridor and found herself at an unfamiliar nurses' station.

A nurse in Day-Glo orange scrubs that could have been seen from space ignored Jo, instead reconciling the medicine cart with an unseen spreadsheet on the computer. Jo looked around for someone else to get directions from. A woman in a perfectly pressed suit the color of mascarpone walked toward her.

"Excuse me. Do you know how I get back to the elevators?"

The woman stepped back and looked at Jo with surprise. "I'm sorry. What did you say?"

"I asked if you could point me back to the elevators. Please."

"Yes. Go down that hall and take a left." Her gaze lingered on Jo longer than was comfortable.

"Is something wrong?" Jo had only asked her for directions. Maybe she was Chattanooga-famous and an earthling had deigned to speak at her. But the woman didn't seem haughty so much as baffled.

"No one usually notices." She pulled out a heavily patinaed silver watch on a chain and glanced at it before tucking it back into the pocket of her jacket. "I hope you find your way."

Jo didn't have time to reply before the woman disappeared past the other side of the nurses' station. Her face was vaguely familiar, but Jo couldn't figure out where she'd seen her before. Whenever that happened when she was back in town, she assumed she'd seen them on the local news. Jackie insisted on watching every evening they were home.

When Jo made it back to the room, her mother looked awake. Her eyes were open, though they were unfocused and staring out the door into the hallway. If Jo were almost any other person in the world, she would have jokingly said her mother looked like she'd seen a ghost.

Jo sat in the chair next to the bed with her hands in her lap.

"Jackie said you were awake." The last time she'd spoken to her mother had been in a dream meet-up arranged by her dead grandmother. It had not been a warm conversation.

Mary looked up at her, away from the expanse of the hallway. "Jackie said—" A fit of coughing interrupted her statement, but she was easier to understand afterward. "Jackie said you were coming. I didn't believe her."

"Well, considering you said I would be kicking the bucket soon, I'm not surprised." Her mother was a Voice of the Dead, not a prophet, but she'd been partially correct in her pronouncement.

"I told you he was coming for us both." Mary went into another coughing fit.

There had been no "he" about it for Jo. She had no idea who her mother was talking to or about, but Jo doubted it was the man with mix-and-match eyes who haunted the dreams she'd had about her Voice grandmothers.

"I am glad you're here." Her mother had developed a knack for sounding completely lucid and like a creepy disembodied voice in another room at the same time. "I need to make a confession."

Jo paged through in her thoughts the laundry list of issues she had with Mary. It was a bit late for a confession or an apology. Jo hadn't forgiven her, but she'd come to a better understanding of why her mother was as she was. Finding out she, herself, was a Voice of the Dead hadn't done much for Jo's sense of sanity and well-being either. If Jackie and her father were right about Mary, there hadn't been much hope for her to live a settled, quiet life. Even with that knowledge, the bruised little girl Jo had been wasn't ready to welcome even a dying woman back into her life with open arms. The bruises had healed a long time ago, but the ramparts Jo built to protect herself were still shiny and spiked.

"You don't owe me anything."

"Everything isn't about you, Jolene."

Jo rolled her eyes. Having an argument about her name, again, was pointless.

Her mother's eyes closed, and her breathing hitched. Her lips were still moving as if she were speaking, but there wasn't any sound. So much for her mother's confession. Jo looked out to the hall. The woman in the impeccable suit walked by without looking in. The crystal face of the watch she'd glanced at earlier glinted in her hand.

Being alone in a room with her mother, being in a hospital, period, made Jo claustrophobic. She stood and walked to the open door. She watched as the woman disappeared down another hallway leaving the corridor empty. Most of the other doors were closed, or at least pulled to. This was the floor of the quietly dying.

"I thought he would be with me forever." The words were clear, without the rasp Mary's voice had been wrapped in earlier. Jo spun around, but her mother was sleeping, her breath coming more evenly with the rise and fall of her frail chest. All that was left of her mother was skin, barely stretched over bone, and a thick rope of white hair, braided neatly and snaked over her freckled shoulder and across her neck. Where had the words come from? They certainly hadn't come from Mary.

Jackie clicked her way down the hall toward the room and waved awkwardly at Jo still standing in the doorway.

"Did she say anything?"

"Only that she needed to make a confession before she faded again." Jo hesitated to tell her the rest, even though hearing voices was nothing new to Jackie. But maybe her aunt could make some sense of it. "And after she fell asleep, she, or someone else, said 'I thought he would be with me forever.'"

The color slid out of Jackie's tanned face. "Mary said that?"

"Somebody said it. Mary was asleep, but it sure as hell sounded like her. The old her."

Jackie crossed to the bed and sat heavily on the chair Jo had recently vacated.

"What?" The hair on the back of Jo's neck stood at attention.

"Nothing." Her aunt wouldn't look at her.

"Is there something going on I should know about?" Could her mother not even die without causing drama?

After a long minute, Jackie finally met Jo's gaze. "No. I mean it happened when Momma died but ..."

"What happened?" Jo took a deep breath. Nothing in her new life was ever straightforward; there was always some dark secret lurking around the corner waiting to further fuck up her peace of mind.

"Voices don't pass quietly." Jackie looked down at her hands and twisted her bracelet around her wrist.

"We're all destined to go screaming into that good night?" Jo had gotten the impression from her dreams that Voices got taken out in the field of battle by a soldier of their time, a knight with a broadsword for Winifred and a Civil War soldier with a musket for Rebecca.

"There's just a bit at the end where the difference between life and death isn't so clear." Jackie started to speak again but stopped herself.

"And?" Her aunt wasn't one to be at a loss for words.

"That's it. Mary must be close now."

That was obvious. It was why Jo had come back.

Jackie stood. "Are you sure you want to stay tonight?"

"Not really, but it seems like I should now that I'm here."

Jackie nodded. "That chair pulls out to a bed, of sorts. The nurse will bring you some sheets." She looked around like she was taking an inventory, picked up her purse, and walked toward the hall. "Call me if you need anything."

Jo needed Jackie to be straight with her, but apparently that wasn't going to happen. At least not at the moment. Jo had had enough of secret-keeping. Secrets in her family—both the one she'd been born into and the one she had chosen— had a way of getting people she loved killed. Or worse.

Jo did her own inventory of the room. It was pale-gray and sterile, despite the floral wallpaper border that made her think of the blandness of funeral homes. She settled back into the chair and thumbed through a magazine Jackie had purchased from the gift shop, marveling at how few fucks she had to give about the season's best red lip.

CHAPTER 4

Leo gathered his dishes and walked them back to the teahouse's minimalist kitchen. How Ivanka and Fred, and Jo when she was working, were able to produce the volume and quality of food they did amazed him. Fred was wiping down the prep counter, and Ivanka stood at the sink washing sheet pans and racking them on the drainboard.

Leo set his cup and saucer with the remainder of the dirty wares. "How are things going with Goran?"

Ivanka shrugged. "Good. Though I'll be shocked if I ever know every weed and twig and what they are used for."

Leo laughed. "Goran has neglected to mention there are reference books?"

"He said those are for study, and 'a witch knows.'" She turned to move the dry sheet pans to the speed rack jammed in the corner between the sink and the reach-in cooler. She slid in water that had dripped on the floor and started to lose her balance.

Leo caught her, and Ivanka grabbed his arm at the wrist to steady herself.

Her eyes went wide with shock.

Leo righted her and let her go. "Sorry. I didn't want you to fall." Ivanka had been through a great deal. He didn't discount the idea that being grabbed by someone, even in assistance, could be jarring for her.

"Thank you. That would have been bad. I just …" She looked deeply worried by her response to the near-fall.

"No need to explain. Now what were you saying?"

"A witch knows." Her face had paled, but she attempted to cover her discomfort with glibness. "I think Goran uses his references quite a lot when setting tasks for us."

"And when doing whatever he does in that little room in the back of the antique shop. Don't let him give you a hard time."

"Witches." Fred shook his head while he undid his apron.

He, like Jo's friend Gregor, was in on the secrets they all kept but didn't have his own. It was another aspect of their situation Bettine would take issue with if she made good on her promise to visit.

"I need to run to the post office. I'll be back in time for family meal." Fred hung his apron on the peg on the office door and walked out past the tea station.

"Are you sure you're all right?" Leo waited for her to answer without further prompting. His question was met with protracted silence.

"What do you know about the lore of the three sisters?"

"I don't have my reference book with me." He chuckled at his own callback, but Ivanka's expression remained one of concern. "Many believe sets of three sisters with the gift of witchcraft are born in times and places of upheaval. Some say they are a counterbalance to the forces of darkness and chaos, but witchfinders have believed they are part of the chaos. The abilities of the sisters reflect those of the Moirae: the spinner, the measurer, and the cutter. Hasn't Goran mentioned this to you all?" Leo would've been surprised if he hadn't.

"He has. He's a little confused by us, though, and thinks we aren't all witches, or maybe not just witches." Ivanka leaned against the counter and looked up at him. The color was returning to her cheeks, but she still looked apprehensive.

"Vesna mentioned he thinks Ana might not be a witch."

"I think he's just frustrated with her. Since Veronika ... well, you know, since the river, Ana has been ... different."

"I don't know her or see her often enough to notice, but I understand you would. It isn't surprising. The shock of her sister's actions, the existence of witchcraft, and everything else she has come to know about in such a short span of time." A great deal had happened to all of them.

Ivanka nodded. "Thanks."

"Anytime." He didn't ask her about Faron. She'd said more to Leo in the last five minutes than she had in all the time he'd known her. Faron had chosen someone like his mother in that regard; Ivanka didn't bend to prying.

Leo said his goodbyes and headed out into the courtyard. There was another reason he had come into town.

He climbed the stairs to Lichtenberg's garret flat. A meeting with the Austrian was low on his list of pleasant ways to spend time, but living behind the Veil often made for uncomfortable liaisons.

Lichtenberg answered at the first knock. He turned his bespectacled face up at Leo with his hello. Gray eyes, gray beard, gray sweater, gray man. The flat behind him looked like something out of an Indiana Jones movie. Bookshelves lined with leather-bound volumes and shiny-spined paperbacks covered the walls where there weren't maps of the city stuck with indecipherable patterns of pins. The spillover was neatly stacked on every horizontal surface except for the crisply made single bed shoved up next to one of the bookcases. Lichtenberg, like himself, wasn't a man who ever planned to entertain a lover in his living quarters.

Lichtenberg stepped aside and ushered Leo in.

"I've made tea, though I suspect you may have already had some this morning?" Lichtenberg fiddled about in his kitchenette.

"I have, but thank you." Leo looked around for a place to sit. He didn't want to protract this visit with the niceties of hospitality, but he didn't want to be rude. There was one chair at the cafe table that seemed to double for dining and as a nightstand.

"Sit in the chair." Lichtenberg poured pale tea into two mugs and brought them to the table. "I know this is not a social call."

"How do we stop Bettine from coming?" Leo took a sip of the tea and set it back on the table. It tasted of grass clippings.

"I think you mean how do we prevent Bettine from coming without arousing further suspicion?" Lichtenberg settled onto the edge of the bed.

"That would be more accurate."

"Bettine is not one to easily manipulate. She has her own idea of how things should be—independent of the Board—and Ljubljana has been of special interest to her for some time." Lichtenberg looked at Leo pointedly.

"Since Berta."

"Your family was of concern to the Board long before that business."

"What concern is my family to the Board? Aren't we on the same side?"

"On the same side of the Veil perhaps, but witchfinders have traditionally been rather public in their dealings with the supernatural."

"I am not my father. Or my brother." Leo knew the weight of the statement and that no matter how many times he uttered it, Lichtenberg wouldn't shift his opinion of the Kos family. Though Leo still followed the teachings of the church, he didn't believe Jo and people like her were in league with Satan.

"She is aware of that fact, but old prejudices linger. However, I do not believe that is her reason for visiting."

"You mentioned the 'unusual' number of witches to Vesna. That seems a pretense." Gustaf had been cagey on their brief phone call and left Leo to fill in most of the details. He hoped his imagination was more problematic than the truth.

"If I am correct, it is twofold. She senses that the gathering of supernatural beings under one roof, or around a Voice and her family, threatens the secrecy of the Veil. And she has suspicions about Dušan Črnigad."

Lichtenberg's words trailed off, but Leo easily finished his thought. If Bettine knew Črnigad was more than the necromancer and alchemist he pretended to be to the Board, then she would be keen to see what abilities his son possessed and make sure he posed no threat to the order of things.

"I know you care for Ms. Wiley and you may fear for her, but a visit from Bettine is more immediately of concern to her son and possibly to his father." Lichtenberg finished his tea and set the mug down.

Gods and the Long-Lived were not to meddle in the affairs of mortals, according to the Board, though Leo was highly suspect of their ability to do anything much about it. The Board's potential interest in Faron was more concerning to him.

The air contracted, pressing the book-lined walls in around Leo. Daylight struggled through the wavy-paned windows and pooled thickly at his feet. He needed air and stood in one hurried motion and made his way to the door in two strides. "Thank you for your time, Gustaf. Let me know Bettine's travel plans as you learn of them."

Out on the landing, Leo took a deep breath, but his body didn't relax. He'd promised Jo he would protect Faron. And though she said she didn't want it, he was determined to protect her too. He had failed to shield her from the baleful magic of witches, including one who had barely scratched the surface of her abilities. Bettine and the Board wielded far more power to do harm. In his rush to get out of Lichtenberg's stifling apartment, he'd forgotten to ask him about Bettine's previous tenure as Observer in Ljubljana.

———

Ivanka stood in the cobblestone courtyard in front of the shop looking up at Leo, his hands on the balustrade. His head was tilted down, but his closed eyes didn't see her. The conversation with Gustaf had not eased his concern, then. What she'd seen when he touched her wouldn't offer any comfort either.

Dušan Črnigad appeared, smoothing his collar, on the walkway below where Leo stood. Leo opened his eyes and saw her then. She smiled but there was no mirth in it—only the recognition that shit was about to start again, and they were both in the middle of it.

She watched as the two men made their way to the stairwell and disappeared before emerging into the courtyard one behind the other. Leo was less imposing without the billow of his black wool cassock and the authority of the Roman collar, but he still towered over the smaller man in the perfectly pressed suit. The two stood facing each other, another moment in their uneasy truce.

Ivanka marveled at the power of Faron's mother's vortex. Good and evil all drawn to her little orbit in an ancient city no one could pronounce or place on a map. It had pulled Ivanka in too. It had taken her mother and father from her and given her Faron. It had showed her what she and her sisters truly were. It had made a god pretend to be a man and a man leave his god. There were those who longed for that much power, who wanted only to be adored, worshipped even.

And then there was Jo. And her. And what did they want?

Mostly for those they loved to be left alone to live as they chose.

The men parted on a nod. Leo disappeared through the arched door onto *Zajčeva*, and Dušan made his way to her across the cobblestones.

"Ivanka, good morning. Could a man get some tea?"

A man could. A god she was less sure about. "I was about to pick out the brews for the day. Is there something you'd prefer?"

"My tastes are simple."

She smirked. "English Breakfast it is."

She waved him ahead, but he insisted on holding the door for her.

It was quiet inside. The music had stopped, and Vesna was in her office calling bands for the next few months' engagements.

"Just you this morning then?"

"Vesna's here. Fred stepped out." She made her way to the tea station with Dušan in her wake. He looked unnervingly like an older version of Faron, except for the shock of white hair at his temple and the eyes. Dušan's glowed like amber with a bottle-green ring at the edge.

Ivanka turned on him and raised an eyebrow.

"How are your studies?" He watched as she turned back to the tea station and rinsed out a pot with hot water from the dispenser.

"I assume you mean with Goran. Fine. It's a lot of theory and correspondences." Strainer. Tea leaves. One for the pot.

Could he please sit down?

"Only theory?"

She whirled around on him. "Why are you here?"

"What did you see this morning?"

"Nothing." She took down a cup and mismatched saucer with a skull and crossbones emblazoned over the blue Willow pattern. The cup clattered on the saucer as her hand shook. "It's none of your business."

He turned to walk to the nearest table and pulled out a chair. "Could I have a cup of whatever soup our Frédéric has put together for this afternoon?"

Bastard.

Ivanka reached over to the iPod, cranked up the volume, and hit shuffle. L7's "Pretend We're Dead" screamed through the shop speakers. Anything to drown him out. She'd practiced the techniques Goran had offered to protect her mind from others capable of prying. She wasn't exactly good at it, though, and Dušan was an expert at getting into her head.

CHAPTER 5

Jo picked her way past the ruined clapboard church and through the overgrown cemetery to where she knew she would find her father's grave. There were no shades about, but a sliver of moon hung so low and close she could've reached up through the flannel of the warm night and wrapped her fingers around it.

Night birds called, and a dog barked over the sound of a faraway train. She didn't remember his resting place being so far from the church. Brambles had taken over the small family plot. She laughed at the idea of late summer blackberries fat on the fertilizer of her ancestors, sure her grandmother would have had something to say about that and about the deer drawn to dance over the shambolic gravestones.

A cloud slipped in front of the moon, and she continued to feel her way along in darkness. Whispers came then from Mary—her mother, not Jesus's—and Grandma Rose. And Winifred, the many greats-grandmother she'd seen in a dream, cut down by a knight with star-filled eyes like Dušan's when he was in full Black God mode. There were other voices she didn't recognize. All whispered her name, barely audible above the tall grass brushing against her dress.

The bramble and the clouds parted to reveal Death seated upon her father's headstone smoking a hand-rolled cigarette. The grave was open and empty, but the more concerning part was Jo knew then where she'd seen the woman at the hospital. It was her fewer-greats-grandmother Rebecca, who'd jumped through her own door before Old Green Eyes could put a musket ball through her heart.

Rebecca smiled up at Jo. "It took you long enough."

Jo woke to a shrill warning from a machine attached to her mother cutting through the silence of the ward.

A nurse rushed in to check. Then others followed with a crash cart. Jo, still mentally coiled in the dream and unable to fully comprehend the situation, was asked to step outside.

The door closed with a soft click as Jo searched her pockets for her phone then thought better of it. Jackie could sleep. There wasn't anything either of them could do at this point. Note to self: living will, do not resuscitate. She leaned her butt against the chair rail, tipped her head back to touch the wall behind her, then pulled back immediately. The hallway held too many memories, and hundreds of miserable faces flashed through her thoughts.

Deep breath. Wake up.

The sound of footsteps at the far end of the corridor brought her back to the moment. The woman in the cream suit stopped at the end of the hall, then walked with a bit of a swagger toward her.

"Should I call you Death, or Grandma?" Jo watched a smile play across the woman's face.

"Rebecca, if you don't mind. Family shouldn't stand on ceremony. Especially ours." Death cracked the door and attempted to peer into the flurry of activity around Mary.

"Are you here for Mother?" Maybe that would be a comfort to Mary, that Death came for her rather than the man, whoever he was, that she feared.

"Not now, but soon, I think."

"That seems to be the general wisdom, though Mary hasn't gotten the memo." Jo shuffled in her lean against the crash rail. Why did hospitals always make her want to smoke?

"She has. She's just holding on, waiting for him." Rebecca watched for Jo's reaction.

"Which him? The knight with the Black God's eyes or the soldier with eyes like Achelous?" Jo's dreams had shown her both options, but they were her dreams. Maybe neither thing was true.

"That version of Death is not coming for your mother. She has never stared into the eyes of the dead as a true Voice." Rebecca's accent was hard to place. It had the lilt of the South with a twinge of Victorian England via Hollywood.

"So I've made my bed, have I?" Jo had opened doors for lost soldiers wandering the Julian Alps. If a Voice's death was based on current warfare methods, was she going to get taken out with a rocket-launched mortar to the sternum?

"You have ample time to uncover that mystery. As for your mother, I think she believes her love will come for her." Rebecca looked at the crack in the door with a mixture of disappointment and pity.

"My father?" Jo doubted John, her father, had procured

passage from Dušan's sad realm of the lost dead.

"Yes. We both know that isn't going to happen, but your mother's mind makes its own realities."

"You know about my father? Wait, of course you do, you're Death." Jo rolled her eyes.

"Death isn't a single entity, it's more of a job description." Rebecca paused and tilted her head. "I guess it's easiest to say Death is my calling."

"So how do I spring my father so he can move into the Next?" Jo's heartbeat thrummed in her ears. If her own however-many-greats-grandmother wasn't going to give her a straight answer, she would seriously consider a good primal scream, hospital or not.

"It isn't like the internet." Rebecca smiled at her like she was a dopey puppy chasing its own tail. "It's sweet, dear, how you think everyone else knows everything you don't. Nothing is as black and white as you'd like to make it."

"So, you don't know how to get him out of there? Or you aren't going to tell me because the princess isn't in this castle?" There wasn't even an attempt at hiding her exasperation.

"Don't be snippy. I'm happy to help you."

"'Don't be snippy?' Are you kidding me? I have moved so far beyond snippy, snippy is a pale dot in the distance."

"You think you want to know everything, but, even if you won't believe me about anything else, know that omniscience is a terrible burden. Not even the gods want it." A shadow darkened Rebecca's expression for a flash, then she smiled at Jo again, a genuine smile that lit up her eyes, gray-blue, just like Jo's. "Your mother will live to fight her personal ghosts another day."

As her words finished their faint echo in the vacant hallway, the machines in her mother's room stopped beeping in alarm. Relieved medical personnel filtered out the door, and the nurse who'd pushed Jo out of the room stopped to talk with her.

"Your mother has stabilized. Maybe you can get some more sleep?"

Sleep was the furthest thing from Jo's mind. "Thanks."

The nurse nodded and walked away. Footsteps sounded from the opposite end of the hall. Jackie was making her way toward them, flushed and disheveled.

"Someone from the nurses' station called me. What's going on?" Her aunt was out of breath. "Rebecca." Jackie nodded at her curtly.

"Mother flatlined, and the cavalry brought her back." It sounded flippant as soon as it was out of Jo's mouth, but it was too late, and, shit, she was rudely awakened at an ungodly hour on virtually no sleep.

Jackie didn't even flinch. "Why don't you two walk over to the Arts District and get some air and some breakfast? I'll stay with Mary for a bit."

Jo went back into the room to get her shoes and wallet and left Jackie and Rebecca not talking to each other in the corridor.

As Jo reached down to get her shoes from where they had been pushed under the bed in all the heroic lifesaving measures, her mother grabbed her upper arm. Jo stood up too quickly and whacked herself on the bedrail, hard enough to see stars. She staggered back and touched her forehead at the hairline. There was blood on her fingers when she looked.

"You have to find John, Jolene. You have to bring him to me. I have to tell him." Her mother's hissing words dissipated into a spate of wracking coughs.

———

Leo's phone hummed in his pocket as he stepped off the bus at Škofja Loka. His neighbor Teja had offered to collect him, perhaps something had come up.

It was a foreign number but stopped ringing before he could fumble the phone out of his pocket and answer. Jo rarely left messages, but maybe she would call back.

Teja and Luka's tiny car pulled into the parking area as Leo slid his phone back into his pocket. Teja popped out of the driver's side, her graying hair in disarray and her sweater buttoned crooked. She leaned across the roof. "Hurry, please. We need you at the house."

Leo folded himself into the car, happy to be on the passenger side and not having to find a place for his legs around the steering column. Teja slammed into reverse before he got his seat belt fastened.

"What's going on?" Teja was usually the calmest person he knew, but something had her hackles up.

"Luka's mother." If Leo had had his niece's gift of seeing auras he would have guessed a cloud of black steam hovered over Teja's head.

"What now?" Leo tried not to sigh heavily. He knew the truce between Teja and Luka's mother was always strained, but the woman had only arrived the night before.

"She dumped the house spirit's millet out for the chickens and then came in and dumped the salt cellar on the floor." Teja cornered the next turn on rails and slung him against the door. "Sorry."

Teja took caring for the local nature spirits very seriously, and Luka's mother thought it was ridiculous. Though she'd never actually interfered before. "I'm not sure I'll be much of a referee."

"I don't need a referee. She's already packed up and left. The spirit shredded her nightgown and dumped her breakfast on her head. She tried to blame me, but I was outside trying to round up the chickens he let out before he took up his anger with her." Teja laughed then. "I'm glad she's gone, but the house spirit, well, he's still very unhappy."

———

Leo usually had a way with Luka and Teja's house spirit, but as soon as he walked in the door a plate from the drying rack connected with the lintel, right above his head. The thing wasn't easy to see. It moved in a way that let it slip between space. The science or logic of it wasn't of as much concern to Leo as was the structural integrity of Teja and Luka's house. The spirit had already taken his revenge on much of the dishware, hurling it against walls and at least one window. Luka had quickly extinguished the cooking fire to keep the mischievous spirit from stealing coals and hiding them in the rafters.

Leo took a breath then shooed Teja back out of the house with Luka behind her. Another plate struck the doorjamb as he closed the door after them. In all Leo's dealings with house spirits over the years, he'd never seen one take up such violent means of revenge. Chasing the chickens, putting out the hearth fire, and hiding socks had been the extent of it.

Leo pulled a kitchen chair into the middle of the room and sat down, mindful that another plate missile could be incoming at any moment. The blur of the creature out of the corner of his eye slowed and settled into a dark shadow under the table.

"Teja and Luka have been good to you, and you know they will both make it right."

The shadow slunk back further under the table and stilled. Luka had already refilled the salt cellar and returned it to a place of prominence on the table. "If Teja can come back in, she can make more millet for you or maybe some fava beans." The shape came closer to the edge of the table, out where Leo could almost see the outline of a cat-sized fur ball with legs.

Leo stood and stepped to the door. He caught the movement of another larger presence out of the corner of his eye before he turned the knob. When he looked directly into the kitchen, there was nothing. He turned back toward the door to open it. A voice that was a more murmur than words vibrated in his ear as claws raked his cheek.

He opened the door slowly and relaxed when he felt the other presence leave. He touched his face where the skin burned. There was blood. Teja questioned him with a raised eyebrow, and Leo beckoned her back into the house, which now smelled of roasting chestnuts and autumn leaves.

Having been served porridge and promised fava beans now soaking on the counter, the spirit stilled and returned to his neither-seen-nor-heard status. Teja insisted on tending to Leo's bleeding scratches and feeding him lunch. They sat around the table enjoying Teja's bread with sweet butter and *pršut* on the few unbroken plates. The discussion avoided the house spirit's tantrum until Teja turned the subject back to the Unseen, as she called it.

"Luka's mother didn't help with her nonsense, but the spirit has been restless for days. Something isn't right; it's never drawn blood before. The forest is unsettled. It's waiting." Teja set the last bite of her bread down on her plate and looked first to Luka and then to Leo.

Luka frowned. "Teja, Leo has enough worry with his Jo away. Why say this?"

Teja leveled her gaze at her husband. "Because, Leo knows these things too."

Leo doubted Bettine's planned visit to Ljubljana would disquiet the Unseen. Teja had keen senses and was rarely wrong in her observances. He wasn't about to dismiss her words or the other presence that had made itself known in their house. He also wasn't ready to admit to her that it wasn't the house spirit who'd scratched him.

CHAPTER 6

Ivanka hung back while her sisters pulled their packs from Goran's trunk and headed out into the woods near Vrhnika.

"Goran, can I ask you a quick question?"

He ran his fingers through his salt-and-pepper hair, making it stick up at odd angles. "Of course. Is something wrong?"

"Not wrong. Troubling maybe."

"Is this about Ana? I don't think she's not a witch. I was frustrated with her not taking things very seriously." He dropped his pack at his feet and looked at her with apologetic concern.

"It's not that. Ana has been hard to figure out lately. It's me."

Goran cocked his head slightly and waited for her to continue.

"When we were working with the *scopolia*, I had that reaction."

"Reaction? You went straight into a trance while Veronika and Ana tried to cough up their lungs."

His kind smile put her at ease, but she still hesitated to

continue. "Yeah. How long can the effects last?"

"A couple of hours at most, why?"

That was not what she wanted to hear. "Something happened. The next day at work. I saw something."

The kind smile shifted back to concern. "In what context?"

"I slipped in the kitchen …" Saying it out loud, wrapping it in words, would make it real and impossible to take back, but she needed to know, needed Goran to confirm the possibility. "Leo was there and grabbed my arm to keep me from falling. When he did, I saw something."

Goran took a deep breath. "That can happen. It confirms my thoughts about your abilities. What did you see?"

That was the thing wasn't it? What she saw was more troubling than the fact that she could see things. "I saw Leo die, and it felt like it was going to happen soon." She paused and looked down at the dirt on the toes of her hiking boots. "What am I supposed to do with that information? Am I obligated to tell him?"

"Visions aren't always what they seem, it could mean a number of things that aren't necessarily his physical death. And as far as obligation?" He ran his hand through the mess of his hair again, creating new defiant angles. "That's a strong word. Everything a person does has consequences, for a witch doubly so."

She'd learned that lesson already thanks to her sister's dabbling.

"If you tell him, it can serve as a warning, and he can be aware of the possibility. Or it could make it easier for it to become a self-fulfilling prophesy. Which it will be, however, is partly up to Leo." Goran turned his head to watch Veronika and Ana. Veronika had stopped to retie Ana's laces before they had even gotten out of sight. "What do you think you should do?"

"I think I should tell him. Faron's father was in the shop right after and wormed his way into my thoughts enough to know that something had happened." Her dislike for Dušan continued to grow, despite Faron and Jo's efforts to make peace with him.

"Better that he hears it from you than Črnigad. I'm sorry this is the way it has begun for you. We should find a divination tool for you to work with more regularly."

That was not how it had begun for her. It had started much earlier, the night her mother, possessed and wild-eyed, had crashed into Faron's dormitory room and slammed her against the wall. She'd seen her father's death in the demon's eyes and her mother's eventual fate. Was it too much to ask that she would see good things, too?

"I like the pendulum you showed me." It had belonged to Goran's mother, Breda. It was a large piece of quartz that had been carved and polished to a point, then suspended on a silver chain connected to a ring decorated with leaping foxes.

"I think that is too simple for you. Today while we are out, look for things in the forest that catch your eye: stones, sticks, even animal bones. It isn't a traditional way here, but I've tried it. I think you might have better luck." He dug through the pack at his feet and produced a black cotton bag and handed to it her. "Put what you find in here, and I'll teach you how to cast."

She nodded and took the bag, being careful not to brush

his hand. She wasn't up for any more messages, not until she figured out how to deliver the first one.

———

Jo dabbed at her forehead. The coffee house's bathroom was dimly lit, but it was clear once the dried blood was gone that her cut had disappeared on the walk from the hospital. She added it to the long list of things that didn't add up: being cold all the time, seeing the past when she touched things, having a preternaturally accurate sense of smell, and getting the occasional glimpse of someone's thoughts or aura—usually Leo's. Both his mind and the colors that swirled around him were especially loud.

Or she was especially attuned to him. She sighed at her reflection in the mirror. He had kissed her goodbye at the airport. The breathlessness of it stirred her when she thought of him. She hadn't heard the words "I love you" in his thoughts, but she'd known it like it had been transmitted through every skin cell straight to her heart. It scared her to be so important to someone. It scared her more than it comforted.

As her connection to Leo grew, she felt it recede from Faron. Her son was still affectionate and protective of her, but he felt like unknown territory. None of them had known what it would mean for him to take on the mantle of the White God, but she hadn't expected it to make Faron more otherworldly than his father, at least not to her.

And now she had her own developing weirdness to unpack.

She threw the tissue in the wastebasket and headed back out into the toasted bakery fug permeating the coffee house.

Rebecca had found a table outside on the small, stone-paved patio. She'd taken her hair down. The tight bun she wore, paired with the masculine cut of her buff-colored suits, had made her look like a stunt double for Tilda Swinton, milky porcelain skin and all. With her hair down she looked more like a pre-Raphaelite muse in jarringly modern clothing.

Jo perched on the petite wrought iron chair opposite. "You look twitchy."

"There's no smoking on the patio." Rebecca smiled at Jo, further transforming her visage from typecast angel to earthy human. "Your cut has healed."

"I was going to ask you about that. I seem to have picked up some quirks along the way. This," she pointed at her damp hairline. "Ice in my veins, weird memories and feelings when I touch things, bloodhound smelling abilities … oh, and I can see auras and hear what other people are thinking, if they are being obvious about it." The woman running the cash register brought her coffee out and set it on the table. Jo nodded a thank you and continued. "Is this a normal thing for Voices?"

"Have you asked Jackie?" Rebecca took a sip of her coffee, black and unsweetened, and set her cup back down.

"No. She's got her hands full with Mother."

"You mean, no, because you already know it isn't normal for Voices, or Portals."

Jo waited for Rebecca to continue, but she took her time.

"I will answer your other questions first and then we will come back to that one. Yes, I am, or was, a Portal. You are the only other one in our line since. What you saw in your dream was real, or at least most of it. Green Eyes is not your well-traveled river god. I'll let you do your own homework on that but will say that the Lady in White folktale at Chickamauga is yours truly in the earliest days of my current role. Those Voices who answer the call to free the dead of war and pestilence and disaster are often taken swiftly by an incarnation of Death. We are not usually given the chance to linger and age. I believe it is seen as a gift to meet Death in that manner." She cocked her head. "I have yet to decide if I agree, but it doesn't matter. We can't outsmart Death. My decision to jump through my own door before I could be shot and killed, that's what led to this ... job I have now."

"You're being punished?" Jo leaned back in her chair. Trying to outthink fate was why she was still alive and her son would never die.

"Punishment is a perception. I have come to appreciate what I do. It isn't so different from being a Voice. Instead of releasing the wandering dead, I help the living who are ready to cross into the Next let go more easily."

"Do you have to do this forever?"

"Forever is too long to think about. In the In-Between, time passes differently." Rebecca took a bite of the quiche Lorraine she had ordered. "Luckily for me, eggs still taste divine. Mmm."

Jo smiled. "And my original question?"

"Being a Portal is different than being a Voice alone. It is why my choice led me here. A Voice would have simply died when she crossed her threshold. You've complicated things quite a bit. Well, more accurately, you and Dušan Črnigad have complicated things."

"Lovely." Jo set her fork on her plate with finality. The bite of fruit salad in her mouth suddenly tasted of cardboard.

"Had you let Črnigad use you to cross into the world, you would have died to give him that mortal life."

"Yes, my life for the life of a god or a shade." Or a demon. Jo knew that entirely too well.

"Instead you carried his child. You bore him a son. One who has now taken his birthright." Rebecca looked at her, her expression serious but not grave. "You gave birth to a god, Jolene Wiley. You and a handful of Portals in human history. You didn't give your life for that life, but there are still consequences."

"Extra party tricks?"

Rebecca laughed. "I think you'll find it is more than that."

"You aren't going to give me a straight answer, are you?" What was it about the otherworldly and their inability to answer a question?

"I'm not the messenger for that information." Rebecca was done with that topic then.

"Well, if that's all I'm going to get on that, why does Mother think she needs John here to 'tell him' before she gives up the ghost?"

"Your mother wants to apologize."

"Apologize to Dad? For what?" Mary needed to apologize for a lot of things, but mostly to her and maybe Jackie. Mary had been violent with Jo after her father's death, but her parents had seemed the happy couple to her before that. Her father had been resigned to an early death when she'd first talked with his shade, and he had sacrificed his peace in the Next in an attempt to save her.

"Your mother needs to tell you this. I won't take that from her." Rebecca stood and brushed non-existent crumbs from her perfectly pressed pants. "Shall I walk you back, or do you need some time alone?"

"I'd like some time with my own thoughts." Rebecca must have other hospitals and places to visit.

"Stay with her today and tonight Jo. Her time is soon, and she needs to tell someone."

Jo closed her eyes in a long blink and nodded. Rebecca was gone when she looked up. Her mother had never been there for her. Jackie had been nurturer and confidant and disciplinarian, to the extent she had that last in her. Jackie had done everything in her power to fill the hole her parents had left, but either the gap was too big to start with or Jo had kept digging on her own. She'd built a wall around the emptiness, picked people with their own distrusting or barren hearts, and used them as proof that everyone was too broken for love to be real.

Becoming Faron's mother had been terrifying. She didn't think she had it in her to be love for anyone else, but she'd taken Jackie's example and done her best. Leo was doing his damnedest to break his way in, and there was definitely a crack, that crack where the light gets in according to Rumi and Leonard Cohen.

Could she fashion that little bit of light into enough to sit with Mary and hold her hand, help her let go? Forgiveness was too big to consider, there were too many scars, but she could attempt compassion. Whatever her mother had done or failed to do, she deserved her only child's compassion. Guilt tugged at Jo's heart again for how long it had taken to get there, but that cloud could rain on her later.

CHAPTER 7

Leo ran his hands over Jo's crown and cupped the back of her head. She pressed in, her pelvis against his thigh, and locked her arms around him. Her lips parted, and behind his closed eyes his mind tumbled forward to undressing her, uncovering all those tattoos he had glimpsed at the river's edge, and feeling her body underneath his.

He stopped and pulled back to look at her. Her eyes opened, gray-blue like the sea on a cloudy day.

"I love you."

With his words Jo closed up like a puzzle box and walked away.

They had met on a high bridge over a wide, mossy river. She climbed the railing as a crowd gathered around them, and she dived into the thick, golden-hour air. She didn't turn to look back at him, not even once. Her body pierced the water without a splash, and blue-green light rippled out from the hole she'd made in the river. It was a last act, a final separation that left him standing at the edge, gripping the guardrail, white-knuckled.

He hesitated, but then he climbed up onto the railing to jump after her. Someone or something grabbed him from behind with claws that dug into the flesh of his upper arms.

No.

Leo opened his eyes in the cool dark of his room. A blade of moonlight sliced through the crack in the curtains and reminded him that it was night; he had only been dreaming.

He sat up and put his feet on the floor, further reassurance that the dream had been only that. It hadn't been a prophecy, that wasn't his gift. But he had carried Jo once, on the edge of death, to the banks of the Ljubljanica to save her and watched her sink beneath the current. He had gone in after her and nearly frozen to death in his efforts. The life they found themselves in meant losing her was always a possibility, and anxiety had gripped him since he'd left her at the airport. Bettine's announced visit and the incident at Luka and Teja's cottage had only added to his unsettled emotional state.

He reached for his rosary and began to pray, holding the three worn beads above the crucifix between his fingers.

Hail Mary, full of grace. The Lord is with thee. Blessed art thou amongst women, and blessed is the fruit of thy womb, Jesus. Holy Mary, Mother of God, pray for us sinners, now and at the hour of our death.

"Protect Jo. Return her safely home. Amen."

Sleep wasn't going to come back, so he stood and walked to the window. The moon illuminated the outlines of Luka and Teja's cottage; there was a light on in the kitchen. He wasn't the only one sleep had eluded.

———

Ivanka spooned into Faron's sleeping form. His breath was light over her ear. She had slept fitfully for a couple hours but had spent the last hour or so ruminating on whether she needed to warn Leo of her vision. There was nothing she could do about it right then.

She slid from underneath the covers and Faron's protective arm and padded to the desk. She'd set the black bag on her altar to charge the items as Goran had instructed. The buildings around the central courtyard blocked out the low moon, but she could sense its pull. She had yet to dedicate her altar to a deity. Despite Achelous saving her sister, she didn't have much use for gods. Goran had said it was possible to be an agnostic witch, but it would require drawing on her own power alone — which was a finite resource. She suspected Goran had some old-fashioned ideas about things. She was happy to draw the power of the moon into her work and let that be enough.

The contents of the bag tumbled out onto the red cloth she had laid on the desk. The bear's claw and a small tumbled piece of pink quartz Faron had given her landed at the front with the claw curled around the stone. A bird skull and an iron nail were off to the side, and the small antique die Goran had included with the gift of the bag showed three irregular black dots. Other bits and pieces had found their places, but those were the things that stood out.

Ivanka jotted down her impressions and outlined a quick sketch to show Goran when she met with him next. She didn't feel any more settled than before, but she climbed back into bed and folded herself against Faron's back, thoughts of a heart stone wrapped in a claw prominent in her mind's eye. Was it protection or warning?

———

Vesna took one last look at Igor curled in sleep around the warm place she had left in the bed. It was good to have him there, but it made it hard to leave in the morning, even though work was only a few steps away. In an hour or so he would find his way downstairs and poke his head into the kitchen to see what was available for a quick breakfast before he disappeared off into his own day.

What she had with Igor was nothing she had imagined possible and everything she had wanted. Jo's embrace of the world and whatever it offered up each day in the way of companionship had never appealed to her, but the life her mother had wanted for her—a husband and house and two, or better yet, three, children—never felt right either. Then Igor had come to the teahouse to paint a mural, and everything had changed.

Not just for her. The day she met Igor had also been the night Jo found out about being a Voice. Vesna had been pulled unwillingly back into her own family's web of secrets and unwanted duties. She wasn't going to argue with the Fates that brought her Igor if they insisted on an even batch of pain for the pleasure, but that didn't mean she was going to sit idly by and let bad things happen to her friends.

Dreams of Jo and Faron being carried off to a horror of a medieval dungeon overseen by Gustaf Lichtenberg and the Observers had pecked at her sleep. She might not be able to keep Bettine from coming to Ljubljana and pressing the claws of the Board into their business, but she was going to do everything she could to protect her friends.

Downstairs, the shop was still dark. Ivanka and Frédéric

hadn't arrived yet. She enjoyed the quiet of having the teahouse to herself. It made sense to her now why Jo liked to beat everyone to work.

The mental list of the day's tasks got transferred to paper while a pot of Ceylon steeped. She needed to remind Fred to double the soup for the day. Liar's Knot was playing that night, and they always drew a crowd. They would probably wind up staying late for an after-party unless Mia and the guys had already made plans to finish their evening at Niko's gallery. It was far too early to call anyone in a band to confirm.

A knock on the door interrupted her thoughts. It wasn't like Fred to forget his key.

"Oh, it's you," Vesna said as she opened the door. She didn't swing it wide enough to admit Dušan and his overly friendly smile. "We're not open yet."

"But you have made a pot of tea. I wanted to catch you before you had gotten too far into your day."

Vesna rolled her eyes and let him in.

"I see why you and Jo get along so well. Neither of you hides your feelings very well." He continued on to the back of the shop and poured tea for both of them before Vesna could object. He motioned an invitation for her to take a seat in her own shop.

She really wished Jo hadn't been so sanguine about Dušan moving into the building. His presence was the mental equivalent of catching a glimpse of a cat in your peripheral vision and looking to see there was no cat there. Dušan the Man had an aura, but Vesna guessed it paled in comparison to the aura of Dušan the God. This morning his for-show, human aura glowed a vibrant, secure orange.

"I'll stand if you don't mind. I have stuff to do." She brushed past him into the kitchen and reached for an apron.

"You really do not care for me, do you?"

"I'd like to think you didn't need to invade my thoughts to figure that out. I will never understand what Jo saw in you." That was a lie. She knew exactly what Jo had seen in him — he was about as emotionally available as a signpost and exuded an undeniable bad-boy charm. Vesna tied the strings of the apron around her waist and stared at her unwelcome guest.

"Have you spoken with her?" He leaned against the door and drank his tea, holding the saucer and cup close to his face.

"No. She said she'd call when she had time." Vesna wasn't keen for a phone call. Jo had gotten very good at telling when she was hiding something.

"Good to know." He reached past her to set the empty cup and saucer on the edge of the sink. "When you do, tell her to say hello to Rebecca for me."

"Who's Rebecca?"

He patted his jacket pocket and looked at her long enough for his eyes to flash black. "Thank you for the tea."

She heard the bells on the door chime as he left. She walked to the iPod and pushed play, not knowing what she would get. Reka and Ivanka had closed the previous night. Something unfamiliar with a husky-voiced lead singer began pouring from the speakers.

She peeked at the screen. Gang of Youths? Didn't matter. Anything to chase out the tendrils of Dušan's presence.

The singer asked himself how the fuck his life had gotten so weird.

How the fuck, indeed. She carried the cup Dušan had poured for her and the rest of the pot to the sink and dumped them out.

"He's not evil, you know."

Igor's voice startled her. She whirled around on him. "I didn't hear you come in."

"Your visitor and I passed at the door." He watched the last of the red-brown liquid drain down the sink. "I guess there's no tea this morning."

"I'll make you a fresh pot. What would you like?"

"Surprise me."

"I don't know how you can think he isn't evil. He—"

"He isn't a man, love. He is beyond our human morality."

Vesna stared open-mouthed at him. "Do you really believe that?"

"It doesn't matter if I believe it. You've seen enough to know that gods do as they wish, mostly without consequence."

"Without consequence to *them*." She took down the tin of Ceylon and banged it on the counter. "No. I won't accept that. Dušan, Achelous, whoever. They have a place and a purpose. You can't tell me that they don't answer to anything or anyone except themselves."

"It's entirely possible. I don't ascribe to the idea that

people, with our morals and human hearts, et cetera, are the superior creation in the universe. If we are, the universe is a seriously fucked-up place." He took the tin from her before she whacked it on the counter again and pulled down a pot to make his own tea.

"You're very cynical." She smiled despite herself.

"Nope. I am a realist all the way. We are too warlike and awful to each other. We aren't even superior to cats."

CHAPTER 8

Jo sat as close to the bed as she could. Her mother's hands were cold. The shift nurse had said that would happen. The body conserved resources to keep the core warm and the organs functioning as it began to shut down from the extremities in. Jo had become an unwilling midwife, watching and waiting for signs of the end.

Jackie had gone back to the house, or more accurately Jo had sent her because her aunt looked exhausted. Her sister was dying, and aside from Michael and Jo and Faron—who were very far away—Mary was all the family her aunt had left. The realization had landed on Jo with a thud. Knowing with certainty that something lay beyond death wasn't as comforting as religions and popular culture would make one believe. The nature of it was still a mystery. Well, except for the part where souls could find themselves pressed into throngs of the lost in the underworld with Dušan. Dead people were still gone. Unless you were a Voice, and even then, your job was to help them leave. God—gods?—her life was complicated.

"Jolene. Is John here?" Her mother's voice was barely

audible above the steady hum of the heart monitor.

"He isn't coming. He can't." How did she comfort her mother on this point when she couldn't even soothe herself about it?

"He has to. He has to come." Jo could see a streak of tears move down her mother's temple in the dim light from the machines.

"I'm sure if he could come to you, he would. He loved you very much." Jo patted her mother's hand. It sounded trite, even to her. But her father had stayed with Mary when she'd gotten pregnant with Jo. He must have loved her.

"Maybe once."

"He did better by you than Faron's father did by me." On so many levels.

"He was going to leave. He told me that day on the river."

A chill slid down Jo's spine, prickling the hairs on the back of her neck.

"I couldn't let him. I stood up in the boat." Mary's voice was steadier now, stronger.

"Please stop." Jo had been so keen to know everything, but now she was certain she didn't want to know how this story ended.

"The canoe flipped, and he hit his head. I didn't panic. I just held him under until the bubbles stopped. Then I lost him in the water." Mary gripped Jo's hand hard enough to cut off the circulation to the ends of her fingers.

Jo couldn't move. She couldn't breathe. A clammy sweat dampened her face and hands and made its way over her chest and back. *Stop talking. Just stop.*

But her mother's voice was loud and clear now. "I wanted him to be with me always. If he was a shade, he could be my guide. He could stay with me. But I couldn't find him. I called and called for him." Her mother was sobbing now. She turned to look at Jo, her eyes were dark, hollow spots in a pale, yellowed face. "I've called and called, Jolene. Where is he?"

Jo stood, wrenching her hand from her mother's grasp. She backed away, afraid now of the thoughts swirling in her own head. She backed right into Rebecca standing in the door.

Rebecca moved by her to the bed and took Mary's hand. Her mother's panicked questions stopped. Pale blue light suffused the room before the heart monitor let out its call that something was wrong. Mary's shade lifted itself from the carapace that remained of her body, and an opalescent smudge of the woman she had been walked through a weathered screen door into the Next. The staff came then, ushering Rebecca and Jo out of the room.

It didn't take the nurses long to realize Mary had gone. They said words to Jo, placid, insipid words about death. They offered to let the two women sit with the body for a moment with looks of real concern on their faces. Jo nodded and stared. Rebecca lifted Jo's phone from her pocket and called Jackie.

It was over.

Her mother was dead, and Jo was a frightened eight-year-old standing on a riverbank with her face wrapped in her aunt's skirt while her mother screamed into the gloaming for the man she'd murdered.

———

Leo ran down the path toward Teja and Luka's cottage. Teja's terrified voice on the phone had begged him to come as quickly as possible.

She waited for him outside with Luka beside her. Both of them had been dragged from bed. Luka's feet were bare.

"What happened?" Leo finished zipping the light jacket he had thrown on over his T-shirt to brave the morning chill.

Teja shook her head and pointed at the front door.

The door was partially open, and Leo pushed it slowly so he could see inside. The kitchen had been ransacked. All the remaining dishes had been pulled from the cabinets and smashed onto the flagstone floor of the cottage. The chairs were tossed away from the table, and everything on the counters had been swept off to join the debris on the floor.

The reason his friends were standing white-faced on the wet grass in their nightclothes was dripping from the dining table. Most, if not all, of their chickens had had their throats cut and were bleeding out onto the floor. A heart had been finger-drawn in blood at the edge of the slowly seeping puddle.

Leo's own blood chilled. This was not the work of a disgruntled house spirit. He crossed himself and walked over the threshold. A presence, no, a memory of a presence, permeated the air. The smell of blood mingled with the scent of rotting leaves, a witch's lingering magic. It wasn't the signature of any witch he knew. Was Bettine right about Ljubljana being full of witches?

He rejoined Teja and Luka outside and pulled his phone

from his jacket pocket. It was early, but it was time to call in an expert.

Goran picked up on the second ring. "Hello?"

"I'm sorry to wake you—"

"You didn't, but why the early call?" Goran didn't sound like he'd been awakened, but he did sound distracted.

"I'd prefer not to discuss it on the phone. Can you come out to the old monastery?" Leo watched Teja and Luka's faces, but they were both guarded and oddly standoffish.

"Sure. I need to pull myself together, but I'm on my way." He hung up and left Leo holding his phone to his face for a second to process the call had ended. He slid the phone back into his pocket.

"We can wait for him in my room if you like."

Luka and Teja started back up to the main house. Leo closed the door behind him, catching the scent of leaves again, and of roasting chestnuts. It was wrong to think he didn't know this witch.

———

Goran ran his fingers through his hair and pulled a clean shirt from the wardrobe. His conversation with Ivanka about her vision played back in his mind's eye. He doubted she had spoken to Leo. He couldn't blame her. It was a devil's dilemma.

The drive to Škofja Loka seemed to take twice as long as usual, and he was relieved to finally pull into the gravel parking area below the scattered buildings.

He walked up to the main house. The butter-yellow

paint had seen better days, but the bones of what had been an elegant baroque abbey were clear. He'd always found it amusing that a man who lived as a monk would choose to live in a derelict monastery overrun with free-love hippies and the marginalized. Given Leo's current status, perhaps the choice had not been so odd after all.

Goran waved at Leo, who was standing in the oversized picture window. The man disappeared and reappeared as the door to the left of the window opened. Leo motioned him inside, into a room too small for comfort. There was only a bed and a straight-back chair, a small night table, and a tall skinny wardrobe. Two people Goran knew only by sight sat next to each other on the edge of the low, narrow bed. They glanced at him as he entered, then they went back to staring into the middle distance.

"I'm going to take Goran down to the cottage. We'll be right back unless you'd like to join us." Leo zipped his jacket up, as if he were going for a quick jog around the block.

The woman, Leo introduced her as Teja, shook her head, but the man stood and followed them, his feet bare, out the door and down to the cottage set into the wooded area on the edge of the property.

Goran sensed something was deeply off before they entered the building. The coppery tang of blood and residual magic, rotted leaves, and roasted chestnuts assaulted his senses as soon as Leo opened the door.

"If it's okay, I'd like to take a look by myself first, before you tell me what you think happened."

Both men stepped back for him to enter. Goran walked to the edge of a pool of blood that had spread from the carcasses of chickens piled on the table like cordwood. The scrawl of a heart had been distorted and covered as the blood had moved over the flags away from the source. The grooves between the stones were stained dark as the puddle made its way outward, thickening as it went.

He touched the heart with the tip of his index finger. It was something a child would draw on a frosted window, incongruous with the evidence of baleful magic that surrounded him.

A flicker of movement caught the edge of his field of vision. He turned but there was nothing in the shadow. He glimpsed a rustle in the air again and was able to follow it to the hearth of the tiled stove. A darkly furred house spirit shook its head at him and disappeared.

Goran joined Luka and Leo, who were still waiting outside as he had asked. "This isn't the work of any witch known to me."

Leo nodded at his pronouncement.

"We have done nothing to bring the wrath of witches upon us." Luka let out a long breath. "Teja, she thinks it is bad spirits. She says there has been an unsettled feeling in the woods, in the Unseen."

"I think your wife is right. Something is wrong here. Your house spirit has left. I suggest you not return to the cottage until it can be cleansed and warded." Goran offered to do the job, thinking Ivanka and Veronika would benefit from the experience.

Luka nodded again. "Teja said she would call her sister. We will stay with her in Ljubljana.

"I'm sorry this has happened to you. I will get to the bottom of it, I promise." Leo put his hand on his friend's shoulder.

"Please, do it swiftly. Teja, as you know, follows the old way. She believes someone has caused this or brought the bad spirits to us." Luka's tone was grave, and his sentiment was directed at Leo.

"Teja said she never believed I belonged to the Jesuits." Leo was stung by his friend's words.

"She did not and does not, but she also believes the ways of a witchfinder can disturb the Unseen." Luka opened the door to the cottage. The other men tried to stop him. "I need to get a few things. I think we will be away for more than a couple of days."

CHAPTER 9

Jackie's excuses still rang in Jo's ears. She had no patience for them and didn't want to be in the same house with her aunt. She had called a taxi and changed clothes. The smell of hospital still clung to her and she wanted a shower, but getting out and away was more pressing.

"Where to, Miss?"

Jo silently catalogued the few clubs she knew about, but she had no idea which ones still existed or what was open on a random weekday. She just wanted to dance in a crowd of strangers until her feet bled or her brain shut off.

"Cherokee Boulevard? Isn't there a club down there somewhere?"

The driver mumbled a name at her, and Jo nodded.

She got out of the cab in front of what looked like a restaurant but had the distinct thumping bass of a live band seeping out into the night.

"Thanks." She handed the driver some bills. "Keep the change."

"Hey, Miss, here's my card, in case you need a ride home."

Jo nodded and pushed the card into the pocket of her jeans.

Past the doorman who'd stared at her Slovenian passport for a really long time, Jo wended her way through the scattered tables and joined the small throng of people in front of the stage. The band was cranking out an aging-punks-do-Americana cover of "Valerie Loves Me."

The bass player looked familiar, but it took her a few seconds to reconcile the shaved head and patchy beard with the Turner of her memory. Fuck. The last thing she needed tonight was a run-in with that asshole. She didn't usually carry animosity for exes, but Turner and Dušan were exceptions. She turned to walk back over to the bar away from the lights illuminating the crowd, but the tempo had changed with the next song—a weirdly grunged-up cover of "Punk Rock Girl"—and the crowd around her morphed into a middle-aged mosh pit.

Nope. Not tonight. She wanted to dance, not get an accidental head-butt to the face.

She finally elbowed her way, as politely as possible, out to the edge of the crowd when someone grabbed her arm. She whirled around to give them a piece of her mind, but the "fuck off" died on her lips.

"Rok? What the hell are you doing here?" She wriggled out of his grasp.

"I would ask you the same question, but I have a pretty good idea."

"What?"

"I said, 'I have—'"

"No. What the hell is up with your accent?" It was

convincing, but it still sounded completely wrong.

"Should we step outside?"

Jo hesitated for a moment. Him being there, the dodgy accent, it was too weird. But it was Rok. She knew him. Or she thought she had. She nodded and followed him out to the patio, where a few diehard smokers had gathered around one of the battered tables.

The two of them took the table farthest from the door. Rok looked at both the chairs appraisingly and pulled out the more comfortable-looking one for her. That was new. The Rok she knew didn't do chivalry, or not exactly.

"Okay. Why are you in Chattanooga, of all places?"

"Looking for you."

"Is this some Secret Squirrel spy mission?"

"No."

"Then why do you have that ridiculous accent?"

"English has changed a bit over the centuries, but it is my mother tongue."

Jo stared at him. The Rok she knew was verbal only when necessary. He also didn't wear Against Me! T-shirts and groom his beard to within an inch of its life.

"Maybe I should back up a bit. What did our friend Gustaf tell you about me after I left?"

"Maybe let's back up a little more than that. Why the fuck did you leave?" She stood up, knocking the chair over in the process. The cheap metal banged on the concrete. All the hurt and anger she had toward him and all the betrayal she'd experienced that day crashed over her and onto him in a wave of fury.

The smokers at the other table nervously stabbed out their cigarettes and made their way back inside.

Rok reached for her hand, but she pulled away. "Do you even know what happened that night?"

"Yes."

"How? Who've you been talking to?" She was shaking.

"It's not like that, Jo. None of your friends are spying on you. People like me, old ones, we keep in touch."

Jo righted the chair and leaned on the back of it, her knuckles showing white against the flaking black paint and rust, trying to steady herself. "Okay, but that doesn't answer my first question."

"I knew what you were when I met you."

"Of course you did." She threw her hands up in the air. Apparently everyone knew except her. "That's why you stuck around? Because it's useful to have a Voice, or better yet a Portal, at your disposal?"

"It wasn't like that." Rok looked up at the string of fairy lights wrapped around the awning. She followed his gaze. Most of the bulbs were burned out, and it added very little light to the gloom of the alley. "I knew what you were, but I knew you didn't."

"So, what? You felt the need to 'protect' me right up until the time I actually needed some fucking help?" Her stomach turned over. She hadn't eaten since breakfast, but she felt like she might lose whatever was left of it. Was there anyone in her life who hadn't lied to her, by omission or just outright?

"No. I … I liked spending time with you, and Faron too. It had been a long time since I didn't have to pretend."

She let out a sarcastic laugh. "But you were pretending. You were pretending to be Slovenian. You were pre—"

"It's hard to explain what it's like for someone like me. That doesn't feel like pretending. Moving along and morphing into a new person is part of the territory. But I didn't have to pretend I agreed with all the modern niceties between men and women. I didn't think I would be breaking your heart when I left."

But he had. He had been another betrayal. She had thought he was her friend, and he had left when she needed him. To be fair she had tried to push others away to protect them, but Rok hardly needed her protection. He was older than dirt and maybe immortal.

"I was wrong. I thought I could walk away and with time …"

"The memory of me would fade away, like however many times you've done this before." She wanted to hash this out with him, but the uncomfortable chair and the relatively calm discussion weren't matching up with the emotional tempest whirling inside her.

"Something like that, but it wasn't that simple." He looked genuinely surprised by his own emotions.

"Can we get out of here? Walk and talk?"

He nodded and stood to open the gate that led into the alley.

She continued. "Then why the gifts, why the cryptic note about 'remembering who my friends are'?" It had taken her a few days to read the letter that had come with the medallion he'd sent her for her birthday, the actual worst birthday ever. When she finally did, the cryptic message had further pissed her off.

"I hadn't realized how tangled up in things you'd gotten, and I was concerned."

"Yeah. Well that was a shocker for me too. How did you know about Achelous?" Her hand went to the pendant he had sent her, with its faint outline of a bull's head, that she wore under her T-shirt.

"You aren't his only devotee." He smiled at her. It was disconcerting. Her Rok wasn't exactly the smiley type either. "The medallion was mine."

They walked in silence for a long while, across the pedestrian bridge, back to the other side of the river, and almost to where her Aunt Jackie's house was.

"How's your mom? I'm guessing that's why you're here?" He still hadn't told her why he was in Chattanooga.

The enormity of his question pressed against her, pushing out whatever reserve of calm she had left. She couldn't answer. She didn't want to. She was running away from him like a petulant child before she realized it. She ran to the stairs on the side of the bluff that would take her back down to the river level. She could walk home from there. If he was so good at tracking her down, he could figure out where she was staying.

Hashing out everything she had learned that day was not on her to-do list for the evening. She'd just wanted to go somewhere with music and disengage her brain, maybe go home with someone. She had felt mildly guilty about that thought, but she and Leo were stuck at "what happens now?" And though the signposts all pointed to something bigger between them, no promises had been made.

Rok called after her, but she kept going, hurrying down the steps as they disappeared below the line of the bridge. She hit a patch of loose stones that had accumulated on the edge of the first landing, and her legs went out from under her, sending her ass over teakettle down the treads to the next turning.

She lay still on the cool concrete, assessing. Everything hurt. Every bony part of her had scraped a stair. Her leg was screaming. She was sure she'd broken it and maybe a rib. The pain on the inhale felt familiar. Fuck. Fuck. Fuck.

"FUCK!"

Rok's face appeared above her.

"Bloody hell, Sunshine. You okay?"

"No. I am not okay." She felt unbelievably stupid. She was broken, inside and out, and lying on a landing in the middle of Chattanooga with a man she didn't even really know. Her mother was dead. Her mother was a murderer. Her aunt was a lying liar who lied to her and … fuck.

"You aren't bleeding. So maybe you just banged yourself up a bit."

"I'm not bleeding?"

"No. Nowhere I can see."

"My leg." She tried to sit up, and, though it hurt, she was able to.

She pulled up her pant leg, expecting to see bone protruding given the amount of pain. But there was only the hint of a bruise that faded as she and Rok watched.

"Did you do something?" Jo stared up at him, open-mouthed.

"Did I do something? Are you kidding me? That is serious magic, Jo. What did *you* do?"

She hadn't done anything. Faron had brought her back from the dead. Did that convey some long-lasting, mystical bubble wrap around her?

Rok got her to her feet and dusted her off. "Are you going to tell me why you took off like that? We can discuss your miraculous healing powers later." By his expression, he wasn't too keen on how that discussion might go.

She was still distracted by the image of a bruise fading in time lapse, distracted enough to let her talk about the other thing without being overwhelmed by it. "Mary died this afternoon."

"I'm sorry. I know there were issues, but she's still your mother."

Yes. Mary was still her mother.

Rok pulled her in for a hug, and she let him. She let him find her mouth with his and kissed him back, losing herself in the familiar smell and taste of him. He ran his hand up into her hair and kissed down to her neck and back to the point where her ear met her jawline. In his familiar voice, he said, "I've missed you, my Jo."

Leo's face appeared in her thoughts, his expression more resigned than disapproving. She would never be the thing he wanted her to be. Rok was easily as fucked up as she was, and, really, had he done anything worse than she had? He was familiar. And safe. He wasn't ever going to ask her for her heart.

The two of them sneaked into her aunt's house like teenagers and crept up to the guest room. Eye to eye, Rok held her face in his hands. "You sure about this?"

She looked down at the sliver of space between them. She'd started shedding clothes as soon as she hit the bedroom door, but Rok was still fully dressed. There were more twinges of guilt about Leo and buckets of anger—at Rok, at her mother, at everyone in that moment—but he was offering forgetfulness, at least temporarily, and that was the thing she most wanted.

She kissed him hard on the mouth and slid her hands inside the top of his jeans.

Rok pulled away again. "I take that as a yes?"

———

Jo knew the path to her father's supposed resting place now, and it was less difficult to move through the old blackberry canes and honeysuckle even though the moon was dark. The star-filled sky made her shiver, reminding her of Dušan's eyes when he first revealed his true self to her when he came to her in the mountains. She shook off the thought. She had other quarry.

The bramble and underbrush spit her out again at the foot of the newly covered grave. Rebecca was not there to greet her. Jo sank to her knees in the soft dirt at the edge. Why had she thought Rebecca would be there waiting? Death had done her job.

She didn't have anything left in her to cry. All the progress she had made to untangle the barbed-wire inside her had been undone by her mother's words. Jackie had known. Her father had, too, when he'd come as a shade to her in Ljubljana. They had both protected Mary at Jo's expense.

She'd run out into the night away from Jackie, one of the few people in the world who loved her despite her spikiness and straight into Rok, whom she'd dragged back to her aunt's to angry-fuck, whatever future she had with Leo be damned.

Jo looked down at the grave and imagined it a more inviting place than the bed she'd made for herself. She sat back on her heels and threw her head back, eyes closed, but she didn't even have it in her to wail into the night. What was the point?

A hand gripped her throat and lifted her head back up.

A shade, thin and drawn, stood on the mound in front of her. Bent over with her neck in his grasp, his face inches from hers, his eyes were dark and empty of the warmth they'd had in life. His stare bored through her as she gasped and scratched at his hand with her fingers. Her breath left her.

Milo.

Jo sat up in a tangle of bedclothes, full daylight streaming through the gauze curtains of her aunt's guest room.

Not him. Not now. There were too many other things to deal with.

But he had come to her, finally, in a dream, and he had come to her angry. It was a reminder that no matter how much she blamed her mother and father, however mad she was at

Jackie for knowing, she was hardly blameless herself. She was the reason Milo was dead. She hadn't found his shade. She didn't know where his soul had gotten to, and there had been so many other things to contend with, including her selfish grief, that she hadn't gotten to the bottom of what happened to him.

As soon as she got back to Ljubljana, that would be the first order of business, even if she had to enlist Dušan to help her.

She got up and tucked the comforter over in a half-assed attempt to cover Rok's sleeping form. She'd forgotten how twisted a bed with a top sheet could get. Her robe was crumpled on the floor where she'd left it when she'd gotten dressed to escape into town. After all the paperwork at the hospital. After the confrontation with Jackie in the kitchen that they had both stomped away from, slamming as many doors as possible between them.

Jo could stay mad at Jackie forever, or she could figure out a way to forgive her and start cleaning up the mess she was making of the part of her life that didn't have anything to do with shades or old gods. It wouldn't serve her or Jackie to isolate themselves from the remnants of their family.

The smells of coffee and fried food wafted up the stairs with some full-throated, Southern rock guitar when Jo opened the bedroom door. She took a deep breath. She wouldn't apologize, but she would try to mend. Then she would have to explain that she had an unexpected guest.

Jackie stood at the stove, turning bacon in a cast-iron skillet. "I figured we could both use some breakfast. It's going to be a long day."

"I won't do that thing you do."

"What thing?" Jackie continued to address the stove while she lifted the contents of the skillet onto a paper towel with a fork.

"That thing where we pretend nothing happened."

Jackie turned to face her then, fork still in hand. "What good would have come of me telling a child that her mother had murdered her father?"

"I haven't been a child for a long time."

"Jesus, Jolene, I didn't have any proof."

"But you knew it. You believed it enough to get me away from her."

Jackie nodded. "I was afraid she would hurt you too."

And she had. Mary's rages in the days after her father's funeral had been terrifying. She had screamed at Jo with every other breath, she had shaken or slapped her for not having answers to questions Jo didn't even understand. Her mother had thrown things, including all the mismatched plates from the cupboards. Jo had walked into the kitchen and a shard of stoneware had hit her in the face, missing her eye but opening a cut above her cheekbone.

Mary had stilled at Jo's cry. She had stared at her for a long minute before walking out of the kitchen. She had walked right out of the house, gotten into the car, and driven away.

Jo had sat on the kitchen floor among the pieces of broken plates with a wad of paper towel pressed against her face until Jackie had showed up and taken her to the hospital for stitches. She never went back to her mother's house after that.

"Thank you."

"For what?" Her aunt looked taken aback at the change in tone.

"You rescued me. I get it." Jo slid onto a bar stool and watched her aunt fiddle with the fork before looking up again. "But after today, no more secrets."

Jackie nodded and turned back to the stove. She cracked eggs into the skillet. They sizzled as they hit the hot bacon fat, and her aunt reached over to turn down the music on her phone.

A cough announced Rok's presence behind her.

"Aunt Jackie, meet my friend ... " What name was Rok using now?

Jackie turned to the counter to slide the sunny-side-up eggs onto a plate. They slid straight to the floor as her aunt's eyes went wide with surprise.

"Michael?"

"It's Harry. Sorry to startle you." He jammed his hands in his pockets and hunched his shoulders.

Harry? Jo was not going to call him that. It was too ridiculous.

Jackie stuttered through her own apology and grabbed a roll of paper towels to clean up the eggs and bacon fat.

"Did you burn yourself?" Jo came around the counter and joined Jackie on her knees sopping up yolk and grease. "I'm sorry, it just kind of happened. We ran into each other."

"It's fine. He just looks exactly like someone I used to know."

He probably was someone Jackie used to know. Jo stood up with a wad of paper towel in her hand and gave Rok, who would never be Harry, a narrow-eyed glare.

Rok shrugged and mouthed, "I'll explain later. Promise."

The Outlaws quietly grinding out "Green Grass and High Tides" in the background struck Jo as just the right amount of what-the-fuck for the moment.

CHAPTER 10

Vesna wrapped her hair up into a messy bun. She needed to wash it, but she didn't want to take the time to dry it. She slid in under the hot water and savored a moment of calm. Igor hadn't stayed the night. He had a gallery opening in Maribor and wouldn't be back until late that evening. She'd missed him, but it was also nice to have the flat to herself for a bit.

She'd spent the evening curled up on the couch with Antony and Cleopatra nuzzling against her ankles, purring, happy to have her all to themselves. She'd thought about watching television on her computer, but she'd hated to interrupt the silence. Instead she'd selected a book from the pile of refresher reading Leo had loaned her.

When she'd told her father she had no interest in being a witchfinder, she'd stopped paying attention to that world almost completely. She hadn't forgotten everything he'd drilled into her head as a child—no one could have, with him constantly railing about everything from yoga to Satanism overtaking the United States and threatening them all—but she'd tried to dismiss as much of it as possible.

The water in the shower seemed warmer than usual. She

tapped the dial to adjust it down a bit. The steam and the warmth were making her light-headed.

Images from the book she'd chosen popped up, unbidden, in her mind's eye. Gruesome drawings of haunted souls with hollowed-out eyes roaming the open spaces of a forest, looking for an unsuspecting person to possess. She shook off the image, but not the thought that the unsatisfied dead meant the living harm. It was a nearly universal belief, cutting across cultures and geographies.

A tiny part of her wished that dealing in the supernatural was more about unicorns and helpful woodland creatures who hung out your laundry for you in the night. The Hollywood versions of fairytale had a lot to answer for, but most people would never know the truth of it. And those who longed for an enchanted life had no idea what the reality they wished for looked like up close and personal. If nature was red in tooth and claw, the supernatural was doubly so.

She dressed quickly and grabbed her shopping bags on the way out. Fred would be waiting downstairs for her to go with him to the market for the teahouse. She'd never bothered with it before, as Jo did most of the ordering and buying. It was one of the few administrative things she enjoyed.

It was possible these tasks Vesna had taken on would become more permanent. Maybe the best thing for Jo where the Board and their meddling was concerned would be to disappear for a bit. She wished she knew how to contact Rok. He'd be the perfect person to whisk her away, if Jo could forgive him.

Vesna snorted to herself. Jo might be able to forgive Rok, but Leo would never forgive her if Vesna were the one responsible for sending his lady love out into the world with another man.

There might not be a choice.

The thought was clear, and that it registered so made her antennae twitch as a chill crept up the back of her neck. Someone or something had a message for her.

She shook it off and hurried down the last steps to the courtyard where Fred was absentmindedly looking up at the square of sky the roof line allowed.

———

Faron had offered to walk Ivanka to work. He'd been quiet over the last couple of days, and she was happy he wanted her company. He held her hand as they nipped through the shortcut from their block of flats into Tivoli park. The cool morning air was heavy with the scents of late spring, a mishmash of high floral notes over the clean melody of grass and dew.

The park was full of families with small children enjoying the clear Saturday weather, and prams crunched along the manicured gravel path. The teahouse would be busy later. Ivanka had finally convinced Vesna to let her set up a few tables in the courtyard so people could sit outside. Jo had always been hesitant because of the noise. The courtyard amplified sound, and conversations outside the shop easily floated to all the floors above.

Now that nobody lived in the building but "family," Vesna had given her the green light. If Goran or Gustaf or Dušan wanted to complain, they knew exactly where to go to do it.

Faron stopped her in the underground ramp that led up

to the small square in front of the Museum of Modern Art. He leaned against the wall and pulled her into him for a kiss.

Being a few minutes late was worth his unexpected attention, and she forgot about her to-do list and drank him in.

He came up for air and ran his hand over her temple. His eyes had changed. They were still a stormy blue-gray like his mother's, but they had taken on a new quality, as if they were flecked with silver. It wasn't obvious or dazzlingly sparkly, but it was hard to miss. The mind behind them was different, too, but that had happened the night his mother and her sister had ended up in the river.

It was a strange irony that the Faron who peered out at her seemed to have aged decades, but the face those lovely eyes were set in would never change. She still didn't fully comprehend how a man became a god. Didn't the god have to be in there all along? Half of Faron's DNA had always been from Dušan. She added several new questions to her list for Goran for their lesson and hike the next day.

"What does your day look like?" Faron ran his hands down her sides and rested them at her waist.

"Fred and Vesna are going to the market this morning, so I'll start prep and then process whatever they bring back." She ran her thumb over his lips. "And what are you up to today?"

"I'm meeting with Dušan, and then I need to work on a paper."

It amused her that he had insisted on finishing his degree. He would have several lifetimes to read and travel, an undergraduate degree hardly seemed necessary, but he'd said it would keep things as close to normal as they had been.

"What does Dušan want to talk about?" She tried not to sound too interested. Her concern, more accurately her worry, about his father being shady frustrated Faron.

"He didn't say. He only asked if I would have some time this morning." He pushed off the wall and took both of her hands. "We should get going."

She nodded and continued to hold one of his hands as they walked into the central city.

Dušan was waiting for them in the courtyard. She offered to make them some tea, but they both refused and headed out onto Zajčeva. She unlocked the door and locked it back behind her before walking to the tea counter and fiddling with the iPod that held the shop playlists.

Vesna had added some new music by moods. Ivanka scrolled down to "Contemplative" and pushed Play.

It was definitely a different vibe than Jo's lists or the ones Reka had put together for after they closed. Ivanka started a pot of strong tea for herself and checked the prep list Fred had taped to the front of the reach-in the day before. She pulled out the *mise* for currant scones before returning to the tea station to pour her morning dose into a staff mug. An unfamiliar voice, raw on the edge of emotion, drifted out over a plaintive piano offering an image of death looking down on everyone like a pale moon in a sunny sky.

The lyric stuck in her conscience like a straight pin. Death was inevitable and inescapable, unless you were Dušan or Faron.

She needed to tell Leo.

———

Faron walked in silence beside his father until they made their way to the river then followed the embankment toward *Trnovo*. A few people noticed Dušan and looked away quickly. Faron didn't understand why someone who had to hide what he was had done so much to make himself famous. Maybe it was easier to hide in plain sight?

"How are your Ivanka and her sisters?" Dušan pierced the silence that Faron preferred to empty chit-chat with his father, or with anyone, for that matter.

"She is hardly mine, and I think they're fine. Goran keeps them busy, but I think he is kind to them as well. They've all earned some kindness." Ivanka especially. She carried the weight of being the oldest.

"Ivanka is the measurer."

"What does that mean?" Faron stopped as they reached the canal and looked at his father. Dušan could sense his mood, but he could no longer read his thoughts now that they were on more even footing.

"The three sisters. Ivanka is the measurer. From what I know of Veronika, she is the cutter. And that leaves young Ana as the spinner."

Ivanka and her sisters were not the Fates, they were a trio of witch sisters. "I don't understand."

"Your girlfriend and her siblings are not the Moirae of legend, but like the weird sisters, they have talents that reflect the Fates. Ana is the spinner. She will have an affinity for the natural world, some ability to communicate with animals, among other traits."

"I guess that makes sense, but what about the measurer and, you said, the cutter?"

"As the measurer, Ivanka will know the length of life and be able to see into time, the gift of prophecy or sight. A heavy burden." Dušan shook his head.

"And Veronika?"

A woman with a pram filled with a bundle of blankets with a tiny pink face passed between them and the balustrade marking the edge of the pavement above the canal. Her gaze flickered to Dušan and then away. Faron half expected her to start humming an "I'm just here minding my own business" tune.

"You already know the answer to that one. Veronika wields the scissors that cut the thread of life. She is a very powerful witch. A witch who can kill can cure as well. As the one who wields the scissors, she will be able to prolong life or end it."

"Does Goran know this?"

"Certainly. Does he believe it in his bones? Not yet, but he will come to."

"What does that mean?"

"It means that the menagerie your mother has assembled, however unwittingly, is a problem."

"For who?" Faron watched his father's face to see if he could learn more from his expression than from his words, but there was nothing to glean.

"Have you had breakfast?" Dušan walked on.

The church bells rang out the hour. With the morning sunshine, the leafed-out trees and scattered blooms, and the foot traffic hurrying along, Faron had the fleeting feeling of being on a film set rather than the familiar streets of his old neighborhood. His life had taken on a layer of fantasy or magical realism, so perhaps feeling distant from it wasn't that surprising.

"I could eat." Faron followed in his father's wake. He wasn't going to get anything more from Dušan on the subject of his girlfriend and her witchy sisters.

Outside the Trnovo church, Dušan stopped to read the plaque honoring the place where Slovenia's national poet, France Prešeren, had met his muse Julija. Faron knew the story as well as anyone who grew up in Ljubljana would. Prešeren had seen Julija at a church service, but she was much younger and under the protective care of her parents. He pined for her, dedicating much of his work to her, but she never returned his affection. Now he stared at her from across the square where his statue took pride of place, looking for all eternity at a bust of her framed by a bronze window casing on a nearby building. Maybe it was romantic, but Faron came down on the side of maybe it was creepy.

"I brought your mother here once." Dušan interrupted Faron's thoughts.

Great. A dating story about his parents. Everyone's favorite thing ever.

"She had lived in Ljubljana for a couple years by then but hadn't seen much outside of clubs and classrooms." Dušan continued to look at the front of the church, as if he was searching for something. "It was a romantic gesture on my part, the story of Prešeren and Julija." His father tilted his head at the plaque.

Faron wondered about the real reason they were out for a stroll and now, he guessed, breakfast.

"Ivanka understands you will not age, you will not die?"

"Yes. As best as any one of us can. I'm not sure I even really understand it."

"You will, but only with time."

An elderly woman with her hair tied in a pale floral scarf waddled down the steps from the church, her lace-up shoes straining to contain her thickened ankles and feet. She startled when she saw the two of them standing there. She made the sign of the cross and hurried away talking to herself and the few pigeons gathered on the edge of the street. "Črnobog and Belinus standing in Trnovo as plain as you please."

Dušan chuckled. "The Veil is thinning." Then he walked on past the Plečnik house in search of breakfast.

Victoria Raschke

CHAPTER 11

Jo sat on the balcony with Helena, looking out over the late-morning sun glinting off the river. After an awkward breakfast, Jackie had insisted that Rok, who would never be Harry, check out of his hotel and join them at the house. He'd happily disappeared to collect his things, and Jo welcomed the few moments to regroup.

"Do you think Rok is Michael's father?" Helena was enjoying the skin-crawling possibility that Jackie and Jo had sexed up the same man.

"But how?" Michael was seven years younger than she. Where could Jackie and Rok possibly have met?

"Well, clearly he's been around long enough." Helena smiled at her.

"Stop it." Jo pulled her knees up and put her chin on them. It was all too sordid to think about, but she would drag a confession out of him when he returned. They were due for a long and possibly ugly conversation. And she hadn't even shared her mother's revelation with him yet.

After grilling Rok, Jo and Jackie had to tend to all the

things dying in the South required. Jackie had relented on the full-on funeral. Mary had no friends to speak of, and it would be depressing to sit in an empty church. Jackie, on the other hand, had lots of friends, and several had come by with casseroles, pasta salads, and mostly store-bought baked goods after breakfast.

She and Jackie had an appointment to purchase a coffin. Wiley women were only buried in old-fashioned pine boxes, and Jackie had spent the previous afternoon calling around to funeral homes trying to find one that had them and that then didn't try to convince her to spring for a supposedly more luxurious, sealed coffin to keep the elements out for as long as possible. The thought of her mother surrounded for eternity by polyester "satinette" in a soup of her own making was too gross. Besides, returning to the elements was the point of burial.

Jackie had written an obituary and emailed it to the paper. Jo was supposed to call the pastor at the church next to the family graveyard to arrange for burial and a simple graveside service the next day. Pastors weren't usually her thing, but she'd come to an understanding with religion, or at least with faith. Rev. Lightfoot must be ancient though. He'd done the service for her father and had looked like the creepy minister from *Poltergeist* then.

"Are you going to sit like that all morning?" Helena pierced her thoughts, most likely wanting to continue to poke at Jo's squicked-out feelings about the whole Rok/Harry/Michael thing.

"No. I need to make a phone call." Jo slid her feet to the smooth wood of the balcony decking and stood up. She pulled her kimono around her and headed back inside.

Helena followed her. "I'm sorry if you think I'm being mean, it's just that—"

"It's just that now I should understand better why you didn't have a problem with shacking up with me and, very separately, with my son?" The thought of it still made Jo a little queasy, but she had forgiven Helena her trespasses in life, as well as the few that had occurred since. "I do, but that doesn't mean I relish the idea of Jackie and Rok getting it on at some point or the idea that I grew up with Rok's son and that Rok then acted like a father to my son." How had her life gotten so weirdly complicated?

"It will be fine. You are all still the same people." Helena smiled at her again, an attempt to be reassuring. Reassuring wasn't exactly Helena's best look.

Jo may have looked like the same person she was before her mother had confessed to murder like she was confessing to leaving the iron on, but she wasn't. The day her father died, something had cracked inside her. It had happened again when Dušan told her he was leaving. She could have sworn she had heard something rattling around inside her the whole time she was pregnant. She'd felt that old fracture widen as her mother's words sank in. She might look the same on the outside, but the inside was damaged.

"I'm going to take a shower. Then I am going to call Rev. Lightfoot and see about a backhoe and a prayer." Jo shrugged off her kimono and stepped into the bathroom.

When she came out, toweling her hair, Helena was sitting on the edge of the bed.

"Can you make yourself useful?" Jo bent over and wrapped the towel around her hair before standing up and tucking the ends under the back.

"I can't make phone calls for you, but I'm guessing that's not what you had in mind." Helena patted the duvet. Jo plopped down next to her.

"No, I can do that. Can you find out things?" She watched Helena's expression out of the corner of her eye. Why hadn't she thought to ask her guide before?

"What kind of things?" A note of suspicion crept into Helena's voice.

"Can you figure out where Milo is? I need to find him when we get back to Ljubljana, and I'd rather not involve Dušan if I don't have to."

"Funny you should mention that … I have been looking for him. Or at least keeping an eye out for him. Maybe he crossed that night?" Helena was trying that voice of reason thing again. It wasn't so much disingenuous as it was ineffectual.

"Maybe, but my gut says no." As did the dream she'd had that morning.

"I'll see what else I can do." Helena put her arm around Jo's shoulders.

Jo shrugged her off. "Second thing. You don't have to pretend to be something you aren't. I appreciate the effort, but grief counseling and nurturing really don't suit you."

Helena laughed her sparkling laugh. "I know, but you do seem dejected. And maybe I teased too much about Rok, or whatever his name is." She put her hand on Jo's thigh; her touch was cold but comforting.

"It's Rok. I have no intention of calling him Harry." Jo snorted and got up. "Thank you for looking, though, even before I asked."

"All part of the gig, for as long as you'll have me." Helena waved then disappeared as if she'd never even been in the room. Jo stood looking at the empty spot on the bed and wondered how long she *would* have Helena. Did she really get to make the choice? Was she keeping her from something infinitely better?

A soft knock at the door interrupted her thoughts.

"Come in."

Jackie opened the door and leaned on the jamb. "Have you called Rev. Lightfoot?"

"Not yet. I just got out of the shower and was talking with Helena."

Jackie made a disapproving face, all narrowed eyes and pursed lips.

"We've been through a lot together." To hell and back even.

"That's the problem. Your spirit guide should have a little more distance and perspective." Jackie shrugged. "But I won't argue with you anymore about it."

"Thank you."

"I'll let you get dressed. Hopefully your friend Henry or Harry or whatever his name is, will get back soon. We need to go pay for the coffin and arrange transportation to the graveyard."

"It's Harry, though it doesn't suit him. So, who is this person he looks like? Not Michael's father? I mean with the name and—"

"No. I met him before I met Michael's father, but Michael is named after him. We met on a trail in the Smokies. He was through-hiking the AT. The sky opened up out of nowhere, freak summer storm, and a bunch of us wound up waiting it out in a ramshackle shelter. He was this interested guy with an interesting accent, and, well …" Jackie was off in the middle-distance, reminiscing about nothing Jo wanted to know about.

Jackie snapped back to the present. "He spent a few days with me in Chattanooga then left. Quite the memorable impression." She smiled at the thought.

"So not Michael's dad. Check."

"It is funny that we have the same taste in men."

Jo threw her head back and let out a huge sigh.

"Sorry. Didn't mean to offend you." Jackie crossed her arms over her breasts and tilted her head at Jo.

"He's the same man, Jackie. He's Harry, and Michael, and my friend Rok from Ljubljana, and god only knows how many other names he's had over the years. Or centuries."

"I thought Rok was Slovenian." Rok and Jackie had never crossed paths on her few visits to Slovenia. Rok had been on the road traveling as much as, if not more than, he had been in town before disappearing altogether.

"Yeah. So did I."

"So, is he a Long-Lived?" Understanding dawned on her aunt's tired face.

"Maybe. Or he could be immortal. I have no idea, but I plan

on dragging it out of him when he gets back. I'm just glad he's not Michael's dad. I don't think I could have stomached that."

Jackie scrunched up her nose. "Well, kiddo, at least he's got good taste in women." Jackie leaned in and kissed her on the cheek. "Get dressed. You can put him through the inquisition when we get back from the funeral home."

CHAPTER 12

Leo watched as Goran and the Novak sisters piled out of Goran's bright-green hatchback. Each of them dipped into the back for a bag and walked up the hill toward where he stood in front of Teja and Luka's house. He had spent the last day burning chicken carcasses and scrubbing the floors. Teja had offered to come back from Ljubljana to help, but he needed to do it alone, especially if she believed he had brought this upon them.

Goran shook Leo's hand and reintroduced him to the younger sisters, Veronika and Ana.

Ana looked up at him. "You are still very tall, Mr. Kos."

Leo laughed. "Yes, I am. And you can call me Leo."

Goran shepherded his charges toward the front door and turned to Leo. "Thank you for cleaning up the mess. I think it would have been too traumatic for Veronika and Ana. They were there, you know, when their father …"

Leo did know. He'd blessed the Novak house at Gustaf's request before the cleaners had arrived, in case there was any lingering baleful magic. The magic at Teja and Luka's had dissipated, but Goran had insisted on cleansing and warding the cottage before the couple returned. Leo didn't disagree with him.

Goran gave each sister a small iron brazier suspended on a triple-chain handle and lit a circular charcoal briquette in each bowl before adding a few beads of frankincense resin.

"Walk around each room clockwise and fan the smoke with your hand. Then come outside and walk around the house." Goran looked back to Leo. "Do you have holy water?"

Leo nodded and patted the front pocket of his jeans.

Goran continued his instructions. "I'll go after the girls, then you can bless each room."

Ivanka entered first but looked back at Leo with an expression he couldn't parse. Her sisters followed her, and he and Goran waited outside.

"Vesna tells me you aren't sure about Ana's abilities."

Goran ran his hand down his beard and looked up at him. "I wish I hadn't said that. I have no doubt Ana is a witch, or perhaps something more, but I don't think I can teach her anything."

"What does that mean?" Leo had only intended to make small talk while they waited for the girls to smoke the house, but he'd touched a nerve.

"She's the most naturally gifted of the three, but it's a wild, natural magic. She's going to have to get a handle on it quickly, or it will get her in trouble." Goran shrugged. "She can talk to spirits and slide into the In-Between with a thought. God only knows what else. And I have no ability to do those things or stop her from doing it."

"She can talk to spirits like Jo or like Helena's mother?" There were witches who could call up the spirits of the dead, but it was advanced magic.

"Neither. She can slip into the In-Between like a cat or a house spirit. She doesn't see any danger in it, and she won't listen to my warnings about what she could meet there."

"Is it you or her?"

Goran laughed. "It hadn't occurred to me that it could be me. Do you want to talk to her?"

"You're asking the local Witchfinder to help you train up your wild baby witch?" It was an odd prospect.

"You are no more the Witchfinder than I am a dolphin."

"I'm sure my father and brother just rolled over in their graves." They had both heartily embraced the Witchfinder role and happily acted as judge, jury, and executioner.

"You aren't them, Leo. I'm grateful for that. We need a protector on this side of the Veil, not another persecutor." Goran watched as the sisters emerged. Ivanka and Veronika were taking the task seriously. Ana followed them, skipping.

"Another?" Leo waited while Goran appeared to be forming his thoughts.

"I know you and Gustaf have come to some kind of detente, if only because of Jo, but don't expect anyone else from the Board to be so accepting."

"I know how Valter and my father felt about Observers and the Board—"

"They only disliked the interference in their work, but whatever Gustaf thinks his job is, his charge is to put down anything, or anyone, who threatens the peaceful sleep of mundanes."

A chill ran down Leo's spine. "He is very fatherly with Jo."

"Jo isn't the only citizen of the Veil under Gustaf's watch." Goran looked down at the path leading to the front door and back up at Leo before walking away.

Leo followed him into the cottage and blessed the peace and calm of the house and its inhabitants, hoping some of that blessing would calm his own thoughts.

———

Ivanka pulled a jacket out of her bag and spread it out to sit on the ground in the front garden. Leo made his way around the outside of the cottage, stopping to bless each window. In her mind's eye, he would always be the tall priest in the long black robes. Maybe that person would always be there, under the façade of his street clothes. People couldn't change who they were, not completely. There was always an outline or imprint of who they were before. She clung to that as she watched Faron change into a stranger in some ways, believing her Faron was still in there, under there.

Veronika packed up Goran's house-blessing supplies. Ana skipped off into the woods behind the cottage. Goran called after her to stay close, but Ana was already in her bubble. She had no more heard what Goran said than she cared how bramble-scratched and muddied she would be when she found her way back to them.

Ivanka had no worries about her sister getting lost in the woods. She wouldn't, though Ivanka would have been hard-pressed to offer any concrete evidence for how she knew that. She took a deep breath and closed her eyes, listening to Leo's even cadence as he prayed. The leaves whispered in the breeze, and there was a moment of peace.

It came to her again, the image of Leo, falling away, leaving this world. The image was different this time though. Ana skipped through as Leo was dying. She skipped straight into the arms of a waiting shadow of a person, twisted and dark against the bright dream.

"Ivanka!" Goran's voice brought her back to the moment.

She opened her eyes to his worried face.

"Where did you go?"

"Nowhere. I was sitting here waiting on everyone to finish."

Goran's frowned down at her. "Your eyes rolled back in your head. I wanted to make sure you weren't having a seizure or something."

She shook her head. "I'm fine. But I have to tell him."

"Are you sure that's the best course of action?"

"Intellectually? No. But my gut says yes." She stood up and stretched her back.

Goran put his hand on her arm. "It's very important to remember that you are not the cause of the things you see."

"I didn't think that was how the Fates worked." She smiled, a little ruefully, at him, and bent over to pick up her jacket.

"You and your sisters aren't the Fates. You're—"

"I know." She walked toward Leo, rehearsing in her mind how she could tell someone she'd watched them die, twice.

"I think we're done. Should we send out the trackers for

Ana?" Leo smiled at her. His mood had lightened since their arrival and the completion of their task. Ivanka hadn't realized he felt responsible or had some guilt about what had happened, but it was clear now.

"She'll find her way back when she's ready." Despite the scary vision, she still wasn't worried about Ana. Whatever that dark thing was, her sister didn't seem to be afraid of it. "Can we talk? Privately."

"Sure. I have something for Goran in my room. Walk with me up the hill?"

"You know when I slid in the kitchen the other day and you caught my arm?" It wasn't the best opener, but she had to start somewhere.

"I'm sorry if I was inappropriate. I know some people don't like to be touched. I just didn't want you to fall."

"No. Thank you for that. My reaction wasn't because of what you did. I saw something." She hesitated. "Something I wasn't sure if I should tell you."

Leo stopped and turned to look at her.

"I don't know how much Goran has told you, but my gift seems to be the sight."

"He did tell me, and I'm sorry. It's a heavy burden."

"Yeah. Look, I don't know how to say this or even if I should, but I saw you die. And I saw it again just now in some trance-like state that freaked out Goran. He said it was up to me to tell you. That it would either serve as a warning or it could be a self-fulfilling prophecy, if you took it that way."

Leo's expression was unchanged.

"I wasn't going to tell you, but seeing it again made it seem important." Ivanka looked down; the toes of her Chucks were hidden in the grass.

"Thank you. I don't have the sight, but my dreams have been disturbed, and Teja thinks the Unseen, as she calls it, is unsettled. I think you just confirmed there is a danger near." He smiled at her again in that mirthless way he had done from the balcony. "We should all be aware."

"Are you worried?" His face was so hard to read.

"Not worried, but vigilant. It's a constant in my line of work." He gave her a genuine smile and continued walking toward the main house.

Apparently it would be a constant for her as well.

———

Ana ducked under a low branch and picked her way through the undergrowth to a natural clearing in the wood. Fallen leaves and the long needles of evergreen trees made a matted carpet large enough for even Mr. Kos to lie down on.

The sun was warm where it had space to find its way through the trees, and she stretched out on the ground to let the light fall on her face. Ana closed her eyes and listened. Small animals of the forest twittered and scurried in the bramble just out of sight—not wary, but curious.

A presence sat beside her on the ground. She knew it was her friend, but he seemed upset. She opened her eyes and looked up at his worried face.

"Ana, you shouldn't be so careless in this place." She liked his voice, it was deep and steady like a drumbeat in a song.

"The animals know me here."

"It isn't the animals you need to worry about." He shimmered in the bright sunlight, like a reflection on water. He was solid but not, and she knew she could touch him but didn't. That would be rude.

"Is it the thing that killed all of Mr. Kos's friends' chickens?" She didn't like that something had hurt them. The chickens hadn't done anything wrong.

"I think so."

Ana sat up and crossed her legs. "Do you think it will come back?"

"Yes. It's an angry thing." Her friend turned and faced her. "I don't want you or your sisters to get hurt."

"Can we stop it or bottle it up like a demon?"

"How do you know these things?"

"Books. They are mostly boring, but they have more in them than Goran tells me." She sighed and pulled the zipper up on her sweater. The sun had decided to hide behind a cloud, and her friend always made the air around him cold.

"I don't know how to stop it."

"I'll be careful." She pushed herself up off the ground. "But what about you? Can it hurt you?"

He looked up at her. His eyes were always dark and kind of sunken, but now they were sad. He shrugged and looked off into the trees.

She didn't know how to cheer up a ghost. "I'll be careful, I promise, and I'll tell my sisters to be careful too."

CHAPTER 13

Jo climbed into the backseat of the Town Car next to Rok. Jackie had already claimed the front seat next to the driver and was buckling herself in.

Rok took Jo's hand. She had forgiven him as much as she could. He was what he was. She wasn't sure if she'd be forgiven by Leo or that she would be able to forgive herself if her return to an old pattern with Rok had ruined whatever chance she and Leo had. Still, she was glad Rok was there; she needed a tether she could touch.

Michael scooted in on the other side and closed his door. The driver turned and nodded at them and waited for the hearse in front to begin the journey to the graveyard in Polk County. At least they had all agreed that they didn't need to drive at funeral procession speed. There weren't any other cars behind them.

A quick service at the graveside and back to Jackie's for lunch—that was the plan. Enough food had appeared to keep them fed for a month. It was one of the strange things Jo hadn't realized she missed about the place she grew up. After her father's funeral, and again when her grandmother died, people had brought food to them for weeks.

Then, everything had been homemade, and Jackie's best friend had brought rosemary pound cake both times. For remembrance, she had said. The pound cake had showed up again the previous night, to honor Mary's death, with air kisses in a cloud of powdered scent. The sweetness of a Southern woman could be as fake as a rubber snake, but when the kindness was real, it was fierce.

The driver turned off the highway to the back roads that would lead them to the white clapboard church Jo had been dreaming of and dreading. The pavement on the other side of the road was faded and had a dripped pattern of tar to seal the cracks. It stretched out for miles and looked like Fred's swirling Arabic hand. She imagined it was a prayer, or maybe instructions that she couldn't read but desperately needed to decipher.

Rok squeezed her hand, and she turned from the window and her thoughts and smiled at him. She welcomed his calm as she tried to process what her mother's confession meant. There wasn't any love to be lost between them, but Mary's admission had revealed her father's secret-keeping, and Jackie's. He could have told Jo the truth when he'd come to her as a shade in Ljubljana. Had he been more willing to sacrifice himself for her because of what had happened between him and Mary? Did it matter? Jo still needed to find him and bring him back from that horrible place, but she was angry with him now too. What else had he kept from her?

"When are you going back to Ljubljana?" Rok laced his fingers in hers as he asked.

"I'll be here a couple more days." She wanted to be home,

but home held another set of worries—least of all how she and Leo would continue to dance around their feelings for each other. He wouldn't be happy if Rok followed her back, but maybe Leo would understand. She hoped he would understand. "Where are you going from here?"

"I have a few things I need to take care of, and then I plan to go to Ljubljana."

"To stay for a bit or for a visit?"

"Mm. Unknown?" He half-shrugged against her shoulder.

Jo whispered in his ear. "Will you be there as Rok or as Harry?"

"Rok."

Jo nodded and laid her head back against the leather headrest. She closed her eyes and fell into a light sleep for the rest of the ride to Benton.

Rok nudged her awake as the hearse and the Town Car pulled into the empty gravel lot in front of the small church. Rev. Lightfoot and Rebecca, dressed impeccably in a pantsuit the color of fresh milk, stood on the front steps leading to the sanctuary. It appeared that they had teleported; there weren't any other cars, and it was a bit of a walk from anywhere.

Jackie shook hands with the minister, nodded at Rebecca, and turned back to look at the hearse as the driver swung open the rear door. "Well, shit. We don't have enough pallbearers."

"Miss Wiley, I would thank you to not use such language on the steps of the Lord's house." Rev. Lightfoot glared at Jackie with a look that would have withered the healthiest of blooms.

The minister's visage had moved straight from creepy Poltergeist preacher to the Crypt Keeper.

Jackie mumbled a half-assed apology, which frankly surprised Jo. Her aunt didn't take to being censored, even by clergy.

Jo, Rok, Michael, Rebecca, and the two drivers wound up bearing Mary to her final resting place, where the edges of the freshly dug grave and the mound of excavated dirt had been covered with bright-green outdoor carpeting. A darkly comic image of the six of them dropping her mother's casket, and Mary's husk of a body tumbling out like something from a Faulkner novel, gave Jo the worst case of church giggles she'd had in a long time, at least since Maja's funeral at *Žale*. But the image of Maja's death, her neck circled with a chain of purpled bruises, sobered Jo right back up.

After the casket was placed on the boards over the hole in the ground, Rev. Lightfoot asked them to bow their heads in prayer. Jo stood next to Jackie, with her aunt's warm sweaty hand in her cold one. Everyone except Jo, Rebecca, and Rev. Crypt Keeper had a healthy sheen on their brows as the sun beat down on them for the longest graveside service in the history of burials.

The good reverend said his final amen, and two men Jo had spotted walking up during the extended soul-saving attempt, shovels in hand, pulled the chucks out from under the casket. They all stayed to watch as the box was lowered by remote control into the ground. Jackie lifted a corner of the green carpeting on the mound and scooped up a handful of dirt. Rebecca did the same, and Jo followed. Each woman dropped crumbles of the damp orange clay onto the brass plaque bearing Mary's birth and death dates.

Rebecca whispered under her breath. "May you find peace in the Next, granddaughter."

Her ancestor's words chipped away at a crack in the plaster that Jo had been layering over her feelings since that first night at Mary's deathbed. Fat tears stung as they ran down her face. It wasn't sorrow for her or for Jackie or even for Rebecca, it was anger at whatever being or deity or chaotic grouping of coincidences had cursed her family to walk the Earth marked by their association with death.

Jo was the first to turn away, back toward the church and the cars, but she stopped at her Grandmother Rose's grave. Rose's death had seemed like a personal affront to Jo after losing her father. Rose had stopped at a traffic accident on the highway on her way to Jackie's house for lunch on a random Sunday. She'd been struck by a car as she tried to help the occupants of one of the vehicles, and she died at the hospital in Chattanooga later that night. Maybe that was her war and the driver had been her soldier, come to take her out before she could age.

Rebecca joined her at Rose's grave as the others walked past. Michael took his mother's hand. For the first time in Jo's life, Jackie looked fragile.

"Rose was a remarkable woman. She never went to the places of the embattled and wandering dead like we have done, but she made it her purpose to care for the dying and take their last words, often given after they had passed, to their loved ones." Rebecca laid a single yellow rose on top of the headstone.

"Why does Jackie dislike you so much?" Jo looked around

at the other graves and the other yellow roses Rebecca must have placed.

"I came for Rose. Jackie begged me not to take her mother from her, from you."

"That's not how Death works, is it?" Jo waited for an answer, assuming that as with everything else she'd asked, she'd get another question or another puzzle to untangle.

"No. It isn't how Death works for most. I will come for Jackie and Michael, and the two drivers, and even Rev. Lightfoot someday. But, Jo, you must know now that Death will never come for Faron."

The tears ran hotter as she nodded her understanding.

"Or you."

CHAPTER 14

Vesna knocked lightly on Dušan's door. She really hoped he was out. She hoped he was gone, maybe forever. Though that was her dark heart wish, she needed him now.

The door opened, revealing Dušan dressed as crisply as always. Did he sit around his apartment in a suit, shirt pressed to a knife's edge at the collar? Of course he didn't. Before she knocked he was probably lounging on the couch in his god-form version of boxers, pondering his next move. Jo would have appreciated the image.

"I was expecting you." He waved her in.

"I'm sure you were." She closed the door behind her.

It was the first time she had been in Dušan's apartment, which was very similarly laid out to Jo's—except with a bigger main area and bathroom. An adjoining studio had been incorporated years before for the previous tenants.

Dušan offered her a seat in one of the plush chairs in the living area and disappeared into the kitchen. "Would you prefer red or white?"

"White is fine. Thank you." Vesna couldn't relax, and her

eyes darted around the flat. Dušan's decorating style wasn't as stark as Jo's, but it was very minimalist—except for the art.

The apartment looked like a chic gallery. There were a few paintings, but mostly there were photographs, and mostly those taken by other photographers. It was easy to tell, as they were in color and featured more landscapes and people than Dušan's more famous photographs.

Then there was a triptych of woman in an orchard. It hung on the wall that made up the long side of the L that delineated the bathroom from the rest of the flat. The three photos were black and white, but they gleamed like glass-plate prints or tintypes.

Vesna stood and crossed the room to get a better look. The first photo was a woman with her hair in a thick braid, walking through the trees in a vintage dress—something from the 1940s by the cut and fabric pattern. Her back was to the photographer, her right arm outstretched and her fingers slightly open as if she were caressing the fruit as she walked by.

In the second photo, the woman was naked, her hair shaken loose and wild. She was seated at the base of a tree with her head turned so the curtain of her hair covered her face.

The last photo was of the woman lying on the ground under a tree. Dappled light played over her skin, and an apple had fallen into the tangle of her hair spread out around her like a crown. The woman's eyes were open and staring directly into the camera with a knowing, pleased look on her face. A tattooed snake wound its way from her upper arm across her shoulder and nestled its smooth head just inside her collarbone.

It was Jo.

"We had the perfect light that day." Dušan handed Vesna wine in a hand-blown glass as fine as a soap bubble and looked at the last photo with her.

She turned to Dušan as if she were seeing him for the first time. "You were in love with her."

"A part of me will always be. But gods and mortals, those relationships never work out."

Vesna couldn't tell if he was being funny or if he was lying.

"She called you then? Rebecca told her. I asked her not to." Dušan took a sip of his wine as calmly as if what he spoke about were as mundane as the wine in his hand.

"Were you going to tell her that you knocking her up made her immortal? Or were you just going to let that ride until everyone else popped off around her?" Vesna's dislike of the man resurfaced with a vengeance. "Were you just going to continue to toy with her?" Vesna moved away from him, back toward the door.

"What do you think the purpose of a Voice is, or a Portal, for that matter? How do you think such a thing as a Voice came to be in the world?"

Vesna clutched her wine glass in both hands. The question had never occurred to her. Voices and Portals simply were, like trees or mountains.

"Now, Vesna, I know you think about the world more deeply than that."

"Stop it! Do not go digging around my head. I came here to ask for your help. I can see now that was a mistake." Vesna backed closer to the door, looking for a place to set down the wine glass. She wanted to throw it at him, but even in her anger she couldn't stand the thought of damaging the art or smashing the beautifully made glass.

"I apologize. Please, sit. We have much to discuss."

She had come to his apartment hoping he would make sense of what Jo had said. Vesna could have gone to speak with Gustaf after the call and Jo's startling revelation, but her gut had said no. Despite Gustaf's paternal affection for Jo, Vesna still didn't trust the Observer—or any Observer—as far as she could hurl one.

"You are wise not to trust Gustaf in this. Not because he would do her harm, but because he is not his own master."

"I said stop it. I won't stay if you keep doing that."

"You think very loudly. Perhaps you should attempt to rein in your thoughts." He laughed, but it was with genuine amusement, not mockery.

"You're right." She sat back down on the chair he had offered her earlier. "Okay, Črnobog, Lord of Darkness and Death, what is the purpose of a Voice, or a Portal for that matter, and how did Voices come to be in this world?"

"Humans have worshipped an embodiment of death as long as they have worshipped the Sun. The two great mysteries of life: how life is sustained and how it ends. Death is busy. There are always those reluctant souls who refuse to cross into the Next when the door opens or the rainbow bridge appears or whatever iconography a people have collectively imagined into being." Dušan swirled the wine in his glass and waited to see if Vesna had any questions.

She was transfixed by the light playing against the fine glass and the legs of the wine as they ran back into the puddle at the bottom. As much as it pained her to admit, she saw then what had attracted Jo to Dušan all those years ago. It wasn't just the bad-boy artist persona. He could weave a spell with his words. "But Voices aren't divine. Where do they come into this?"

Dušan laughed. "Aren't they?" He set his glass on the table between their chairs. "I know you have a low opinion of gods, Vesna. And you are right, to a point. We do sometimes get bored, and a bored god is a dangerous thing. Those early gods of death had a penchant for dallying with the living mortals they were tasked with shepherding into the great beyond. The children of those unions became two things, the Long-Lived and the Voices."

Vesna's mouth dropped open to a surprised O before she snapped her jaw shut again.

"The Long-Lived had the capacity to avoid a meeting with Death, some to the point that they are effectively as immortal as a god. Some Voices, the Portals, gave the gods an opportunity to give up their immortality and move into the Next at the end of the mortal lives they took."

"But to do so, the Portal had to die." Vesna finished her wine and set her glass next to Dušan's.

"You can see where this leads?" He was enjoying his role as lecturer, quizzing the student who hadn't read ahead.

"Where do the gods come from? If they all decide to hang

it up, who is left in charge?" Vesna hadn't read ahead, but she was logical.

"Very good. Portals had another ability. They could bear a child to a god. Horus and Osiris, Mithras, Tammuz, Jesus. There were others, lost to time and the millennia of human existence, but you get the idea."

"Faron." His name, said in the context of the many others, changed it forever in her mind.

"Faron, born of the union of a mortal woman, but a Portal, and a god—to take the place of a divine being who was done with being a god." Dušan's gaze bored into her, and his eyes flashed black and star-filled as Jo had once described, both beautiful and horrible.

"But Isis, Anahita, Mary, the others all became ..." Vesna's voice trailed off into her thoughts.

"Divine in their own right. Immortal and exalted. They carried the child of a god. The blood of a god flowed in their veins, through every cell, and rested there."

The enormity of Dušan's words pinned Vesna back in the chair. "You used her." Contempt and bile climbed up her throat.

"No. She was chosen."

"Ha. According to Gustaf there was no one left to choose. Jo is the last of the Voices and Portals. You just had to track her down before someone else did." A more-disturbing thought occurred to her as she spat the words at him. Dušan hadn't chosen Jo or used her; Jo had found her way to Ljubljana and Dušan. It had been predestined.

"And now you see."

"Don't do that." She had been thinking very loudly though. "But the gods, you, you can do whatever you want without consequence. You answer to no one but yourselves."

Dušan's laugh made the wine glasses vibrate on the table. "No, dear woman. You have that completely wrong. There are mysteries beyond my knowing. I knew when I met Jo what she was and saw how our fates were intertwined."

"But you fell in love with her. Didn't you want to protect her then?"

"Love is no more rational in a god than it is in a mortal." His expression changed. Whether it was regret or longing she saw there, she would never know.

"And now what will the gods do? There are no more Portals for their murder-suicides or baby-making." Vesna was still disgusted, but she saw now why Igor's dismissal of human superiority bothered her so much. The gods weren't superior either. They were all equally broken.

"If the Board had its way, all the gods would fade into the twilight. Witches would die out, or be stamped out. The occasional Long-Lived would still emerge in a bloodline. They would become the most powerful beings—humans with incredibly long memories and plenty of time to turn the world to their wishes, a world without a trace of enchantment."

"So, they are what? A bunch of undying atheists demanding everything be explained by science?"

"You think a witch can't be explained by science? Gustaf has told you and Jo that the Voices just died out. He might believe that, though I've tried to warn him about Bettine and the Board as it exists now. The Board has been hunting down and disappearing powerful witches and Voices for centuries. Families went into hiding, but some things are hard to conceal."

"The Board can't use magic to find them?"

Dušan laughed. "Do you think Gustaf is the only Observer with some kind of gift? They aren't above using magic to achieve their ends. Tsk tsk, Vesna, you should know that despots are excellent at being hypocrites."

"But Jo's family?"

"Underestimated. Her mother wasn't well. Her aunt doesn't take the role seriously and only bore a mortal son, and Jo appeared to have not carried it on to the next generation. They were still watching her though. And Gustaf let them know she was a Portal as soon as he realized it. That's why Bettine is coming."

Vesna sat up and looked up at Dušan. "Aren't you, aren't gods omniscient, omnipotent? Can't you just make all of this stop, rip open the Veil?"

"We, I, do have great power, but I am not omnipotent. My vision into the past is long, and I can see many futures, all of them equally possible."

"What future do you want?" What future did she want?

"A re-enchanted one."

Vesna looked at the wine in her glass. All the futures she imagined, in which the world was free of the Board and Observers and Witchfinders who acted as executioners, were achieved only by sacrifice. Dušan had to see that as well. And who demanded order in that world? Could she put any more faith in an anarchy of witches and pantheons of gods than she had in the Church and the Witchfinders?

———

Ana skipped the bus and walked to school. She would be late, but it didn't matter. Aunt Olga had given up driving her to school, though she'd insisted on it after the last time Ana had disappeared. Her aunt would be mad if she was late again, but that didn't matter either. She had dreamed about her friend, and he was feeling lost in a park somewhere closer to the center of town. It felt like the one off *Tavčarjeva*, and her feet took her in that direction, away from school altogether.

She hated the busyness of the city in the morning. It was loud with too many cars and buses and people hurrying to get to a desk at school or a desk at work. They didn't even notice how, when the sun made it up over the top of the buildings, all the dew on the grass and trees sparkled like diamonds or how the little brown sparrows huddled together to look for breakfast in the cracks in the pavement. They just walked or biked or rode, their thoughts all jumbled with who had said a mean thing to them or how they were going to pay a bill or what they needed to buy at the market for dinner.

Occasionally she heard someone ask themselves, "Why?" very loudly. She'd heard an old woman practically shout, "Enough!" in her head before throwing her bags in the nearest waste bin and turning the opposite direction from where she had been going. But most people's thoughts all muddled into the same noise.

She couldn't hear Breda's thoughts, but she had figured out that some people knew how to keep their minds closed and quiet. Her other friend's only thoughts were, "Why?" even when he told stories or asked her about her day. It was like he still had a heartbeat, but it made the sound of the same word over and over again, ticking away forever, asking for an answer.

She crossed the street to the park. She didn't have an answer for him, but she wanted to. She had never seen anyone as sad as he was. Except maybe Veronika, but Goran's lessons had helped with that. Her sister's thoughts had changed from "Why?" to "What if?" Ana's had changed too. But there were usually more answers than questions, and that was a strange thing.

Her friend was sitting on a bench on the other side of the small park. There was a woman sitting next to him smoking, unaware her friend was there and watching the people pass as if he were looking for someone in the crowd.

Ana waited until the woman brushed her cigarette against the ground and walked to the nearest waste bin. She looked at the butt to make sure there was no fire and then threw it away.

The bench still held some of her warmth and loneliness when Ana sat down.

"I found you."

Her friend turned to greet her with a half-smile. The bruises around his neck hurt to look at in the morning sunshine. He had died very violently, and that made her sad. He was too kind to have been hurt so badly. There were a lot of things in the Now that were not fair, but it surprised her how many things in the In-Between were also unfair.

"Shouldn't you be in school?" His voice sounded like putting her ear right up to a guitar while someone was playing, even in the rush of the city around them.

"Probably. But I felt you were lonely today, and I thought you could use the company. I already read the whole book we are supposed to talk about." Ana shrugged out of her backpack and set it next to her on the bench. "You said you'd tell me your name someday. It would make it easier to find you." Names were powerful things. Breda had taught her that.

"If I tell you my name, it has to be our secret."

Ana nodded. Some names had to be secret. You could call a person with their name, and if you could call them, you could hurt them. Breda had given her her name without hesitating. Ana still hadn't decided if it was because Breda trusted her not to use the name for harm or if Breda was too strong to worry about how it would be used. Either way, Ana treated names with care.

"It's Milo."

"Milo." She said the name again in her thoughts, stretching the syllables out: *Mee-low*. "That's a nice name."

CHAPTER 15

Jo lay in the tub surrounded by the scent of damask roses and myrrh, courtesy one of Jackie's expensive handmade bath bombs. The bathroom lights were off, and a few candles flickered around the edge of the garden tub. One-way glass gave her a view of the dark river and the lights twinkling on the other bank.

Her aunt's house and the other houses perched over the river had always seemed like lairs to her. They were bigger than anyone needed, but they were also tucked into the trees and looked to be hiding when you saw them from a boat or from the opposite side of the river.

The candles, the bath, and the view from her hideout should have been relaxing. She had wanted to be alone with her thoughts, but now Rebecca's words tumbled, uninterrupted, over each other—mingled with images of her mother holding her father underwater while his life ebbed out into the Tennessee. Flashes of Milo standing on her father's grave and her father disappearing into a black hole of inky wings and eyes joined the rumination.

Her conversation with Vesna had not put her at ease, but

it had been good to talk to someone who wasn't there in that same soup with her, paddling through her mother's death and all that it had brought with it.

Jackie had offered Jo some cucumber slices for her eyes. Her face should have been puffy from lack of sleep and crying, when she had finally let the tears come, but she looked fine. Immortality appeared to offer a few tiny perks.

A soft knock on the door interrupted the next downturn of her spiraling thoughts.

"Mmhm."

Rok's voice was muffled by the door. "May I come in?"

"Mmhm." She sat up in the tub, water sloshing with her movement.

He opened the door wide enough to slip in and closed it softly behind him.

"Is there room for two?"

"Mmhm. I need to let out some water though." She slid down to the tap end of the tub and pulled up the lever for the plug. A few gallons of pricey bath glugged through the pipes, and she pushed the drain closed again.

Rok undid the ties of his mustard-yellow, kimono-style robe. It was printed with fauns and satyrs prancing through patches of forest. She'd given it to him for a birthday not long after they met. Did birthdays still matter when they were infinite?

He joined her in the water, sliding in behind her with his legs alongside her hips so she could recline against his chest.

"You've been in here awhile. I was … concerned." He ran

his hands down her arms, resting them in the crooks of her elbows. His fingers felt warm even in the hot bathwater.

"Mmhm."

"I thought I was the non-verbal one?" He kissed her lightly behind her ear.

She snorted.

"Are you okay?"

"Let me see. My son's father turned out to be the literal Slavic god of darkness. My too-many-greats grandmother is gigging as Death, and she came to collect my mother who murdered my father, whose soul was pulled into Dušan's limbo realm by a demon. Oh, and a former lover who was killed by the same demon tried to choke me out in a very realistic dream, probably because I've been too busy trying to figure out what it means that my son is now the White God to figure out where his soul had gotten to. And I'm probably not going to die. Did I leave anything out?" She closed her eyes and laid her head back on his shoulder.

"I'm glad you didn't tell me about your mother being a murderer before the funeral. I might have had to object to her being buried in sacred ground. But you left out the part about your friend and longtime fuck buddy turning out to be a Long-Lived who wasn't actually Slovenian and who hit the road the night you almost died."

"The first night I almost died. I guess you don't know about my birthday twofer." It should have been funny, but neither of them laughed. "And, yeah, fuck you for leaving."

"You also left out that you're kind of in love with an ex-priest and you have no idea what to do about that so you're fucking the friend you may also still be mad at."

"Shit. I can't keep all these things straight. Maybe I need an assistant?" She smirked at the ceiling.

"I'm glad you can find some humor in it."

"Dark comedy at best. *Variety* gives it three stars." One of the candles extinguished itself in the puddle of wax that had accumulated in the jar.

"The *Variety* reviewer clearly didn't empathize with the lead character. What's-her-name from *The New Yorker* gave it a rave, calling it an intimate portrait of one woman's triumph over unbelievable odds." He moved his hands back up her arms, cupped her shoulders, and gently pushed her forward so he could massage her shoulder blades with his thumbs.

"Pauline Kael? That doesn't sound like her, and besides, I'm pretty sure she's dead." Jo snorted again. What did she know? Maybe there was an afterlife market for banter-y movie reviews.

"I've been around awhile; the pop culture references get a little fuzzy." He repositioned his hands and ran his fingertips along her collarbones absentmindedly, tracing her snake tattoo. "But seriously, kiddo, you've got a ton of shit on your plate. I just wanted to remind you, you aren't alone."

"Says the man who has already announced he's about to disappear again." She slipped out of his grasp and turned over in the water like a seal, sliding her feet past his hips so she could sit facing him.

"I said I'd be back in Ljubljana after you get home. You also have Jackie and your cousin—"

"Yes. My cousin, Michael. Should be easy for you to

remember his name." Jo cocked an eyebrow at him.

Rok glared at her before continuing his enumeration of Jo's ground team. "And Faron, and Gregor. Vesna. Leo. Fred and Reka and Ivanka at the shop. Goran and Gustaf. Oh, and Helena and, probably Matjaž still, right? I mean he is definitely your type."

Jo splashed him, stirring up the heavy scent again. "Matjaž and I are just friends. No benefits." She couldn't say she hadn't been a little bit disappointed by that, but it was better for all involved. "I see your point. But Helena is, in fact, dead, and I don't think she is going to want to hang around with me forever. Aside from Faron, everyone else you named is going to die, and I am just going to go on. Like you." She could say it. She knew what the words meant, but she still hadn't wrapped her head around the concept.

Rok nodded thoughtfully.

Jo pulled herself closer to him, making an X of their legs. "Did you know all this when you met me?"

Answering her needed a big breath and a pause. "I knew you were more than you appeared. The Long-Lived develop some extrasensory skills over time."

"What magic powers do you have?" Jo ran her fingertip down his sternum, stopping at the gap in his chest hair that marked a fine, silver scar.

"Like you, I heal quickly, but a serious injury will leave a scar—like that stab wound you just pointed out." He took her hand and brought it to his mouth to lightly kiss her pruned fingertips.

"And I have some powers of premonition and psychoscopy."

"Psychoscopy?" He was being very distracting. She shivered as he kissed the inside of her wrist where a tattooed sparrow played over her blue veins.

"I get a sense of something or someone from touch."

"And you knew what I was?"

"I knew you were different, but not what exactly." His lips had made their way to the inside of her elbow.

"And what can you sense now?" Somewhere in the back of her thoughts, she knew he wasn't being completely honest with her. He'd spent a whole week with her aunt and had failed to ever mention that to her. How many of her other forebears had he had trysts with?

"That you are troubled by everything that has happened." He stopped teasing and kissing and looked up at her. "I never presume from there, Jo."

She cocked her head at him.

"I never assume what will happen next with you."

"But …"

"I don't always know if what I see is what will happen or if it is what I want to happen. We still have choices."

A cynical laugh escaped her, partially dampening the cocoon he had spun around them with his words and feathery kisses.

"The Fates have a general outline of how things will go, but the players and scenes can change, and our days, our hours, still belong to us."

She pulled him into her and kissed him, hard, sealing that hour for the both of them.

———

Goran dusted the end tables and breakfronts in the public section of his shop. He watched through the front window as Ivanka and Frédéric set out café tables in the courtyard. He liked the new busyness of their private little square, though he did wonder how much longer it could last.

The Board didn't care for clusters of those like him, like Jo and her son, who lived with the secrets of things beyond the average person's understanding. Jo had amassed a coterie. That was surely a problem.

Before his mother had died, she had told him stories about places and times where witches had been safe in communities protected from outsiders. She had wished for that sense of community, so far removed from the solitary, lonely lives that modernity and the Board enforced. She had said the isolation made it too easy for witches to turn inward and twisted.

He had to wonder if that was what had happened to Avgusta, Helena and Matjaž's mother—one of the few other witches he had known in Ljubljana. She had definitely made bad choices, had taken action without input or advice from another soul only to fulfill her own desires. It wasn't that a witch wasn't allowed to do things to bring about personal happiness, but taking whatever one wanted had consequences.

Avgusta had paid the price. He hoped it was a lesson his current pupils remembered well, especially Veronika. If he was right, she would be more powerful than Avgusta had ever dreamed of being. That level of talent needed to be wielded with a great deal of caution.

Ivanka, like many witches he had known or read about, had only one gift. It wasn't one he would wish on his worst enemy, but now he was tasked with teaching her to control it and not let it control her. Thousands of years ago, she would have sat at the center of a temple, waited on by handmaidens, and dispensed foreknowledge to royalty and military leaders. Now she was unstacking chairs and making brownies in the teahouse across the courtyard.

How could he teach her to fit an outsized gift into her single life?

Ivanka carried out the sidewalk sign and balanced it on the cobbles before disappearing into the teahouse again.

Veronika and Ivanka were trouble enough, but they were trouble he fundamentally understood. The third sister, Ana, was something entirely other.

He had been somewhat serious when he'd said he didn't think she was a witch. She was beyond that—more a force of nature than a practitioner. And it was getting more difficult to keep that quiet. When he met her, she had been an unassuming child. She was somewhat traumatized by the events her sister had instigated, but thoughtful and observant.

She was still thoughtful and observant, but there was a wild electricity about her. He'd watched random people take notice of her when they were out hiking. And he knew from Vesna that Ana's aura was a difficult one to miss. He couldn't see the colors that swirled around living things, but he could sense when a person's aura was more in line with the supernatural. Ana made the hair on the back of his neck stand up.

And the girl had brought his mother back to him, briefly. Like Jo she was a conduit for the dead, but unlike Jo she could sustain that connection only temporarily. He had had a chance to talk with his mother, to find out what had really happened to her after the Observers disappeared her. Her brief presence had been a warning, or so he believed, about the Observers, but it had also solidified the need to protect Ana until she could fully protect herself. A being like Ana, whose aura glowed in the Unseen, tended to attract things, and not all of them were benign.

He finished his dusting and returned to his workshop in the back of the store where he kept his library, which included his mother's handwritten spell books. Maybe her words could guide him in his search for a way to shield Ana awhile longer.

———

Gustaf paced the short length of his flat waiting for the mail application on his computer to ping with notice that Bettine had replied to his message. Perhaps he should have called. He hadn't because he was sure she would discern any hesitation or trepidation about her visit in his voice.

He wanted to point out that the visit was unnecessary without revealing that it was also unwanted. If he could convince her to postpone her arrival, he would have more time to arrange for many of the people she had an interest in to be out of town, either temporarily or permanently.

He wished he had not been so good at his job previously. His diligence about recording and reporting every arrival and departure, every action, however small, that might be of concern to the Board, had meant that he told Bettine about

Jolene Wiley as soon as her status as a Voice and Portal emerged. He had believed unquestioningly in the mission of protecting mundanes from anything behind the Veil.

Now he was more uncertain. The Board was quick to eliminate any threat, by a number of means that he now saw through Vesna and Leo's eyes. To destroy or imprison a person or being because of their natural ability was more troubling than the consequences of an errant spirit spooking schoolmarms and window washers.

The computer chimed, and he scurried to the lone chair parked beside the table he both worked and ate at.

Dearest Gustaf,

I am of course looking forward to my visit. It has been years since I have seen you in person, and it will be a treat to catch up as friends. Please do not feel that you need to make special arrangements on my account.

I will arrive by train on the last day of the month. There was some disagreement on whether I should fly or drive, but you know my distaste for airplanes and a driver seemed an unnecessary expense. There were only a few complications in making the connection from Paris, but the trip will be an opportunity to catch up on my reading.

I have booked a room at the Grand Hotel Lisica. I'm looking forward to being in Ljubljana again after so many years. To think the last time I stayed at the Lisica, Tito himself was still in power.

Please let the former Brother Kos know that I am very much looking forward to discussing the situation in Ljubljana with him. I believe we will find him invaluable in keeping the quiet.

As always,

Bettine

Gustaf closed his laptop. Bettine was ever the politician. In less than two hundred words she had reminded him of their previous romantic dalliance before she had elevated through the ranks of the Observers and reminded him that if he could not handle the situation in Ljubljana, she was happy to call upon the services of the local Witchfinder.

If she found his attachment to the denizens of the Veil troubling, she would be shocked by the Witchfinder's predisposition toward them.

Perhaps Ms. Wiley's mother would live for some further weeks, delaying her return. Leo could not pretend disdain, and Bettine, learning that Ms. Wiley had ensnared the affections of a witchfinder, would have her carted off to the catacombs for invented crimes before he or Leo could devise a plan to stop her. Bettine would probably take Leo, as well, despite her fondness for the bloody methods previously employed by the Kos family.

CHAPTER 16

Jo accepted another peck on the cheek from her aunt.

"Is someone picking you up at the airport?" Jackie patted Jo's shoulders and looked around. "Did you really only bring that backpack?"

Jo nodded and said yes for the fourth time in their conversation.

"Are you and Michael, I mean Harry, on the same flight?"

The nodding was going to be replaced with eye-rolling if this went on much longer. Jackie was acting like Jo had never traveled overseas before.

"No. He's not going straight back to Ljubljana." Jo picked up her backpack and shrugged into the straps.

Jackie put her hands on either side of Jo's face. "Be careful, and let me know when you're home."

With Jackie's touch, a sense of sadness and foreboding washed over Jo. It took her breath for a moment.

"You okay, hon?" Jackie's scrutiny turned to concern.

"I'm fine. Still processing everything that's happened." As

far as Jackie was concerned, the only new information Jo had was about Rok's personality swaps and the truth about how her father had died. Jo had decided not to share Rebecca's revelation with Jackie. She'd promised not to keep secrets, but there wasn't an easy way to bring up the fact that she was probably immortal and explain to Jackie what that could mean. Fuck, Jo didn't even really understand what it meant yet.

Jo also chose not to tell Jackie this would be the last time they would ever see each other. That was the source of the foreboding. Jo hadn't seen beyond that. She just knew that she would not see Jackie again, at least not on this plane of existence. How much more could a person lose or have taken and keep it together? The Fates could kiss her ass.

Rok, who would never be Harry, appeared at the door to the kitchen. "The car's here."

Jackie nodded and then pulled Jo into another hug that nearly crushed her ribs. "I love you."

"I love you too. And thank you for everything. I was angry, but I know you did what was best." Jo kissed her aunt on the cheek. "Take care of yourself."

Jackie nodded again. "I will." Her eyes were wet. If the tears came, Jo would be crying with her, and that was not the last image she wanted to leave Jackie with or hold of her aunt.

"I'll text you along the way as I get to New York and Amsterdam, and I'll video call when I get home so you can see I am alive and well. Just remember I have a layover in New York." It was a white lie, but not an unbelievable one. No one could fly from Chattanooga to Ljubljana without killing time in an airport somewhere.

Jackie nodded and squeezed Jo's hand.

Rok ushered Jo out to the waiting car and joined her in the back seat after stashing their bags in the trunk.

"Airport?" The driver put the car in gear and rolled forward.

"Yes, thank you." Rok answered.

"No. Would you take us to Coolidge Park?"

The car stopped, and the driver turned around to look at them.

"Why do you want to go the park?" Rok looked at her, confused.

They weren't going to be late for their flights. Rok had reserved a room for them in a hotel near the airport so they could spend a night alone before he left her again. But she needed to make a small pilgrimage before she headed back to Ljubljana. "I'd like to go to the park first."

Rok shrugged and waved the driver on. "I'll still pay you for the fare to the airport."

The driver shrugged and put the car back in gear. He turned onto Battery Place and then made the turns to cross the river at Veterans Bridge over Maclellan Island. Jo couldn't see much except the treetops from the car, but she could sense the dark island beneath them. It would be slightly easier to get out there from Coolidge Park.

The driver dropped them among the bustle near the shopfronts that faced the river. Rok paid and tipped the driver and took their bags from the trunk.

"Are you going to tell me what's going on now?" Rok handed her bag to her as he adjusted his on his shoulder.

"I need to go out to the island." It didn't sound like a crazy idea, yet.

"Achelous?"

"He let me know he was here the night I arrived. I think he knew the truth about me, and I need to ask him a few questions." She absentmindedly played with the bull medallion on her necklace.

"Can we rent a boat?" He didn't seem at all perturbed by the idea.

"Maybe, but it's a nature preserve, and you have to apply for a permit to go out to the island. That takes some time …"

"Are suggesting we swim to the island?" Now he was perturbed.

"It's the best way to sneak over."

"Jo, that water can't be safe to swim in."

"You'd be surprised. I wouldn't necessarily eat fish out of it, but it's safe to swim in. Besides, I'm immortal, remember? And you? Well, you're whatever you are. We'll be fine."

He looked exasperated but resigned. He gave her a funny half-smile. "Where can we leave our stuff?"

"Let's get some food first. We should probably wait until it's dark."

They wandered around and found a tapas place with a decent menu. Jo wanted a glass of wine but decided she'd rather be clearheaded when, or if, she got a chance to chat with Achelous again.

Rok caught her playing with the medallion on her chain as she looked over the menu. "You know, you could probably just go down to the river and shout out to him to meet you over here."

"I thought of that, but … we have a complicated relationship. This is better." She closed the menu and pushed it aside. Swimming out was a small sacrifice. She didn't want to owe him for anything other than answers, if she could get those.

The server covered their table with small plates of vegetables, Spanish sausages, and marinated cheeses. Jo picked at a few things. Her appetite had been bigger when she was ordering.

"You can still change your mind. I can call a cab to take us to the hotel now." She sensed he was teasing. He knew her mind was made up.

Jo watched him finish his wine but didn't reply.

"Before we go on your mission, can we ride that carousel? I've been wanting to since I got here." He dragged a cube of feta across his plate with the tines of his fork and jutted his chin in the direction of the park next to the river. It had a carousel that was filled with hand-carved horses and fantastical animals.

"Why didn't you ride it already? When *did* you get here?" There still hadn't been a satisfactory answer about why he was in Chattanooga.

A shout from across the restaurant interrupted his reply about not looking like a weirdo riding a carousel by himself.

"Jo? Jo Wiley?" The man with the shaved head she'd recognized as her ex, Turner, made his way across the small dining room to their table.

Jo couldn't put any words together before Turner pulled a chair from a nearby table and sat down.

"I thought I saw you at the show the other night but figured my mind was playing tricks on me. Then the bouncer said he'd had some chick named Jolene with a weird passport come in." He took a breath. "And here you are."

"Harry." Rok stuck his hand out.

"Sorry. Yeah. Nice to meet you, Henry." Turner immediately turned his attention back to Jo. "How long has it been?"

"A long time." Not long enough.

"It has been. It has. Are you still living in Slovenia? I mean I guess you must be if you have a weird passport, right? Why are you in town? How long are you staying?"

Rok stared at her. "Who is this asshole?" flitted through his thoughts and hers. Jo ignored the fact that she had heard someone's thoughts besides Leo's and returned to the problem at hand.

"I do live in Slovenia, but my aunt still lives here. I was in town because my mother was ill."

"Oh. I hope she's feeling better."

"She died." Jo looked at her empty plate and then back up at Turner's bewildered face.

She continued. "*Harry* and I were having dinner before I fly out tomorrow."

"Cool. How do you two know each other?" Turner was nodding his head like a dashboard dog with a spring neck.

Jo ran through a number of explanations in her head, but Rok answered before she could light on a satisfactory answer.

"We met at a club a few nights ago, and when she wasn't at the hospital or burying her mother, I've been fucking her brains out." Rok ignored Turner's shock and motioned to the server for the check.

Turner recovered after a protracted, awkward silence. "Well. Have a good trip, I guess. It was nice to meet you, Henry." He stuck his hand out to Rok again. "It was good to see you, Jo. It really was." He put his hand over Jo's on the table before he left. He didn't return the chair he'd borrowed.

"That was rude." She offered Rok a half-smile. If that was the only penance Turner ever paid for leaving her high and dry with twenty Deutsche marks and a sleeping bag in Ljubljana, he'd gotten off lightly.

Rok stared at her for a long minute. "That was Turner? That was the man who dragged you to Slovenia?"

"He didn't drag me. I was up for the adventure." Jo pursed her lips at Rok.

"I'm grateful for whatever role he played in getting you there." Rok shook his head. "But what could you have possibly seen in him?"

"He wanted to take me away."

CHAPTER 17

Vesna wrapped a jar of apple butter from the shop in a clean tea towel and nestled it in a market basket next to some of Ivanka's cheese scones. Her mother's mood was always softened with a small gift. The guest she was bringing with her should be gift enough, but goods needed to change hands to make sure things went smoothly.

Igor picked up the basket from the bottom and tucked it under his arm. "Ready?"

"No." Igor was practically living with her—he would be officially doing so by the end of the month—but he still hadn't met Mrs. Kos. Not by design, necessarily, but because Mrs. Kos didn't live in the city. Her few visits to Ljubljana had coincided with Igor attending a show or a gallery opening out of town.

Vesna knew her mother wouldn't approve of her seeing an artist, even a successful one. Even though she wouldn't approve, she would start asking her usual questions: When would they be married? When would they have children?

"It can't be as bad as that?" Igor's voice was soft. He knew not to tease when it came to her mother.

"It probably isn't. Just promise me you won't let her get to you. One of us has to be calm enough to drive back without smacking your car into a tree."

He shrugged. "It'll be fine."

The drive to Ribnica was quiet, with only Billy Bragg's back catalogue to fill the silence in the car. Vesna had introduced Igor to the English singer, and he'd developed a bit of an obsession. An image from "Tank Park Salute" caught in her thoughts as she watched the countryside go by—death watching them like a pale moon in a sunny sky.

Vesna replayed Jo's phone call in her head for the hundredth time. Her friend was immortal, or so Death had revealed to her. Death—who was also her many-greats grandmother. Jo and her son would live forever as everyone around them faded. Everyone except Dušan. How convenient for him. Had he known all this to be true from the beginning, or had he put the story in motion? There was no way he was above a long con. Which was more of an affront, fate or machination?

Igor found a spot on the street near the Kos home. It was quiet in town, even for a Sunday. The house Vesna grew up in was within a stone's throw of *Ribniški grad*. The images from the exhibit on display there, of Slovenia's last known witch trials, flitted through Vesna's mind. Her family had a hand in that dark time, and as far as Vesna could see, they had never atoned for it.

The first time Vesna had visited the museum, a group of noisy school children, equally fascinated and repulsed by the torture devices, had offered cover for the overwhelming shame and guilt that had gripped her. Her family's crimes were on display, and the shadow those horrors cast spread far beyond those of the castle towers.

"Vesna?" Igor's voice brought her back to the moment.

She shook her head to clear her thoughts. "Sorry. This place."

"You aren't them."

She wasn't. Nor was Leo, but the blood of those men, who had taken such pleasure in the witch stool and the thumbscrews, ran in her veins.

"I know." Could her family make amends for centuries of torture?

The chalking from Epiphany was still clear above her mother's front door. The parish priest must have done it for her this year. Vesna instinctively touched the lintel as she had seen her father do so many times. He had been the one to write out the year and initials of the Magi in the strange equation. He had blessed the door with holy water and said his own prayers, the prayers of a witchfinder, to protect his family from the demons and devils he hunted, from the haunted souls of the witches he and his family put to death. It was the same kind of magic Goran had used to protect their enclave on Zajčeva, and her father had never seen the irony in that.

Mrs. Kos opened the door and invited them in. Igor paused briefly at the threshold. A thought flitted across his features, darkening them briefly, before he smiled broadly at Vesna's mother's welcome.

Lunch had already been laid on the table, and Mrs. Kos ushered them to their seats. Miha, Vesna's younger brother, and his fiancée, Inesa, would not be joining them. Mrs. Kos offered a flimsy excuse for their absence, but Vesna knew her mother wanted fewer people there to interfere with her interrogation of Igor.

"Igor, you should sit here." Mrs. Kos pulled out the chair to the right of her seat at the head of the table.

Igor did as he was told. Mrs. Kos sat, and Vesna took her place on her mother's left, across the table from Igor. He tapped the point of her shoe with his, a small reassurance that he was up for whatever her mother planned to serve them alongside the Sunday lunch.

"Igor, will you say a prayer before we eat?"

"I defer to you, Mrs. Kos. That is not my way."

She gave him a disapproving look and said a quick prayer thanking Jesus for the bounty of her garden and his general protection. Vesna watched as Igor waited to pick up his fork until her mother had begun eating, as if Mrs. Kos were a queen. In that house, she was.

"Vesna tells me you are an artist. Do you paint or are you a sculptor?"

"I paint." A mischievous smile tugged at the corner of his mouth.

"Portraits? Landscapes?"

"Social commentary, but also murals."

Mrs. Kos set her fork on the edge of her plate. "What does this mean, 'social commentary'?"

"I'm a graffiti artist. I do some commissioned work, murals mostly, like the one of the Boston Tea Party at Renegade Tea."

"Yes, I have seen that one." Mrs. Kos turned her steel-eyed gaze to Vesna. "You didn't tell me that your friend painted that mural."

"You didn't ask." Mrs. Kos asked very little about Vesna's business unless it was about their financial health or to comment on the dishwasher issue. Vesna set her jaw to avoid commenting on the "your friend" remark.

She turned again to Igor. "That piece is well executed, but derivative, I think, from a Japanese artist?"

"Yes. Jo wanted the Boston Tea Party, but done like *The Great Wave*."

Mrs. Kos nodded. "And your social commentary? Isn't graffiti the same as vandalism?"

"I don't deface monuments or historic treasures." Igor continued to enjoy the roasted homegrown potatoes, unperturbed by Vesna's mother's questions.

"Were you drawn to Vesna for her taste in art or because she is the daughter of a witchfinder?" Mrs. Kos didn't even look up from her plate for this last salvo.

Igor set his fork down soundlessly on the rim of his plate. "Neither. I appreciate Vesna's intellect and her loyalty to her friends. She is also uncommonly beautiful."

Vesna's face burned.

Mrs. Kos brought the full power of her glare to bear on Igor. "I find it difficult to believe you didn't know who Vesna was. It isn't the first time your family has encountered ours."

Vesna looked from her mother to Igor and back to her mother. What the hell were they talking about? She searched

Igor's face for some surprise, but there was nothing. "You knew?"

"I knew of the Kos family, but I didn't realize that's who you were descended from the day I met you. My family is from Tabor and Ptuj."

Vesna stared, her mouth slightly open.

"The Witchfinder at the time was eager to drown a witch on Herman II's behalf, even one who had been acquitted. He didn't know then that Veronika had a child in secret in Ptuj, when she fled there after the first trial and acquittal. Her family, my family, hid the child, a daughter, when they came for Veronika and put her to death." Igor picked up his fork and continued eating.

"You're descended from Veronika of Desenice?" Vesna looked at Igor trying to read his face. Had he been with her only to mock her and her family?

"You would know this if you had continued your studies with your father. He took a special interest in tracing the bloodlines of Slovenian witches." Her mother spat out the word "witch," as if it were bitter. "And you wouldn't have invited one to your bed so easily."

Vesna stood up. "We're leaving."

Mrs. Kos stood then too. Anger radiated off her like a shimmering red thundercloud, but there was something else there, too—shame. Vesna had been blind to her mother's secret for her entire life.

"Did Father know?"

Her mother's anger evaporated as quickly as a summer storm, and she collapsed back into her chair. She put her head in her hands for a moment and then looked up at Vesna. Her mother looked old and humbled.

"He did not. I waited for the signs to show in you or Miha, but you both seemed to be spared."

Igor looked unsurprised by this revelation. "What better place for a witch to stay hidden than in the house of the Witchfinder."

Vesna sat back down and pushed her plate away. "I didn't come to ask for your blessing, and I sure as hell didn't come asking for this."

"When you refused to continue your studies with your father, I suspected." Mrs. Kos looked at Vesna again. "You hid it well."

"What choice did I have? Father made it clear that anything supernatural was from Satan. I knew he wasn't above exorcising his own daughter."

"I prayed from the time I was little for the Devil to leave me, but I was in his grip."

"So you took up with a witchfinder?" Vesna looked from her mother to Igor, who was still picking at his potatoes as if the bomb that had just gone off hadn't left shrapnel everywhere.

"He didn't see the evil in me."

"Jesus, Mother, you aren't evil. I'm not evil. Igor isn't evil. If witches are born, and you believe in God, then surely God must have had a hand in making all of us witches?" Vesna tossed her napkin into her plate.

Her mother stared at her as if the thought had never

crossed her mind.

"Have you talked to Uncle Leo about this?" Vesna was angry at and sorry for her mother. Self-loathing was a pointless waste of energy.

"Why would I tell the Witchfinder I am the thing he hates?"

"He doesn't hate you, or even what you are."

"How could he not? The Devil took the woman he loved."

"No, a vampire revenant took the woman he loved because my father was too busy trying to exorcise the demons out of Berta instead of tracking down the thing that was harming her. If Leo is mad at anyone, it would be Father." And himself. Self-loathing seemed to run on both sides of her family.

Mrs. Kos started to defend her husband but saw the futility in it.

"What is your gift, Mother?"

"She's a weather witch." Igor finally pushed his plate away.

Both women turned to stare at him.

He shrugged. "Witchfinders aren't the only ones who keep track of the families."

"Show me." Vesna would have happily traded the ability to part clouds for the foreknowledge that often made her miserable.

Her mother sat up in her chair and gazed into the middle distance. An unfelt air current lifted the loose strands of dyed-black hair at her temples. Igor and Vesna turned to the window as a breeze picked up and rustled the trees outside, turning the leaves of the linden tree in the yard to the silvered undersides. Her mother sighed, and the tree stilled almost instantly.

"All those times I thought storms made you angry ..." Vesna had dreaded thunder and lightning as a child because her mother would scold her, and the house had crackled with her rage. The black clouds Vesna had always seen around her mother had been literal as well as figurative.

———

Igor opened the door to the car for Vesna, but she didn't climb in. She turned instead and searched his face to see if anything had changed between them. For a moment at the table, she hadn't been able to decide if she felt more betrayed by her mother for hiding the truth from her, or by Igor for knowing so much he hadn't shared.

"You really didn't know who I was that first morning, when you came to talk about the mural?" Vesna waffled between wanting him to say yes or say no.

"I put it together later that day."

"Did you know what Jo was?"

"No, I knew her life was about to change when I started painting, but not how or why. My sight doesn't work like yours, remember?"

Igor could see into the future, too, but only through his art. Vesna thought of the mural he had done for Jo's birthday at Niko's gallery in *Metelkova*. He had seen Jo's connection to Achelous, and he had known that she would end up in the river. It wasn't only Death that looked down on them from sunny skies, waiting, it was the past—both the secrets and the sins.

"I want to grill you on why you fell in love with me. Is it really for me, for those things you said to Mother, is it because we are the same, or was it an accident in a long-delayed plan for revenge? But I don't want to know, and, in the end, I don't think it matters. I know that you do love me, and I need that to be enough."

"I won't answer your question then." He pulled her into him, wrapping her in the ephemeral hint of violets and paint that clung to him like its own kind of aura. He kissed her, and she forgot about witches and why they might be drawn to her and Jo like a gathering storm.

CHAPTER 18

Jo and Rok finished their dinner and walked out into the noticeably cooler night air. Rok convinced her to take one ride on the carousel before they went for their illicit swim. They walked down to the park, figured out where to buy tickets, and stood in line with the families and dates waiting their turn. The lights and music swirled against the darkness surrounding the pavilion.

Rok followed the fantastical creatures and traditional horses that spun by them in time to the calliope. His face glowed with a childlike glee she had never seen in him before. When she took his hand, hoping to join him in his excitement, she saw another version of him in her mind's eye: a slightly thinner man in a striped vest selling tickets to a crowd of billowing skirts and parasols.

"You worked at a carousel before?"

"There aren't many secrets with you now, are there?"

She shrugged.

"Carnivals were an easy place to hide. The people who ran them didn't ask questions, and we moved around a lot. I repaired the wooden horses and sold tickets."

"And then you moved on again."

She hadn't intended to dampen his mood, but a wistfulness settled over his joy.

"How old are you really?"

"I don't know what year I was born."

"Okay, where were you born?"

"Outside Pons Aelius."

"I thought you said you were English?"

"I said English was my mother tongue, which was a bit disingenuous. Pons Aelius is Newcastle upon Tyne now."

"So you're, what, *two thousand* years old?" The quick math in her head came up to something like twenty-five lifetimes.

"Probably closer to eighteen hundred. Hadrian's wall was completed when I was a young man."

The calliope stopped, and the riders began to dismount the brightly painted animals and leave.

"Gustaf thinks you're, like, maybe three-seventy."

"There's a lot the Board doesn't know." Rok nudged her to follow the couple in front of them through the turnstile.

Jo scanned the available rides and chose a colorful fish. Rok moved on past her and chose one of the stationary horses on the outside, a black charger in medieval armor. Had he been a knight too?

The other riders scrambled for their mounts, and the bell sounded. The carousel began to turn slowly as the calliope whistled a Sousa march. Jo watched Rok, knowing he was far away in another time, then turned to look out at the few people who gathered at the edge of the railing to watch. As her fish bobbed up and down, she caught a glimpse of a Middle Eastern woman with glowing olive skin and a nimbus of light at her crown. On each turn, the woman caught her eye and smiled.

Mary, Mary of the Crossroads, Mary of the Various Sorrows who had saved her from a witch's fire, had found her way to Chattanooga. Mary who had told her to return home, to be there for her mother, the other Mary. Impatient for the ride to end, Jo looked for Rok. He was gone, moved, she assumed, to another horse though the sign said not to change while the carousel was in motion. After eighteen hundred years, safety rules probably didn't mean much.

The song finally wound down as the turning slowed, then stopped. Parents pulled their sleepy children off unicorns and merhorses and headed for the exit. Jo let them leave in front of her as she searched the crowd for Mary, but she was gone.

Jo left the pavilion, unconcerned with where Rok had gotten to, and looked for that floating cloud of light she'd seen hovering over Mary. She spotted a glow receding in the darkness toward the river. She caught up to the Blessed Virgin in a stand of trees under the deep shadow of the Walnut Street Bridge.

If Jesus had brothers and sisters, was Mary still a virgin? Those kinds of thoughts were the reason she had gotten in trouble at Sunday school. "I never know if I should be happy to see you."

Mary laughed. "I do appreciate your irreverence. Most

people start crying or prostrate themselves."

"I could do the prostrating part if that's protocol, but I can't say my heart would be in it." It was strange to speak with Mary. Their previous encounters had mostly been visual with a few words exchanged in Jo's head. There was still a part of her that wondered if maybe this was all a grand hallucination she continued to build upon as she disappeared further down her own personal rabbit hole.

"Prostration isn't necessary. And, really, it's a bit awkward." Mary cringed a bit and looked past Jo, back toward the lights of the park and the carousel. "Rok is looking for you."

"I lost him in the crowd, after I saw you." Jo looked over her shoulder and back to Mary. "Would it be rude for me to ask why you're here?"

Spring peepers and cicadas sang in the trees behind them, and boisterous voices drifted down from the pedestrian bridge overhead. Mary looked up at the superstructure and undergirding of the bridge and back at Jo.

"I would be surprised if you didn't. I had hoped to catch you at the hospital, but you had Rebecca. I'm sorry about your mother."

"Sorry she died or sorry she was a murderer?"

"Both."

Jo was sorry about both, too, but mostly sorry she couldn't harangue answers out of her mother now that she had crossed into the Next.

"I wanted to see you before you visited Achelous."

"Is this about making a choice about who I should venerate?"

Jo avoided the word "worship." The obsequiousness of it made her skin crawl.

Mary laughed again, but it came out as a snort. "No. That doesn't matter to me. You can worship, excuse me, *venerate*, whomever you choose. I wanted to tell you I'm here. If you need me."

"I think I already knew that?" Mary was verbally pointing at something Jo couldn't see, at least not yet. The supernatural world was chock-full of beings who couldn't give a straight answer if their afterlife depended on it.

"Good." Mary looked out again past Jo to the lights and sounds of the park closer to the pavilion.

"That's it?" Why did she feel like she was missing something really important in this conversation?

"Yes. That's it."

Jo couldn't hide the incredulity on her face.

Mary took an audible breath and pursed her lips. "Look. Nothing I tell you now will make any sense to you. I don't think Rebecca's words have had time to sink in; you've had too many other things to deal with."

That was a fair assessment. She had no idea what it meant that Death would never come for her. Well, she knew what the words meant and the general sentiment, but not what it would mean to her. "Can you help me with any of those things?"

"I said I would be here for you."

"You did." Jo turned at the sound of her name. Rok had found them.

When she turned back to ask Mary what happened next, she was gone.

"Who were you talking to?"

"Mary."

He looked confused.

"Jesus's mom."

"You … you talk to Jesus's mom?" Confusion had deepened to incredulity.

"It's a long story, but yes." Maybe she would explain the whole thing to him when he came back to Ljubljana, whenever that turned out to be.

"You are full of surprises, my Jo." He leaned in for a quick peck on her cheek. "Let's do this thing."

Jo took his hand and walked with him deeper into the stand of trees where they could undress. The banks were steep there, but they couldn't just walk half-naked into the river from the kayak launch. She wasn't worried about getting in as much as she was worried about getting back out.

Rok lowered her down the embankment then followed her. The water was cold, much colder than the air—but nothing compared to the last river she'd been in. The two of them looked out for barge traffic and pleasure boats and headed for the island. She felt stronger in her body than she had in a long time, but it was still an effort to swim out to the island against the current.

Perhaps this hadn't been her best idea.

They made it to the narrow landing beach after overshooting it in the dark. A lantern shining through the trees and a woman's laugh caught them off guard. It hadn't occurred to Jo that there might be people on the island. She'd forgotten there was a campsite.

"What do we do now?" Rok spoke softly and pulled himself most of the way out of the water next to her on the beach.

Jo shrugged and played with the medallion around her neck. She wanted to take off her bra and wring it out, but that seemed like a bad idea. They'd kept their underwear on so they wouldn't also get charged for public nudity if they got caught.

"Maybe we can just wait here a second and see if he shows?"

As soon as the words left her mouth, a hand gripped her ankle and dragged her down the sandy bank back into the river.

"What the fu—" Water went up her nose and choked her.

Fully in the water, her lungs burned. She hadn't had a chance to take a breath. She groped around in the darkness for Rok and tried to kick her ankle free, but whoever had a hold on her had vise grips for hands.

Her face finally broke the surface, and she gulped air in preparation for being dragged under again.

Achelous popped up next to her with a finger to his lips. Rok surfaced behind him.

"Sorry to frighten you. Well, maybe a little sorry, but I couldn't have Karen scream down the police on you two."

Rok looked puzzled. "Do you know that woman?"

"No, nor her companion, but isn't Karen the name used for random white women here? Or is it Becky?"

Jo laughed and got a mouthful of river water in the process.

Rok still looked confused.

"I think Achelous has been enjoying the local scene." Jo coughed again.

"I appreciate my dedicants seeking me out in their travels, but I don't think the two of you came out here to pay your respects." Achelous turned in the water to face Rok. "Linditus, it has been a very long time."

"Linditus?"

Achelous turned again to face her. "Your Rok was once a priest of mine on the River Tyne." He grabbed Jo's wrist and plunged them all back into the river.

They moved through the water at speed, and Jo found herself on the opposite bank again where they had left their clothes, the scent of orchids strong on the warm night air.

"Dress yourselves, and let's go find a beer." Achelous was dressed in what could best be described as a hipster costume, right down to the heavy-rimmed glasses that helped soften the unnerving green glimmer of his eyes.

She'd never seen him in his true god form, but one afternoon's quick internet search of Greek and Roman archeological finds had given her an idea. Depending on the artist, he was either a snake, a bull with a missing horn torn off by Hercules, or a saucy merman. Jo preferred the Slovenian version of Achelous in his fitted sweater and soft jeans to the slightly more obnoxious American one, but at least in Chattanooga he wasn't above using his magic to deposit them back on land, dry.

The three of them walked back across the park, threading

their way among the couples spread out on blankets chatting or making out. The carousel's music floated from the pavilion, adding a festive melody to the hum of the downtown traffic.

Rok lead them to a hole in the wall he'd discovered farther down Cherokee Boulevard and snagged a corner away from the crush of customers at the bar. A round of beers loosened Achelous's tongue but only to talk of himself. Jo couldn't find a gap in his long-winded observations of twenty-first-century Americans to ask questions about Dušan or what his plan may have been.

Rok excused himself to go to the toilet, and Achelous scooted closer to her on the banquette.

"You can ask your questions, but I don't have any information for you. I've done my part." Achelous drained his beer and looked around for the server.

"What does that mean?"

"I promised to keep you safe."

"Safe from what?"

"Safe in the skirmishes before the war."

Rok slid back in on the other side of Jo. "What are you two looking all conspiratorial about?"

"Nothing. But you two should call a cab and get some rest." Achelous paid the server, who had finally appeared, for the beers. "You have a long day tomorrow."

"And you?" Jo watched Achelous pleat the receipt into a fan without even looking. His eyes were drawn to a dark-haired woman at the bar who returned his gaze with an interested smile.

"I'm sure I'll find a way to occupy my time."

Jo cocked her head at him. "Will you go back to Ljubljana then?"

"Who says I'm not there now?"

The nature of gods and their abilities was still beyond her.

She and Rok walked out onto the sidewalk to wait for their ride. The lines from a song followed them out the open door, something about Death watching them all, like a pale moon in a blue sky.

CHAPTER 19

Leo stopped by to see Teja and Luka on his way to the airport to collect Jo. They had decided to stay in town a few more days. Without the chickens to care for, there was no need to rush back, and Teja was reluctant to return—even knowing the cottage had been cleansed and blessed by witches and a priest.

Luka walked with Leo out to the car he had rented.

"You should've borrowed ours. We don't need it in the city." Luka frowned at the gleaming white estate car.

"Thank you. I appreciate the offer, but I wanted something a little roomier."

Luka laughed. "You have plans then?"

"I arranged a room—well, two, in case—in Bohinj for tonight. A soft landing for Jo's return after burying her mother." Leo had felt it presumptuous, but Vesna had insisted it was a good idea and that Jo would appreciate the gesture.

"Was this your idea?" Luka laughed. His friend knew him well.

"Jo's friend Vesna, but I'm glad she suggested it. And she

told Jo, so it won't be a surprise." Or a shock.

"Vesna is a smart woman." Luka clapped him on the shoulder. "Drive carefully and enjoy your evening." Concern drifted over his expression, but he smiled through it.

"There's something else?"

"Teja. She does not believe this business in the woods, with the Unseen, is over. She is worried for you." Luka looked reluctant to share his thoughts.

"You aren't burdening me with insight, friend. I agree with Teja. There is more to come." Leo's concerns lay more with Bettine's impending visit than with Teja's unsettled spirits, but each was worrisome in its own way.

Luka ran his hand through his short gray hair and sighed. "Be careful. I am concerned, too, for you and your Jo."

Leo nodded. "I will take every precaution."

Luka stepped back to let Leo get into the car and stood watching as Leo drove out of the small parking area and onto the street. He was standing there still when Leo looked in the rearview mirror.

Leo kept the radio off on the drive to Brnik. A scant half hour to be alone with his thoughts was not unwelcome. He had tried not to think too long on what seeing Jo again would be like. The death of a parent could change someone. Priorities could shift.

He had asked himself what he wanted to happen that evening. It came down to a sense of connection, an idea that this thing between them was possible. Could it live and breathe on its own? Perhaps it would take the shape of a heartfelt conversation, or perhaps it would be more physical.

The thought aroused him and made him anxious. He had not been with a woman since Berta, and that had been a very long time ago.

———

Ana curled up in her bed with Goran's book of supernatural beings. She thumbed again through the gods and goddesses and stopped at a detailed line drawing. Morana, the goddess of winter and death, and Vesna, the goddess of spring and fertility, filled a page opposite a story of young girls taking an effigy of Morana to the river to drown her so Vesna could take her place at the turn of the season.

The two goddesses couldn't exist at the same time, according to the book. Ana thumbed past it to the page she'd marked with a candy wrapper and a pine needle. That was silly, to think Vesna and Morana couldn't exist at the same time. They were two sides to the same coin, or like the Sun. It didn't stop existing at night, it just shined its light on the other side of the planet, and it was the same with those two goddesses.

The page she had marked was on wandering spirits. Milo had said there was something bad in the woods that had killed the chickens. Ana didn't think it was a spirit like Milo or Breda. They didn't hurt people, even though they were sometimes sad or even mad about being dead.

The evil spirits in the book were lost souls, those who had not been buried properly or who had been killed by demons or vampires. They roamed about frightening and possessing or killing people. Ana didn't like the idea of that, but it was closer to something that would kill the chickens. She closed the book. She wanted to talk to Breda. It would have been easy for her to slip into the In-Between, but she was tired. Breda would be there tomorrow. She put the book down and snuggled under the covers. She closed her eyes wondering if Breda or Milo could meet her in her sleep like before, so she could ask about the bad spirit. Could a spirit be good and bad?

———

Gustaf stood on the walkway in front of his apartment, looking down into the courtyard. A woman came in from the street and wound her way through the busy tables set up outside Renegade Tea. The heavy brass bells on the door handle inside the shop clanged up through the sound funnel the courtyard created. A gray mist clung to the woman, but he didn't need to see her aura to sense her sadness. It was there in the cast of her shoulders.

He made his way to the stairwell and to the courtyard below, carrying his own mist of worries.

At the door, he set off the bells again and gave a small wave to Ivanka as she set a full tea service down at a table of smartly dressed, gray-haired women. She conversed with them in English. It amused him that she had picked up a slight twang from Jo. He preferred the clipped accents of older Brits, but there was charm in the way Jo and others of the American South spoke. Gustaf took a seat at a table next to the women.

"Are you hungry or just tea?" Ivanka half-smiled at him when she got to his table. She didn't trust him, and he couldn't blame her. He had done his job well, and his reporting had given Bettine an excuse to come.

"I would take some of Frédéric's soup, if it is still available. And a pot of green tea, please." He had forgotten to look at the chalkboard outside to see what the soup was, but it hardly mattered; he had never had one there he hadn't enjoyed. "Would you ask Vesna if she has a moment?"

Ivanka nodded and walked back to the tea station. She had a quick word with Vesna that he couldn't hear over the music. The song was almost a dirge with menacing choral voices droning on about knowing "who you are." The staff had better taste in food and tea than in music.

Vesna walked over to greet him. Her aura had an unsettled quality that pulsed like a heartbeat. "Hi." She looked back at Ivanka before continuing. "You've got your order in. Did you need something else?"

"I wanted to speak with you. I had hoped to speak with your uncle, but I understand he is collecting Ms. Wiley from the airport this evening."

Vesna cocked her head at him. "And how did you know that?"

"Dušan. Will they return to Ljubljana tonight?"

Her aura pulsed faster. "No. But I don't think that's really any of your, or Dušan's, business. Why did you want to talk to Leo?"

"I wanted to see if he would go along with my plan." He thanked Ivanka, who brought his soup to the table with a small pot of sencha and a heated iron cup.

Vesna pulled out a chair and sat down as Gustaf took his first bite of Frédéric's curried stew. "Ivanka, would you bring me a cup of something? Whatever's brewing or easy." Ivanka checked on another nearby table and went back to the tea station. The chatter from the British ladies crescendoed in shared laughter. Vesna turned her attention back to him.

"What's this plan?"

"I would like Jo and Faron, Dušan, and possibly the Novak sisters to be out of town when Bettine arrives." He turned the cup in his hands, enjoying the heft of it.

"Won't that make her suspicious?"

"Perhaps. But it will thwart her, if her reason for coming is to inspect the more prominent figures who live behind the Veil."

Vesna shrugged. "She'll just come back, won't she? Are you suggesting we send them away for good?" He could see the thought had occurred to her as well.

"Possibly, but I doubt it. This is the first time she has been here in many years."

"About that. Why did you never mention she was the Observer in Slovenia before?" Ivanka returned and handed her a cup. "Thank you."

Ivanka hesitated before turning to leave them again.

"I hadn't?"

Vesna leaned in very close to him and spoke very quietly. "Gustaf Lichtenberg, I know that you know I can see auras. Don't try to lie to me. Why is she coming, and why were you secretive about her being here before?"

Gustaf's chair had become uncomfortable. Vesna Kos would make a very good Witchfinder if the title should come to her. "I was secretive about it because I did not want to upset Goran, but it is too late for that." The professor had already accosted him, asking why a member of the Board was visiting Ljubljana. Gustaf had not known that Bettine was responsible for Goran's mother's disappearance and eventually her death. Bettine had taken Mrs. Kralj with her when she left her post in Ljubljana, the post that had stayed empty until Bettine had assigned it to him.

"I think there's more to it than that."

There was more, but he wasn't ready to examine his feelings about it or share them with anyone. "There is a personal history I will not discuss at this time, but that is of little importance. I believe the bigger concern is Bettine's intentions once she arrives."

"Do you think she wants her old job back?"

The thought had not occurred to him. Though he found the idea preposterous, it was also concerning. Bettine was advanced in age. She had been older than him by some years when they met in Vienna. The age difference had been her reason for ending the affair. He had suspected there was another reason but never confirmed it. Many Observers had small gifts, nothing like a witch might have, but an ability that helped in their jobs. Whatever Bettine's was, she didn't want it revealed.

"She intends to bring the power of the Board down on what I think she believes is Dušan's menagerie." In truth, Jolene Wiley seemed to be the center on which this collection turned, but the Board would not see it that way.

"Don't they think he's an alchemist or a necromancer? I mean, they don't know he's actually Črnobog, right?" Her voice had dropped so low that he could hardly hear her above the din of the shop.

"That's what he's led them to believe. But the Board has a long memory."

"Longer than a god's?" She snorted.

"Perhaps not. But if they know Dušan is not what he says he is, they will go after the mortals he's collected around him."

"Even the Board won't take on a god?" Vesna made the face a mother would give to an errant child and finished her tea, pushing the cup to the side. She, too, knew more that she would not share. The chatter of the customers began to change around them as more students filled up the remaining tables.

"They see themselves as the very fabric of the Veil. Their stated goal is to keep the everyday people of the world protected from the knowledge that the supernatural is as real now as it was in the past. The old gods, like Dušan, are firmly part of that past reality. The Board would like to keep it that way."

"But why? There are reconstructionist religions popping up all over the place. People seem to desperately want the thing the Board is trying to shield them from." Vesna shrugged. "I understand keeping demons and vampires and the like at bay, but—"

"You think Dušan is less dangerous than a demon or a vampire?"

"He's an asshole, but he can be reasoned with. Revenge demons and *vampirji*? Not as much. Couldn't the Board just focus their attention on the bad actors and leave people like Jo and Ivanka and her sisters alone?"

"Who decides which is evil and which is good? Avgusta was a witch, the same as Veronika or Goran, and did measurable harm to Jo and many others." Gustaf preferred a more black-and-white approach but perhaps a less heavy-handed one. All who lived behind the Veil were capable of evil, as were most humans.

Vesna tilted her head and looked at him for a long moment. He could imagine the thoughts locking into place like puzzle pieces as her aura, a brighter red now, continued to pulse ever so slightly. "Why does the Board exist? Father often spoke of them as an enemy to both the minions of Satan and to witchfinders, but, well, you know how he was."

"How much do you know of the origin of the Board?" There were many things the Board had done to keep its existence and founding in the shadows. Accounts from errant Observers or citizens of the Veil had been sought out and destroyed as soon as they came into existence.

"Only what I know from Father and later conversations with Leo. My father believed the Board has existed since before recorded history. Leo is more skeptical on that point."

Ivanka returned to the table with fresh tea. The shop was busy enough that she should have asked for Vesna's assistance, but she didn't.

"Your uncle is a very clever man for a priest."

"Technically, Leo is a former priest." She frowned at him.

"The Church has hidden much, even from its learned members. I did not mean to insult Leo's intelligence." Her feathers were soothed, and she looked at him again expectantly. He had not intended this to be a lesson. He had only come to find out when Leo and Jo would return so he could arrange a conversation with her about leaving again as quickly as possible.

"The Board formed originally as the Council in the autumn of 810 after Charlemagne called the Council of Aachen. They were a group of clergy Charlemagne trusted to not only root out paganism in Western Europe but also to bring the supernatural realm under his control where it could be hidden. Charlemagne sought to consolidate the power of the state and the church, and that would be more difficult if his subjects worshipped different gods and believed that supernatural beings outside the church could aid them against the Holy Roman Emperor."

"But why then also persecute witchfinders?" Vesna's eyebrows knitted themselves together.

"The goal of the Council—by the time of the burnings they were already the Board—was to keep the supernatural hidden, even the supernatural elements of Christianity. The rise of scientific thinking, which had first been seen as dangerous, was then welcomed as it smothered and ridiculed belief in the old gods, the Fae, and superstition. The Witchfinders wanted to keep fear of the pagan supernatural in the light. The panic they fanned had very little, in the end, to do with finding real witches. You know this. Most of the families were clever enough to stay hidden, though not all." He took a sip of tea and let his words settle before continuing.

"A schism developed in the Board between those who wished to stamp out belief in superstition and anything supernatural and those who wished to retain the services of those who still communed with the old gods or who had innate abilities. They assumed the supernatural and belief might eventually die out on its own if the Veil shielded everything from view, but they were willing to take that risk. And then there were those who wanted the Church to keep its power in the various states that had arisen after the fall of the Empire. These became the self-appointed Witchfinders who believed the supernatural was truly of Satan and should be eradicated, all while ignoring that it was at the root of their own religion."

Vesna sat back in her chair. "And my family, they sided with the zealots? They had been part of the Board, as Observers or what? And then decided that secrecy wasn't enough?"

"Yes. The witchfinder families finally split from the Board in the 1500s."

"Disgusting." He thought Vesna might have spit if they had not been sitting in her tearoom. "Okay. So, what does this all have to do with Bettine?"

"There are still those on the Board who believe the witchfinders were right but hadn't taken things quite far enough."

"So, Bettine wants to come to Ljubljana and lay waste to everyone she sees as a threat to the secrecy of the Veil?"

"If that were the case, my concern would be much less. Bettine is a zealot, but she is far more interested in her personal power. Those who live behind the Veil are the reason for the little power she has. Her concern is more with people like Dušan, who are pleased that the old gods are gaining believers as these 'reconstructionists,' as you call them, increase."

"But she doesn't know Dušan is Črnobog, right?" Vesna looked confused again.

"She may. And that is my worry. The Board has been able to put down wars and demons, quietly disappear powerful witches to remote islands in the North Sea, and murder lesser beings to keep them from disturbing the secrecy. Even with all their power, they cannot overtake the old gods. They can only hope for their continued twilight as they seek to become mortal and die through Portals, like Ms. Wiley."

Vesna sat quietly for a moment, looking at him with her mouth slightly open. "Dušan managed to replace one of those gods who had chosen to die. That would be the worst possible thing in Bettine's eyes?"

"Reason enough for her to come to Ljubljana and put down the rebellion herself."

CHAPTER 20

Jo pulled her backpack down from the overhead bin and slung it onto her shoulder. Her skin was sticky, and her clothes stank from travel and the close press of other bodies. Leo was waiting –for whatever romantic evening Vesna had maneuvered him into planning—and all she wanted was a shower or a long soak. She already missed Jackie's tub.

The passengers ahead of her took their time collecting their bags and shuffling down the aisle. When Jo finally got off the plane, she headed to the toilet to run a comb through her hair and splash some water on her face. She tried to ignore the nervous flutter in her stomach, but it was persistent.

As refreshed as she could get, she walked out to the public area of the small airport. Families clucked hellos at each other in tight little circles of luggage and embraces. Leo was near the exit. Jo looked out the glass door past him, out into the world away from the liminal places of travel where a person was never here nor there. Staying in the airport forever wasn't really an option, however tempting.

She made her way to Leo through the tangle of people and bags and surprised herself by falling into him. His arms circled her, and she buried her face in his chest without a word. There was relief, but also an overwhelming sense of being home, of being safe.

He held her back from him to look in her face. She took the opportunity to stand on her toes to kiss him—a passionate, open-mouthed kiss that led directly from the kiss he had left her with when they parted. She no longer felt the need to hold back. After all the anguish and worry, she knew the moment he'd embraced her. Death would not come for her, but it would come for Leo. She wanted to be here with him for the time they had. Despite all the crap that had happened with her mother and her trying to escape her own feelings fucking Rok, she just wanted this, wanted Leo, if he would accept her.

"We should go. I think we are disturbing the grandmothers." He nodded toward a woman in a bright floral scarf standing off to the side watching them with an inscrutable expression. Her face was familiar, but it was the face of a dozen older women she had passed in the street, their gray hair hidden under brightly printed scarves.

Leo took Jo's bag from her and gestured for her to walk ahead of him to the parking area. He opened her door for her and closed it softly. She watched him walk around the front of the car and pause briefly before getting in next to her.

"I got Vesna's message, but she didn't say where you were taking me." She smiled at him, but he seemed unnerved by her presence.

"Bohinj. I booked rooms at the hotel on the lake." He said it to the steering wheel.

"Rooms? Is someone joining us?" That had not been part

of Vesna's message.

"No … I … I didn't want to assume."

Jo laughed. "I hope you don't have to pay for both."

His shoulders relaxed. "You're sure? You don't mind sharing a room, a bed?"

"Do you mind?"

"No."

"Okay, then. Let's head that way. This place has a restaurant, right?"

"Yes." He smiled finally.

"Good. I need a shower and some food. And then we'll see where things go."

They spent most of the ride in companionable silence, though Jo was certain she had dozed off a few times because it didn't seem to take them an hour to get there.

As they pulled into the parking lot, the sun sank right to where it balanced on the edge of the mountaintops.

"Would you like to stretch your legs a bit first?" Leo pulled into a spot at the hotel. "We can watch the sunset from the bridge."

"Sounds good."

They walked down the road toward the church then made their way down to the water's edge where the river Sava Bohinjska emptied into the lake. Jo had a flutter of nervousness that Achelous might think it was a good time to take her for a dive, but there was no green glow in the water and no scent of tropical flowers.

As the sun sank below the mountain peaks, the lake caught the reflected fire in the sky in streaks of orange and gold. Leo reached for her hand, and they stood without speaking, watching the colors darken and then fade into twilight.

"I am glad you wanted to be here." He turned to her and cupped her face in his hands. "I didn't want ... I never know with you. Not in a negative way."

"You don't have to explain." She'd given up on trying to figure out the map the Fates were following. She was there now, and these hours belonged to her and to Leo. "But I probably do."

"Not if you don't want to. You are who you are. You don't owe me an explanation." He was sincere. And it was hard-fought. She had seen his disappointment and hurt the night he had showed up at her apartment with Matjaž standing on her doorstep.

"I don't know what else to say but thank you." She stretched up and kissed him again. Again, it took her breath, but he pulled away.

Jo rolled her eyes. "Hey, there are no grandmas here to scandalize."

"No, but I want to make sure the restaurant doesn't close before you can get some food. There's not much else around."

———

Jo ran a ridiculously small hotel towel over her wet hair and stepped into the room. At least they had robes. The room was neat and basic and also empty. She hadn't heard Leo leave and had no idea where he could have gone. Maybe he needed to take a piss and wasn't ready to be that familiar.

She laughed to herself and walked out to the balcony.

The room might have been basic, but the view was phenomenal. They could have watched the sunset from their balcony, though they wouldn't have gotten the full effect of the water lapping gently at the shore. Bright stars were visible, and a few soft voices from people walking or sitting outside drifted up to her.

Leo returned with a basket with a wine bottle peeking out. He set it on the dresser by the television and joined her on the balcony.

"We could have watched the sunset from here." He stood next to her and put his arm around her.

"I had the exact same thought, but your idea was better."

"Your hair smells nice. Like rosemary." He turned to face her and ran his fingertips through the front of her hair to the damp ends.

"I filled up my travel bottle with my aunt's shampoo." She laughed. Jackie had expensive tastes in everything but insisted on some crunchy herbal shampoo from the health-food store. Jo just liked the way it smelled. Rosemary for remembrance.

She hadn't yet shared everything she'd learned in Chattanooga with Leo, and she'd asked Vesna to keep their conversation to herself. She wanted to reconnect first. There would be time to relay all the drama and angst over breakfast or on the drive back to Ljubljana the next day. She wanted tonight to be for the two of them. Leo had gone to the trouble of arranging it, and she was relieved to have this time to put those things aside for a moment, however loudly they continued to knock on her thoughts when she was still or quiet.

"I'd like to kiss you again." His voice was low and close to her in the dark, and she could almost feel the bass of it in her chest.

"You don't need to ask."

"You seemed far away." He ran his hand over her hair again, stopping at her neck. He rubbed his thumb over her jawline.

"I was for a second. But I'm here now."

"Do you want to talk about it?"

She shook her head against his hand, and he tilted her head up so he could kiss her. She leaned her head farther back as his mouth covered hers, and she ran her hand up the front of his shirt and to the back of his neck. There was no Roman collar there to stop them.

She started to undo the belt of her robe.

"Let's go inside." His whispered words pulsed to the end of every nerve in her body. She took his hand and pulled him back into the hotel room. Her robe was open, and he stopped and looked at her.

"I had seen the tattoos before ... may I?" He held his hand out ready to touch the dark circle of the eclipse under her breasts.

She nodded. The beading from the scar had disappeared. Along with the lines on her face where a demon-possessed Katarina had tried to take her eye out. The only scar that remained was the one her mother had given her. Fitting.

Leo traced the flame that ran up her sternum and moved

the shoulder of her robe down her arm so he could follow the body of the snake whose head rested in the hollow of her clavicle.

"It is a symbol of Achelous, the serpentine river. But this tattoo is older than the others?" He looked into her face then.

"Yes. Older than Faron." She'd gotten it on an impulse late one night, out with Dušan. They'd met another artist friend of his, and he'd offered to do it then. The three of them had drunkenly careened through the city, back to his studio. Now she wondered if she had been the only one drunk that night.

"They are beautiful, your tattoos, their stories."

He kissed her again, and all the tentativeness between them was gone. Jo's robe fell to the floor, and she helped Leo out of his clothes as quickly as possible, drinking in every inch of his long body with her eyes and her hands.

Leo threw the bedclothes back with one hand and backed her to the edge of the mattress. She scrambled back, trying to pull him with her, but he stopped and went to the basket.

He returned and threw a silver-foiled condom on the nightstand. Bless Vesna; she'd thought of everything.

She pulled him down next to her on the bed. She couldn't touch enough of him or kiss him deeply enough. She wanted to wrap herself around him like the snake and devour him.

She gasped when he finally pushed inside her.

He paused. "Did I hurt you?"

She shook her head and arched against him. They disappeared into each other then. It didn't matter that it was their first time. Any awkwardness was burned away by her need to get to the center of him. She wanted to curl up in his chest around his heart and protect it forever.

Afterward, they lay there with his head on her chest, her legs wrapped around his waist. She would have stayed like that until the morning, but even the deathless had to pee.

When she got back from the bathroom, he had straightened the bed and pulled the duvet back up. She slid under and up next to him, face to face. He was the one lost in thought.

She ran her fingertips over the gray at his temple then placed her hand on his chest over the St. Mary medal he wore on a silver chain. "Where did you go?"

"Not far. Today on the drive to the airport, I'd had this image of an intimate conversation over dinner, discussing our feelings and where we should go from here." He wrapped his arm over her waist with his hand in the small of her back and pulled her closer.

"Followed by a chaste kiss in the hallway before we went to our separate rooms?" She smiled.

"Where did you think this night would go?" He kissed her softly on the forehead.

"I tried not to think about it too much. I wanted to see you. I was grateful you made space for me to land without rushing back to Ljubljana into whatever is going on there." Vesna had filled her in about the chicken incident and Bettine's impending arrival.

"And that's why I love you, you are in the moment and in your body." He seemed surprised the words had come out of his mouth.

She didn't stiffen against him or turn away. She let the

words wash over her and felt what they meant as they tried to reopen that crack her mother's truth and Rebecca's words had sealed over.

She closed her eyes. "I love you. I don't know if the words mean exactly the same thing when I say them as they do when you say them. But I mean them. And I wanted to be here, I want to be with—"

He stopped whatever else she was going to say with another kiss. Their bodies reignited, she moved her leg over his, and he took her with him as he rolled onto his back.

When she pulled her hair out of her face, she could see his aura bright against the white hotel sheets. A cloud the color of Mary of the Crossroads' carnations—the clear red of fresh blood—enveloped them both. She wanted to tell him, but he shook his head and touched her lips with his fingertips.

"We can talk in the morning."

CHAPTER 21

Jo made a face in the mirror while she brushed her teeth. Leo was still sleeping, snoring softly. Part of her wanted to wake him and pounce on him one more time before they had to go back to town, or even just wake him up to talk before she had to share him with the world again, but he looked so peaceful, she didn't want to deny him a good lie-in.

"Whatever Lola Wants" drifted through her thoughts, and Helena appeared next to her in the mirror's reflection.

"Good morning, or should I say good night?" Helena smiled broadly.

"Please tell me you weren't slinking around." Jo shuddered at the thought of being watched.

"No. But I knew where you were and who you were with." Helena leaned into the mirror to inspect her face more closely. She pinched her cheeks and shrugged. "Your priest is sleeping the sleep of the just, so I assume things went well."

"He isn't a priest anymore, and, not that it's any of your business, it was a good night." Jo blushed.

Helena laughed her clear bell-like laugh. "It must have

been."

"Are you here to check on my love life?" She had become someone who had a love life. That thought could wait until after breakfast.

"Though I am fascinated by the way you twist yourself into knots about things, I did not come to find out about your night of passion. I came to report." Helena put the toilet lid down and sat, settling her toga-like dress around her.

"On?"

"Our friend Milo. He is still about. The dead have seen him moping about in Ljubljana. He seems to have made friends with one of Goran's witchlettes."

Jo spit out the last of the toothpaste and rinsed her mouth. "Which one?"

"The little one. Ana?" Helena didn't care much for Veronika. She believed she should have received more than the slap on the wrist she'd gotten from Gustaf for her attack on Jo.

"Ana can speak with the dead?"

"It is something witches, well, some witches, can do. My mother for instance. It's uncommon, but unsurprising." Helena tilted her head at Jo, waiting for a reaction.

"Do you think he would hurt her?" He'd come to her in a dream, angry and violent.

"I don't know, but I think it is probably time to send him on his way."

Jo nodded. "Do you still want to be here?"

Helena was taken aback. "Where did that come from?"

"I don't know. It's just this idea that the Next seems like a peaceful transition, and I don't want to keep you from that."

"If I was ready to shuffle off, I'd call up my own door. I'll know when my work is done. Are you trying to get rid of me?" Her eyes narrowed at Jo.

"No. But I'm still trying to figure a lot of this stuff out. Like am I supposed to release you after a certain time? Or if you leave, how do I get a new guide?" She had all the time in the damned world to figure it out.

"Your guess is as good as mine. I suspect it is like everything else; we figure it out as we go." Helena waved and disappeared.

Leo knocked on the bathroom door. "Could I use the toilet?"

Jo opened the door and kissed him, his morning breath and all. "Of course."

"Were you talking to someone?" He looked beyond her into the tiny bathroom, a little baffled.

"Just Helena."

"She doesn't give you much privacy, does she?"

Jo laughed. "More than you'd think, thank goodness."

———

After a quick breakfast, Leo and Jo headed back to Ljubljana. Jo connected her phone to the rental's sound system and made him listen to a Nineties playlist that Gregor had put together for her. She was quiet as they drove out of Bohinj. She would tell him her story when she was ready.

At a busy traffic circle, Jo took a deep breath and turned down the music. "I can't decide what order to tell you these things in. So, I'm going to go with chronological, if that works for you."

"I don't know what else to suggest, so that's fine." He put his hand on her knee and squeezed gently.

"Before my mother died, she told me she drowned my father."

Leo glanced over at her. She was looking straight out at the road but unseeingly. He didn't know what to say.

"He was going to leave her. I think she was probably already mentally ill at that point. She thought if my father was dead, he would be her spirit guide and he couldn't leave her. Apparently, it doesn't work like that. When my dad came to me after Helena was killed, he said my mother's mental illness broke the connection she had with him. Turns out he lied too."

"I'm sorry."

"Yeah. Jackie suspected, but she wasn't sure. She got me away from Mother. Jackie said she never knew how to tell me." Jo touched her face where the scar marked her cheekbone.

"I can imagine. How do you tell a child her mother is a murderer?" He had to keep his eyes on the road, but he kept glancing at her. Her calm in telling the story worried him.

"I knew this trip would be difficult for you. I hadn't expected it to be so difficult."

Jo laughed. "That's not really the worst part."

They were going through a village, and Leo turned onto the next side street and stopped. "What could be worse than that?"

"Rebecca, one of the great-great-whatever grandmothers from those weird dreams? She's Death. Or working for Death. I don't really understand it. At Mother's funeral she told me that Death would come for Jackie, my cousin Michael, and the others there—I can't remember if she mentioned Rok—but that she would never come for Faron, or for me." Jo stared at him. It was as if she were saying words that she didn't understand the full weight of.

"I don't understand. Are you like Rok?"

"I don't think so. Rok thinks he is a Long-Lived, and Death will come for him eventually."

Words had completely escaped him. Had Dušan done this to her?

"The last thing you need to know is that Helena thinks she found Milo, and apparently he's made friends with Ana. Do you think he's the chicken killer?" Her calm was unnerving, but he sensed it was also fake.

"Can we go back to the part about you not dying?"

"I don't know what else to tell you. I tried to get information out of Achelous in Chattanooga, but he was being cagey as fuck. I'm hoping Dušan will give me a straight answer."

"Why was Rok in Chattanooga?"

"I'm sorry. After Mother … he just showed up, and I was freaked out about what she'd done and … I am sorry. I just didn't really know how to deal with what was, or wasn't, going on with us."

"I don't care. I understand your relationship with Rok is … complicated. But how did he know you'd be there?" All these pieces fit together, he was certain, but he had no idea how. The thought that Dušan might be the common thread bothered him much more than the thought that Jo had been with Rok. He didn't like it, but he could accept it.

"I couldn't get him to tell me." She leaned back in her seat. "So now you know what I know. Which is more than I wanted to and not nearly enough to figure out what comes next."

He took a deep breath and started the car again. They made it to the highway before his phone rang.

CHAPTER 22

Ana walked barefoot into Luka and Teja's cottage. The heavy scent of rotting leaves and roasted chestnuts made her nose twitch. All the dishes were broken on the floor, and the chickens were on the table, their throats cut. Blood seeped out and dripped onto the floor, spreading along the gaps between the flagstones.

She bent down next to the table and drew a heart in the spreading puddle to release the spirits of the chickens. A handful of sparks, like embers from a fire, came together over their bodies and streaked toward the door.

She stood up, dragging the hem of her nightgown through the gore on the floor. The house spirit had gone, but a presence lingered. She glimpsed a darkness, like a patch of night in the forest, from the corner of her eye.

When she turned, a figure stood in the door to the cottage. It wasn't anything like the spirits Ana had met. Even in the In-Between it appeared smudged and blackened on the edges. Its eyes were dark holes in a face as pale as milk, and Ana could taste the bitterness that came off it.

"Why did you kill the chickens?" Ana wasn't sure if she

actually wanted to hear it speak, but she had to ask.

The figure didn't answer her. Instead, it drifted closer. Ana could see that it had been human once but was now twisted with anger. It grabbed Ana's forearm and pulled her up to its face.

The smell of decay choked Ana. She tried to pull away, but the spirit's grip didn't slip at all. The figure turned and bolted out of the cottage, dragging Ana behind it. She couldn't keep her feet underneath her or keep up, and her knees and shins scraped over the grass and rocks. The spirit was taking her into the woods, past the clearing into the part where it was dark even at noon.

Ana closed her eyes and tried to block out the pain in her legs and feet. She called to Breda and Milo to help her, but no one came. When she opened her eyes, the spirit was dragging her toward a hut made of branches and dead leaves held together with vines and cobwebs. It didn't look big enough for one person, let alone two, but they passed through the door together and into a larger space.

Still gripping Ana's arm, the spirit opened a chest in the corner. Dry leaves blew out on a fetid, warm wind. The figure lifted her into the chest, more gently than she'd dragged her there, and closed the lid. Ana fell to a hard, stone floor. The box, like the hut, was larger inside. Ana pushed her senses out to the edges of the walls and discovered she wasn't alone.

"Who's there?" In the darkness, fear gripped her for the first time. This wasn't just a dream where she had slipped sideways too easily into the In-Between. She had shifted time and she was no longer in the Now. Her bloodied feet told her that.

"Ana?" Breda's voice called to her. Ana felt her presence next to her in the darkness and reached out to find her hand. Breda squeezed her fingers. "Are you hurt?"

Ana nodded in the darkness. "What is that?" Now that an adult was there, she felt like it was okay to be afraid.

"I don't know, but in life it was a powerful witch and not a kind one."

"Am I going to die?"

Breda pulled Ana to her chest and ran her hand over her matted hair. "You don't need to be afraid of Death, child."

Ana wasn't afraid of Death, she was afraid of what might come before it.

———

Goran asked the voice on the phone to slow down and start over. It was early, and he hadn't even had coffee yet.

After a ragged breath, the voice tried to explain again. "It's Veronika. Ana's gone."

"What do you mean 'gone'?"

"She hadn't gotten up for school, so I went to wake her up. She wasn't in her room and her bed looks like … I don't know what it looks like, but the sheets are torn up and there are leaves and pine needles everywhere." Goran heard a whispered *fuck*. "There's blood. How is that even possible?" Veronika stopped and took another breath. "How am I supposed to explain this to Olga?"

"Stay there. I'm on my way." He started to hang up but heard Veronika's voice.

"It smells like magic in here, but it's not flowers or plants—

not exactly. It smells like dead leaves and chestnuts, maybe?"

"I'm on my way."

Goran hung up and dialed Leo's number.

Jo answered. "Hey, Goran. Leo's driving. What's up?"

"You're back? Good. Can you put me on speaker?"

Goran heard the sounds of the car and music being turned down, then off.

"Everything okay?" Leo asked.

"No. I just got a panicked call from Veronika. Ana's disappeared."

There was a pause.

"She's taken off before. Is this different?"

Goran relayed what Veronika had told him about the bedroom.

Jo gasped. "Fuck! If Milo hurts her ..."

"Milo?" Goran knew Jo had been looking for her former lover's spirit. He'd given her a working to try to call him to her. "Why would he hurt Ana?"

"I don't know. I just know Helena said he's been seen with her."

"Where are you?" Goran wanted to begin the search, but he had no idea where to start.

"Almost to Ljubljana."

"I'll meet you at Renegade Tea." He hung up and walked down to Vesna's flat.

———

"We don't know it's Milo. Why would he want to hurt Ana?" Leo wasn't doing a very good job of soothing Jo.

"Who else could have taken her? He came to me, finally, after the spell and Helena looking for him. He came to me at my father's grave and tried to hurt me." Jo looked out the window away from him. He empathized with her guilt, but it wouldn't find Ana.

"Sometimes dreams are just dreams, Jo."

"Are you really going to say that to me? It's my fault he's out there wandering around, snatching up little girls."

Angry Jo was better than Guilty Jo. Anger could be focused. "I know you feel responsible for Milo's death, but you didn't kill him."

"I sent him away. Twice."

"I don't think you would have been with someone who would take his disappointment out on a child."

She snorted. "Have you met Dušan?"

"That's different." Sarcastic Jo wasn't his favorite, but it was still better than Guilty Jo.

"So, who or what else would take her?"

"I don't know. When we get to the teahouse, we can think through it with Goran and Vesna and figure out where to go from there."

———

When they got to Ljubljana, Leo parked the car in the first place he found, and they walked quickly into the old quarter. Fred and Reka were at the teahouse finishing up the prep work.

"Vesna said to tell you to meet them upstairs." Fred came out of the kitchen, wiping his hands on a side towel.

"Upstairs?" Jo cocked her head at him.

"In her flat." Fred looked concerned but was calm, as ever.

"Yeah. Are you sure you've got things under control here? We could close."

"Reka and I can handle it. Go do what you need to do."

Jo had become an absentee owner. Maybe it was time to relinquish her stake in the teahouse, but that was a discussion for later.

Leo took the stairs two at a time ahead of her and knocked on Vesna's door before she could get to the landing.

The flat was full of people. Goran, Ivanka, Veronika, and Faron sat on Vesna's comically large couch. Vesna was pacing, wearing a track into the floor, while Igor and Gustaf chatted near the kitchen.

Vesna ran to her as soon as she walked in the door and tackled her in a hug. "I'm so glad you're here. Glad you're back."

Jo nodded. "So, where are we?"

Goran seemed to be the leader. "We're coming up with a list of places to look. We've put together places I know Ana has been where she could have encountered a spirit. Are there places where Milo's spirit might be?"

Jo rested her forearms on the back of the wingback chair at the end of the couch. "He was murdered in the plaza on *Slovenska*. He caught me in that park off *Tavčarjeva*. I don't know, my apartment? Maybe his old apartment?"

Goran ran his hand through his hair, making it stick up like he had been electrocuted. "That's a lot of ground to cover. We'll check off your apartment, Jo. Ivanka and Faron, you two can check the plaza and the park."

Ivanka nodded. "How do we check?"

"I'm hoping that between you and Faron, you'll sense if something is going on in either location. Igor can go to Milo's old apartment. Veronika and I will go to Vrhnika. Vesna and Gustaf can find the hiking spot in Škofja Loka." Goran was numbering the locations on his fingers. "And that leaves Jo and Leo to go back out to the monastery and Teja and Luka's cottage."

Jo still wasn't sure how they were going to find Ana if something supernatural had ripped her out a dream, but she checked her apartment on the off chance Milo was holed up there. She and Leo dashed back to the rental car, Jo lagging again in Leo's wake, and headed to the highway to get to Škofja Loka as quickly as possible.

Leo's quiet allowed her to stew in her guilt. She should have made finding Milo a more pressing concern. It was easy to say too much had happened, but she could have found time to track him down and help him into the Next.

"This isn't your fault, Jo." Leo's voice pulled her out of her looping thoughts. "Guilt won't help us find her."

"That doesn't make it go away." Jo looked out the window. She couldn't see beyond the highway barrier.

"I know."

She studied his profile. Leo carried his own burdens over the things his family had done, and especially about the last woman he had loved. They were more alike than she had realized. They both had the sins of their families on their hands, and in their own ways they had both tried to outrun them. Jo hadn't known that's what she had been doing, but it explained why Leo had felt so familiar, even that first day at the cathedral.

Leo pulled the rental car off the drive into a gravel parking area across from Luka and Teja's cottage and down from the main house where his room was. The wind picked up as they got out of the car, and Leo looked up at the darkening sky.

"It looks like it's going to storm."

"The weather doesn't care much for what we need to do." Jo rubbed her upper arms with her hands. The sun was still out, but she was cold.

Leo met her at the back of the car and took her hand. "Cold hands, warm heart."

Jo smiled. It was an odd saying that she'd never really understood. And she definitely didn't know how to explain that the cold she felt came from inside.

The two of them walked to Teja and Luka's to begin looking. The grass around the cottage had grown without attention, even in the brief time the couple had been away. Their little home looked cheery, though, with windowsill planters full of herbs and early summer blooms.

The door was unlocked. Leo, cautious, walked in ahead of her and checked the rooms off the larger main room from the kitchen and sitting area. Everything had been righted and cleaned from the scene Leo had described to her. The scent of pine cleaner lingered in the house, but there were other scents layered under it—the damp, musty smell of rotting leaves and, weirdly, bergamot. She would recognize it anywhere as the defining floral note of Earl Grey tea.

Leo stood in front of her by the table. "Notice anything?"

"It's very clean. And empty."

"The house spirit fled after the chickens. I doubt it will come back before Teja and Luka." Leo looked around as if he could find a clue to Ana's whereabouts in the air.

"It also smells like witch magic."

"The rotting leaves? You can still smell that?" Leo looked at her funny. "All I can smell is what I used to scrub the floor."

"The leaves, but bergamot, too, and chestnuts roasting." Jo had had the opportunity to discover firsthand what the magic of a few witches and gods smelled like, and none reminded her of the teahouse or Ljubljana's streets at Christmas.

"I can't smell it." He was frustrated, but he'd paled at the mention of the chestnuts.

Jo hadn't had the chance to tell him about all the weird things that had developed since her birthday. No. The bloodhound sense of smell had started before that, and the psychoscopy, too. They could talk about it after they found Ana.

Leo went to check the other rooms one last time. When Jo turned to go outside to wait for him, she saw a face looking in the window.

Milo.

CHAPTER 23

Ana woke up with her head in Breda's lap. The air in the room was oddly warm, like the breath of an animal, but the floor still drove cold into her bones. Breda stirred awake as Ana sat up. The room was in complete darkness. There wasn't even a spark of light so her eyes could adjust.

"Can I make a light?" Ana leaned against the wall right next to Breda, feeling the cool of the older woman's body through her thin nightgown. Her friend wasn't as cold as before though. Ana ran her hand down her own thighs to see if she was warmer or colder in the In-Between. It was hard to tell.

"You would have to be very careful. A bright light will blind us both. Would you like me to show you?" Breda took Ana's hand and brushed both of their fingers through the air in front of them. A pale blue light, almost too dim to see, appeared.

Breda cupped her hand underneath and lifted it out of the air. She brought it to her belly and held the light there in the bowl of her two hands. Ana watched as it slowly grew brighter. When it was as bright as a single birthday candle and shed enough light for Ana to make out Breda's face in the darkness, Breda hung it back in the air in front of them.

"Things are easy in the In-Between. It would have been nice to have that much magic when I was alive."

"You didn't?"

"No. I was very talented at a few things: herbal remedies, finding lost things, keeping lovers together, or not." Breda smiled and laughed softly.

"What were you the best at? Goran said every witch has a special thing they are the best at." Ana snuggled back up to Breda and watched the little light, now the pale yellow of butter, flicker and bob in the air.

"Goran is a good teacher." Breda put her arm around Ana's shoulders. "My special gift was seeing the heart's truest desire."

"Like telling the future?"

"No. Not everyone's truest desire becomes their future." Breda looked down at her and back up at the light.

"That's sad."

"Not always. Sometimes it's a good thing. The heart doesn't always want what's best for us or good for other people."

"What did your heart most want?" The light dipped for a moment as if it would sputter and go out.

"That's a very personal question, but I will answer because we are in a very personal situation." Breda ran her hand over Ana's crown and put her arm back over her shoulder.

"When I was a little girl, my heart wanted nothing more than to be a better witch than my grandfather."

"Your heart wish changed?" Ana turned this thought in her mind. She had never thought about what her heart wanted.

"Yes. The world changed, or I saw it differently, as I got older. I learned well from my grandfather and my mother, but being a talented witch doesn't guarantee happiness. If anything, it brings other people's burdens to your door. My heart wanted Goran to be happy, and I thought the best way to do that was to make sure he never became a witch."

"Your heart did not get its wish."

"It did not, and that is a good thing. Goran had work to do, and because he is a witch, you found a good teacher." Breda's voice wavered for a moment as if she would cry.

"I'm glad Goran is my teacher. The teacher Veronika started with didn't want her to learn." A bad teacher could make you a bad witch. Ana was sure of that.

"Avgusta was too much alone. There are people who think all witches should be solitary, but I believe witches are meant to be together. There are times to be alone, everyone needs that, maybe especially witches. But witches can do more when they put all their gifts together. Our collective power has been fractured for too long."

"Like the three sisters?" Ana had paid close attention the day Goran told them what it meant when witches came in threes. Ana hadn't decided if she and her sisters were there to control the chaos or cause it, or if maybe it was some of both.

"And what has Goran told you about the three sisters?" Breda turned her shoulder to the wall to look at Ana.

"He told us about the Moirae, the Three Fates. They're the

spinner, the measurer, and the cutter who weave the cloth of life. I think it's more like embroidery though. The Fates don't make the cloth, but they design the pattern that goes on it."

"And Goran told you, you are the spinner and Ivanka the measurer and Veronika the cutter?" Ana shifted under the weight of Breda's gaze. It was a test, but not of her.

Ana nodded and bit her lip.

"Goran is partially right." Breda turned and leaned back against the wall.

"What does that mean?" Goran wasn't always right. That wasn't a surprise. No one was always right, however much some adults wanted her to think they were. But she had believed Goran about her sisters.

"It means I will tell you a story."

———

Jo ran out the door, leaving Leo to catch up for once. She crashed into the woods behind the cottage where she'd seen the shade go. Leo called to her, but she didn't have time to stop and explain. Branches scratched at her face, and she lost her bearings. She couldn't hear Leo's voice anymore and could only catch the movement of Milo, or what she assumed was Milo, among the trees. She heard someone walking in front of her and followed the sound into a clearing where the sun, despite how dark it had gotten, broke through the heavy canopy.

Milo stood in the center. He wasn't as wan and dark-eyed as he had been in her dream. And he wasn't angry, he was anguished.

"I don't have her, Jo."

She was ashamed she had even for a moment believed him capable of hurting a child.

"It has her."

"What has her?" The shade version of Milo was much less talkative than he had been when he was alive. "The thing that killed the chickens?"

Milo nodded and looked behind him. The forest changed beyond the small clearing. There was no light among the trees, and they seemed to twist in on themselves. Jo wasn't sure she should go there, but if it meant Ana's safety she would do whatever needed to be done.

"Take me to her."

"He won't be able to follow you." Milo looked past her, the way they had come. She could hear Leo calling her name, but it sounded like he was much farther away than she could have run from him over the roots and undergrowth.

Milo held his hand out for her. His palm was cold but no colder than hers.

"I'm sorry I didn't come looking for you sooner."

"You're here now, and you came to help Ana." He looked ahead and moved the occasional branch for her.

"I made excuses." They had left the real forest. She had discerned that much. Milo was of that place far more than she was, and she was grateful he knew where they were going. Each tree looked more gnarled and broken than the last, and they all looked the same.

"I was angry, at you, at the demon, but I see now that it

wasn't anyone's fault. I had more I wanted to do. You made it clear there wasn't a future for us, but that didn't mean I didn't want a future at all."

Jo's eyes blurred, but she didn't have time to cry. There would be tears enough if they couldn't get Ana back to safety.

After what felt like an hour of hiking in circles, another clearing opened up in the woods. It was nowhere near as inviting as the one she'd found Milo in. A ramshackle hut made of rotted leaves and twisted branches lurked at the edge, its doorway stretched open like a maw.

"Ana's in there?"

Milo nodded and pulled her toward the hut.

"Shouldn't we make a plan or something?" Jo searched the edge of the clearing for whatever Milo had referred to, but there was nothing except the forest that circled in tighter on them than the last time she'd looked.

"The spirit's not here, but it will be back. We have to hurry."

———

"There's nothing here." Vesna called out to Gustaf, who was trailing her along the path.

"You're certain?" He caught up to her, his breath quick— though it seemed more out of fear for what they might find than from exertion.

"As sure as I can be. I can't see any human auras, and I don't have that chicken-skin feeling I get when there's something off in a place."

He nodded. "I don't think this is where they came either." She knew he could see auras as clearly as she did, but she doubted he had the other senses. Fear in those without the sight was a different temperature in the aura than those who had an inkling of what was coming.

"So, what do we do now?" Vesna put her hands on her hips and looked back down the path toward where they had parked Gustaf's car.

"Let's walk back. We can call Goran and see if he's heard from the others." Gustaf led the way along the trail as rain started a slow patter around them. They stayed mostly dry under the forest's canopy right until they got back to the car and the torrent began, drenching them both.

Vesna closed the door with a tinny thud and ran her fingers through her hair to get the wet tendrils off her face. "I doubt anyone's found anything. Goran or Jo would've called us."

After a nod and few quick words, Gustaf slid his phone back into his jacket pocket. "The only people Goran hasn't heard from are Jo and Leo. They are all heading to the monastery."

"We're the closest." Vesna's stomach sank as that chicken-skin feeling crawled all the way up into her hairline.

———

"I wish I had enough magic to make us some cushions." Breda wiggled against the wall and sighed. "Do you remember when I told you about Morana?"

Ana nodded and wished she had a cushion too. "The Goddess of the Witches?" After Ana had met Breda, she had made Veronika promise to light a black candle for Morana every time she tried to do magic. Her sister's spells had a way of going wrong in the worst possible way.

"Yes. She is also the goddess of winter and of death."

"Goran gave me a book. It has a picture of girls drowning Morana in the river, so the spring can return." Ana wrinkled her nose.

"You didn't like the story?" Breda smiled at her.

"It said Vesna, the spring, and Morana can't exist at the same time. I know it can't be summer and winter both, but the seasons are one thing, a cycle."

Breda's smile broadened. "Well done. In older stories, Morana was first the goddess of life—that whole cycle, as you said, from birth to death. Dažbog, the Sun God, loved her—and she loved him as all life loves the Sun. But she was the goddess of every living thing and had many lovers. In jealousy, Dažbog cast her into Nav, the place of the dead. He still loved her though and had to be with her, even there. So for half the year he joined her in the Nav, bringing winter."

"Kind of like Demeter and Persephone?"

Breda nodded. "I think most of our stories of the gods and goddesses come from older stories still. Different peoples told and retold those stories, giving them names in their own languages."

"So Vesna and Morana are the same goddess?" Ana pulled her knees up to her chin and tucked the hem of her nightgown under her toes. Her shins and feet were still cut up and swollen, but Breda's magic had taken most of the pain away.

"They were. But the gods become, to some extent, what we believe them to be. For many years people believed Vesna and Morana were separate goddesses and they became so:

Vesna bright and beautiful, a young woman with flowers in her hair, and Morana, the old hag who carried all of our fears of death and the darkness." Breda stopped and looked at the witch light that still hung in the air.

"Is that what took me?" Ana felt sorry for Morana, but if that thing was her, she was pretty scary.

"No. That was the shade of a person. Morana was never the awful thing we made her in our fear. There is no life without death, no light without the darkness. But sometimes people embrace only the darkness, and that darkness overwhelms them."

Ana nodded. Goran had said the same thing about magic.

"The world got darker as the fear of death took hold, and a time came when witches were hunted and killed. The same woman who had helped deliver a healthy baby was blamed for the death of livestock. I will not say no witches ever cursed their neighbors, but it was a rare thing. A panic grew, and witches and innocents alike were tried and killed. The darkness of her people separated from the truth finally broke Morana."

"She couldn't save the witches?"

"There were some who still believed in the old way, but fewer and fewer—and they had to do so in secret. In her heartbroken state, Morana found a woman, a Portal like your friend Jo, who was rotting in a cell waiting for execution. Morana offered her the peace of death and went to the fire in her place."

"But we still have winter. The Sun wouldn't have to visit her in the Nav anymore."

Breda laughed. "Yes, we do. Other gods and goddesses took Morana's burdens."

"What does this have to do with the story of the three sisters?"

"During those times when Morana chose her own death, all executions were public."

"That's gross." Ana wrinkled her nose again.

"It was a horrible thing. Before the flames took Morana, she made a prophecy, before the Witchfinders and everyone who had gathered to watch her die, that three sisters would come to bring the witches together again. And we've been waiting, lighting a candle for her until she returns."

———

Jo followed Milo into the hut. She'd never been much of a *Doctor Who* fan, but *it's bigger on the inside* was her first thought.

As big as it was, there was no Ana. There was a very sturdy trunk in the corner, though, just big enough to fold a girl into. The thought of Ana's broken body locked away brought the taste of bile into Jo's mouth.

Milo walked to the chest first and tried the lid, but it was locked tight.

"That would have been too easy." Jo looked around for a key, but, unless it had been shoved into the rotting walls, it wasn't there; the room was bare except for the chest.

"Can't you open it with magic?"

"I can't do magic."

"Aren't you a witch?" Milo looked at her, confused.

"I think under the broad definition, probably yes, but …" She could intimately describe the way that place smelled, down to the fact that the majority of the leaves rotting in the walls were chestnut and oak. She'd be great at a swingers' party because she could probably tell you who every set of keys belonged to. But she couldn't pick a lock magically or even with the only tool they had—twigs.

"We need to figure out something, fast."

"I know, I just don't …" Jo stopped, then she smiled and started humming "Whatever Lola Wants."

Milo looked at her like she had cracked wide open. But no sooner had she made it through the first bar, Helena appeared, dazzling in her toga-like dress.

"Yes?" Helena smiled broadly. "Oh, hello, Milo. I see you two have found each other."

"We can catch up later. Can you still do witch things?" Jo didn't have time for Helena's snappy banter.

"Yes. Why?"

"Can you pick a lock?" Jo pointed at the chest.

Helena stepped back and looked at the trunk. "Yes. What's inside?"

What did Jo want to be inside? If Ana was in there, they had failed to save her. And if it was empty, where did they go from there? Either way it was bad. "Nothing good, I'm guessing, but we need to find out."

Helena squatted down in front of the trunk and laid her hand on the latch. The lock clicked softly, and Helena flipped the lid open as she stood back up. "That was so much more complicated when I was alive. I guess there are a few perks to being dead." She smiled at Milo and then looked down into the trunk. "Oh."

The three of them stood peering into the chest as an unpleasantly warm air current blew away the orange blossom scent of Helena's magic. A faint glow from the room inside the trunk illuminated two upturned faces, one of which was Ana's.

Jo let out a sigh of relief. "How do we get you out of there?"

Helena reached into the trunk as the older woman stood and lifted her hand to her. Before Jo could figure out what was going on, or how Helena had managed it, both the woman and Ana were standing with them in front of the trunk.

The older woman slammed the lid shut. "We have to go now. It will know the chest has been opened."

———

Leo stood in the clearing, turning in a circle trying to find any trace of Jo among the trees. He called her name but only got the quieted woods in return. Even the insects had gone silent.

He caught a blur the size of a person out of the corner of his eye, but it was gone when he tried to look at it head-on. He pulled his phone out of his pocket to call Goran, but there wasn't enough signal to even send a text message. If the others had found anything, perhaps they would come there. Something was close, but he didn't know if it would lead them to Ana or not.

Breath, warm and moist on his neck, startled him. When he turned to see who or what was behind him, the blur flew at him and knocked him flat on his back. The leaf litter softened the blow to his head, but he still saw stars for a second. When he sat up, he was alone in the clearing again.

The presence had been too large to be Teja and Luka's house spirit, or any house spirit for that matter. He got to his feet, turning slowly again in the clearing, trying to see it before it attacked a second time. The forest was still too quiet, as if every rodent and bird was holding its breath. The air had changed, though; it carried the scent of autumn leaves and roasting chestnuts and with it a guilt he would carry with him to his grave.

———

"Let's try to get back to the first clearing. We can find Leo and get Ana back to town." Jo walked point and held branches for Milo along the way.

He carried Ana so she didn't have to walk through the forest on her injured feet, though Ana had said they no longer hurt. Breda, as she had introduced herself, and Helena walked behind, eyeing the gaps in the trees for the spirit. Jo expected it to return and give chase from the hut as she and the others made their way out of the In-Between and back into the waking world, but they had yet to encounter it. With her spirit and witchy companions, Jo had to wonder if she belonged in the "real" world anymore.

"Milo, when we get to the clearing, would you like me to open your door for you to go into the Next?" She could never make up for what had been taken, but she could offer him that peace, or what she believed was peace.

"I want to be sure Ana is home safe." He hitched the girl up gently on his hip. She had managed to fall asleep with her arms wrapped around his neck. Milo's tenderness with Ana broke Jo's heart. She had been right to end their relationship; she could have never given him the things he wanted. But because of her, or being connected to her, he would never be a father. She didn't know the nature of the Next, but she prayed that it involved reincarnation.

The forest began to change around them, and Jo sensed they were at the edge between the planes of existence. She could look out to the trees farther down the path and see dim sunlight, and she could smell the rain coming.

Leo stood in the clearing, his back to her as he rubbed his neck as if he were in pain.

A smudged figure came between them on the path and raced at Jo, its face becoming clear as it loomed at her. It was a woman, a woman with pointed teeth and her eyes and mouth blackened, and she wanted Jo to get out of her way.

Jo stood her ground. This was not Death come for her. Rebecca had said that would not happen. And whatever it was, it wasn't getting Ana again. The spirit got close enough to her face to kiss her and glared at her eye to eye before it threw its head back in a guttural laugh.

"I didn't want her. I wanted him." The woman's voice echoed in Jo's head like a hundred people speaking at once.

It turned through itself like smoke and shot toward Leo.

Leo spun around and saw Jo but didn't seem to see the thing crashing toward him.

Jo ran after the spirit, but Milo caught her by the arm and

jerked her back. "I won't let it hurt you."

She struggled against him, screaming. "It can't!" She wrenched her arm free and ran to Leo.

The spirit reached through the membrane between the world Leo stood in and the world Jo and the others were in and pulled Leo through.

His eyes were wide in shock as he looked from Jo back to the spirit. "Berta."

He said it with such resignation, Jo felt the shame he felt about the woman's death as if it were her own shame.

Jo tried to get between Leo and Berta, but the spirit wouldn't let her.

Breda called to Jo from the edge of the clearing. "Say her name. Open her door."

Jo gathered her voice. "Berta Horvat." The words traveled out into the air in swirls of mist as they had done when she had opened the Novaks' door before. She watched as the spell of her speech swirled around Berta's spirit and moved beyond to the edge of the clearing.

An ornate archway opened behind Leo and pulsed with a dim blue light. If Berta went to the door, she would take Leo with her. It would be the easiest way to kill him, if what she had come for was revenge. Jo grabbed Leo's arm and tried to pull him away, but Berta still had the front of his shirt wrapped in her bony hand.

Milo tried to help, but Berta was strong, surging with the bitterness she had carried for so many years in the In-Between. Jo could feel the woman's anger and torment every time the spirit brushed against her in their struggle.

It shouldn't have been difficult to pull Leo away. He should have been able to wrench himself free; he was bigger than either of them, bigger than Milo, but he wasn't fighting against the spirit.

Berta let go of Leo, knocking Jo off balance so she stumbled and fell hard. Milo offered a hand to help her up.

Before Jo could get back to her feet, Berta's shade punched her fist through Leo's chest and ripped out his heart, veins and arteries dangling as the muscle pumped in her hand. The color drained from Leo's face, and he fell back—back through the membrane and onto the matted leaves and pine needles.

Time slowed as Leo's body landed and bounced. A circle of leaves pushed into the air as he landed again, limp on the forest floor. A scream like an animal came up from Jo's gut.

Berta turned on Jo, menacing her with Leo's heart clutched in her fist. Helena bolted across the clearing and tackled the spirit, pushing her toward the open doorway. The two of them fell together into the darkness beyond, before Jo or Milo could reach Helena and pull her back to them.

Jo scrambled over the leaf litter to Leo. His eyes were open and staring into the canopy without seeing.

"No. No. No. No." She ran her hand over his face, his chest. There wasn't a wound, but there wasn't a heartbeat either.

Breda knelt beside her. "His heart has gone into the Next." She reached up and closed his eyes before Jo pushed her away.

Another door opened in the clearing. It was tall and wooden, with wrought-iron hardware. Another presence knelt next to Jo, and a cold hand on her cheek turned her face.

Leo's shade beamed at her.

This couldn't be happening. This had to be a dream, and her grandmothers would appear and tell her it was a warning or that she should be searching for her father. Leo could not be dead. It was unacceptable.

Jo stood up. "This isn't real."

Leo's shade stood and walked a step toward her.

"No. You get back in that fucking body right now. I'm not waking up until this has a happy ending." She couldn't breathe. She could barely make out the others still standing in the clearing watching this nonsense unfold. She would wake up at the hotel on the edge of the lake and walk down to twenty-seven kinds of muesli on the breakfast buffet while Helena offered color commentary on her sex life. That thing hadn't … not both of them.

Leo's shade took both her hands in his. "This is right. I failed Berta, my family failed her. She was out here all this time." He looked off into the dark part of the forest that Jo and the others had come from. "We didn't do the proper things to let her go to her rest. I deserve this."

"What the fuck is wrong with you? You don't deserve this. We're going to wake up at the hotel and   "

"Please stop."

Jo stared at him for a long moment before she went at him, her fists against his chest. How could he choose to go? How could he choose that now?

Leo's shade pulled her into him and ran his hand over her

hair, trying to soothe her. He lifted her face up to brush his lips over hers gently, before he whispered in her ear. And then he was gone. The door closed and disappeared as silently as it had come.

Jo fell to her knees next to his body and wailed as the bottom fell out of the sky.

———

Vesna ran through the rain and the low-hanging branches as fast as she could. Gustaf tried to keep up with her, but she sensed he was some distance behind. A human cry ripped through the trees and pierced Vesna's heart. She staggered on the trail and had to lean against a lichen-covered tree trunk to keep from collapsing to the ground.

In her hesitation, Gustaf caught up to her. "What was that?"

Vesna took a gulping breath. "You mean, 'who was that?'" She felt Jo's heart break in her own chest, but Jo wasn't physically hurt. Someone had died. There was a hole. Vesna gulped in air and pushed on, praying to whoever was listening that she was wrong. Gustaf kept up with her, and they made it to the clearing.

Leo was lying on the ground, his eyes closed. Jo had curled up next to him and Ana stood over them both, her tattered, bloodied nightgown drenched and sticking to her skin. Vesna sensed there were other entities in the clearing and guessed one was Helena, Jo's spirit guide.

Vesna ran to Jo and sank to her knees beside her friend, whose shoulders shook with wracking sobs. Vesna had no idea how to comfort her or how to get them all in out of the rain. She heard Gustaf on his phone. How it still managed to work was a marvel.

Gustaf knelt next to her. He was too awkward to offer physical comfort, but his words helped. "I've phoned Dr. Struna. She is arranging transport for … Brother Kos's body."

"Take Ana back to the car and ask the others not to come up here when they arrive."

Gustaf got up without replying and offered his hand to Ana. "How are your feet, child?"

Vesna looked at the girl. Her feet and lower legs were swollen and covered in cuts and scratches. She looked up at Gustaf. "Can you carry her?" Ana was small for her age, but Gustaf was neither a big man nor a person Vesna would've guessed was particularly good with children.

He nodded. "We will manage." He crouched and instructed Ana to climb onto his back. "Hold tight." He stood straight and hooked his arms under Ana's legs. Vesna watched as they picked their way gingerly back down the narrow trail. Gustaf had depths she had never imagined.

She turned her attention back to Jo. Her friend had quieted, but she still clung to Leo's body.

"Is Helena here?" Vesna looked around as if she would be able to see her if she looked carefully enough.

Jo shook her head and took a long, ragged breath. "She's gone too."

Vesna sat back on her heels. There were no words that could make any of this right. Nothing could bring back the dead from the Next, and given Jo's state, that's where Leo had to be. She laid down next to Jo in the wet leaf litter and held her, as Jo held Leo, and waited for Dr. Struna's team to come for them.

CHAPTER 24

Ana woke up in Dr. Struna's secret clinic tucked into the neighborhood between the public hospital and the castle hill. She looked out the window and into the street. Dr. Struna had told her the last time she was there that the glass was made so that she could see out but people couldn't see in. She stood at the window and watched a woman zip past on a bike.

Her feet felt better. Between Breda's magic and Dr. Struna's medicine that smelled strongly of the room in Goran's shop where he kept all his herbs, she could stand and walk without them hurting.

Breda joined her at the window. Ana didn't have to slip In-Between anymore to call to her or find her. A song popped in her head and Breda was there, or Ana could hum it and she would appear. Breda had said it was her favorite Beatles song. It wasn't one Ana had ever heard before, but she liked the little song about a blackbird.

"I think Dr. Struna will let you go home today." Breda didn't turn to her when she spoke.

"I hope so." Ana was ready to be home. Though she wasn't

sure things could ever go back the way they were. Her Aunt Olga had come to see her when she'd first arrived and sat on the chair next to her bed that whole first night. Ana had thought it was backwards that she was the patient but had to hold her aunt's hand while she cried.

A knock on the door made them both turn away from the window. Breda disappeared as Dr. Struna came in.

"How are you feeling?" Dr. Struna looked Ana up and down but mostly checked out her feet.

"A lot better. Can I go home today?" Ana walked back to the bed and sat on the edge.

Dr. Struna sat in the chair next to the bed and looked at Ana for a long minute before talking again.

"I think you know this already, but I wanted to talk to you about it before you went home."

Ana waited for the doctor to continue. Ana knew a lot of things, sometimes things other people didn't know, and she could hear Dr. Struna's thoughts trying to organize themselves.

"It isn't something I have seen before, and I haven't been able to find anything about it in the literature ..."

"I'm a Voice of the Dead now, like Jo." Breda had already explained it and said she would be her guide, if she wanted her to stay.

Dr. Struna looked relieved. "Yes."

Ana nodded while Dr. Struna explained that her family wasn't a family of Voices. Ana knew that already too. What Dr. Struna didn't know yet was that Ana's family were witches. Or they had been. Her grandmother had hidden it from her daughters, Katarina and Olga. Aunt Olga had always suspected she was different, but she was having a hard time accepting the supernatural as natural. Her aunt's thoughts about it had churned over the ideas so much that Ana had finally fallen asleep in exhaustion. She needed to ask Breda if there was a way she could turn that off.

Dr. Struna continued, trying to explain a thing Ana already knew there wasn't an explanation for. Ana tuned her out until she said, "go home."

Ana smiled and stood up and then stopped in the middle of the room.

"I don't have any clothes." She wasn't ever going to put that nightgown on again.

"Your aunt and sister are bringing something. They should be here soon." Dr. Struna crossed to the door. "Why don't you rest until they get here?"

———

Vesna sat at a table at the back of the teahouse. Her apartment had felt too small to hold her thoughts and all the things she needed to do. The list she had made had a few things that had been marked through, but she'd written as many new items at the bottom of the original list as she had completed. She frowned at the paper and picked up her teacup, but it was empty.

A sharp knock at the front door startled her as she poured more tea. When she turned to the front windows, she was surprised to see her mother standing there, peering in with her hand cupped to the glass.

Vesna opened the door for her.

"Here you are." Mrs. Kos was slightly out of breath. She slung a large leather bag onto the first table inside.

"Where else have you been looking?"

"Your flat."

"You could have called my mobile." Vesna frowned at her mother.

"I didn't want you to make an excuse not to see me. Igor told me you were here. He is a good man, for a witch. You could do worse."

Vesna had seen everyone in her family at Leo's funeral the day before. The frippery of the service had annoyed her. She knew it was Leo's and her mother's faith, but it just underlined for her how differently she felt. Her brother and his fiancée had been there out of duty, but Miha didn't care for the trappings of the Church any more than she had; he hadn't had much of a relationship with Leo because of it.

"Thanks. What makes you think I wouldn't have wanted to see you?"

"You didn't come to the house after the funeral." Mrs. Kos gave her the same face Vesna had seen every time her mother had disapproved of anything she had said or done in life. This wasn't new ground, except it was.

Vesna had needed to get out of Ribnica, away from the graveyard where the Kos men, generations of witchfinders, were buried in hallowed ground. They had dumped the bodies of women and children they accused and tortured into unmarked graves their families couldn't find. She had to leave before the urge to claw them all up out of their smug sleep with her bare hands took over.

"I was worried about Jo." Jo had not gone to the funeral. She had said her goodbye to Leo in the clearing and had said she couldn't face a line of po-faced church officials passing judgement on him for leaving the Order for her.

Mrs. Kos pursed her lips. "Are you her keeper?"

"No. I'm her friend. She's—"

"I didn't come here to talk about her. I came here to talk about you. Sit." Mrs. Kos sat in the chair in front of the bag and began to unpack a stack of books, a worn wooden box, and a gilded crucifix.

Vesna squinted at the spines of the books. One of them was an honest to god *Malleus Maleficarum* in the original Latin.

"What is all of this?"

"Your father's things. I assume the rest are at Leo's … room." Her mother straightened the stack and placed the crucifix, a rather detailed and gruesome one, on top.

"Why are you giving me this?"

"I would have thought with your godforsaken gifts, you would already know that." Mrs. Kos arched an eyebrow at her, and Vesna couldn't decide if her mother was trying to be funny or not.

The bottom fell out of Vesna's stomach as the reason for her mother's visit dawned on her. She shot up from the table, knocking the pile of books over and the crucifix to the floor.

"No. You can pack all of that up and give it to Miha." Vesna continued to back away.

Her mother picked up the crucifix without looking at her and put it back in the bag.

"Your father's wishes were clear."

The weight of her mother's words threatened to push Vesna through the floorboards under her feet. Her father had been tradition-bound in every aspect of his life and belief, why had he strayed so far afield on this one thing?

"The title of Witchfinder falls to you. What you are to do with that title was not in your father's directive and isn't any of my business. Leo chose to ignore the family edicts. I believe that leaves the way quite open for you."

Vesna approached the table and her mother again. "What are you saying?"

"Has grief really made you so dense?" Her mother shook her head. "I thought about what you said about God making us who we are. If you are to be the Witchfinder, perhaps it means something new in that light."

Vesna sat heavily in the chair. She reached out absentmindedly for the wooden box that looked as if it were held together by the will of the splinters it was made of. She opened it, expecting vials of holy water or her father's heavy onyx rosary. It contained a small leather-bound book with an ornate brass latch. Whatever words or images had been embossed on the cover had long been worn away. Vesna turned it in her hands and looked up at her mother.

"It was my father's, his spells and charms. I think you might find it more helpful than directions on how to find a witch's teat." Mrs. Kos shrugged. Her mother's heart had shifted, something Vesna would have never believed possible.

———

Jo rolled over in bed and looked out the gauzy curtains of her bedroom window. It was daylight, but she couldn't tell if it was dawn or dusk. She didn't know or care what day it was. She ran a hand through the hair at her temple only to have her fingers catch in knots an inch from her scalp. Her pits stank, and the sheen of sweat from her nightmares made the sheets stick to her.

None of it mattered. If she couldn't die, if Death, in the form of her great-grandmother or Dušan or whoever the hell had the job that day, wasn't going to come and offer her relief, maybe she could just rot there in that bed. She scrunched up her pillow and curled around it. If she'd had anything left, she would have cried again, but a numbness had crept into every cell of her body.

She punched the pillow and sat up. She had to pee, and though she was happy to rot in place, she'd prefer it not be in a puddle of ammonia.

Milo was still sitting on the futon. She held up one finger as he tried to speak to her again and continued to the bathroom. After she'd run her hands under the faucet and looked at herself in the mirror, she had to wonder why he hadn't run screaming the first time she'd gotten up. She could easily relieve the Medusa of her curse.

But there he was, sitting on her futon, looking slightly less like the depressed wreck she'd met in the clearing. The bruises around his neck still made her flinch when she looked at them. She wished he had the power to alter his appearance like Helena or Henry, her ghost of the Slovenian Alps, had, or the will.

Henry. Another brick in her masonry heart.

Jo sat on the futon next to Milo, close enough to feel the cold of his form against her thigh.

"Can I open your door now?"

He frowned at her. "I told you—"

"Look, I'm okay as I'm going to get. This is the new me." She struck a "ta da" pose with her arms and flopped back against the futon.

"You've been in bed for four days, in the same tank top and pants."

Jo pulled the tank top down to the top of her underwear. "So?" Her orchid was dead. Figured.

Milo let out an exasperated huff, or the best impression of one someone who didn't breathe could do.

"Can you not do this?"

"Do what?"

"Retreat into that razor-wire enclave where you pretend you don't feel anything."

"It's the only place that's safe."

"It isn't safe. I'll admit I was jealous, standing there in the rain watching you collapse over Leo. But part of me was just glad you'd let yourself love someone."

Her eyes burned again. "Yeah. Look where it got me."

"I'm going to go. Either my door will open on its own, or I'll find you when you're in a better place. This isn't how I want this to end."

Before Jo could say anything, he was gone.

Well, she'd fucked that right up. Again. She crawled back to bed and fell into an oblivion dotted with the hellscape dreams she'd had since Dr. Struna and her helpers had ripped Leo's body away from her in the forest. Her father, Helena, Leo, Milo, Henry, Maja, and the Novaks were all drowning around her in a river gray with ash. She couldn't get to them to save them. She couldn't move because something in the water had her by the ankles and pulled her straight down to the riverbed. Screams and cries made it to her ears even through the water, and she'd wake up again to find the screams were hers.

———

Vesna closed the door behind her mother and locked it back. She stood looking out into the courtyard. The sun had risen almost high enough to be seen above the rooftop of their building. It was going to be hot, unusually so. The teahouse was going to be closed for the week. Ivanka had hand-lettered a sign for the door. A death in the family had closed them twice now, and a thought of how many more times that could happen threatened to drag her into a darker mood.

She walked back to her table and sat down. The teahouse was a different place without the bustle of the kitchen or music blaring over the house speakers. Could she run a business and be the Witchfinder? And what did it mean to be a witchfinder now? What had it meant to Leo?

She had a building full of experts she could ask. Dušan surely had ideas about the nature of witchfinders. Goran had made his thoughts clear on more than one occasion. And Gustaf, Gustaf seemed to be struggling with the same thorny problem as he prepared for his boss's imminent arrival. In a battle between those who wanted to keep them all swathed in secrecy until there were too few behind the Veil to matter and those who wanted them all gone, wiped from the earth, so they didn't have any competition, she'd have to choose the secret-keepers. But there had to be another option.

What would Bettine make of the changed situation? She had said she was coming to meet with Leo, the local Witchfinder, to discuss the situation in Ljubljana and, Vesna assumed, enlist his help in … what? Rounding them all up into some kind of supernatural black site?

She guessed she would be the one meeting with Bettine now. And what would that look like? The daughter of a witch and a witchfinder, meeting with a member of the Board who loathed the very existence of the people she cared about the most. What would she give for another conversation with Leo? Probably not half as much as Jo would have given.

Her phone buzzed on the table. The screen said unknown, but she had an inkling of the caller's identity.

"Vesna, I'm glad I caught you. I stopped by your flat, but Igor said you had gone out." Dušan's voice lost none of its richness over the connection.

"I haven't gone far. I'm at the teahouse." Had she summoned a call from him in thinking of him?

"I thought you were closed for the week."

"We are, but it was a quiet place to think." It had been, briefly, anyway.

"May I join you?"

Vesna tapped the screen to end the call, surprised that

Dušan had asked. She would've expected him to know exactly where she was and show up with little thought about whether his presence was wanted or needed.

She started another pot of tea and waited.

It didn't take him long to make his way to the courtyard from wherever he had gone. Vesna let him in and made the niceties of offering tea. There wasn't any food prepared in the kitchen, so she had nothing to serve with it. Dušan was unbothered.

"Have you spoken with Jo today?"

Vesna shifted in her chair. She'd expected this conversation to be about the Witchfinder business.

"I looked in on her after the funeral yesterday and again this morning."

"And?"

"And she's a mess. What would you expect?" Vesna frowned at him.

"You can unknit your eyebrows. I expected she would take Leo's death hard. But she can't stay in bed forever."

"It's been four days." What was four days to someone who couldn't die? "Did you come down just to ask me about Jo? You could've knocked on her door yourself."

"You are a clever one, Vesna."

"Whatever. What is it? What do you want?" Vesna pushed her teacup away and braced herself for another onslaught of Dušan's bullshit.

"Bettine will be here tomorrow."

Vesna leaned across the table. "I thought she was coming next week?"

"The death of the Witchfinder seems to be reason enough to arrive early." He took a sip of his tea and looked at her pointedly over the rim of his cup.

"I guess that means you know I've had a visit from my mother." The call and the request to join her at the teashop had been false politeness. No surprises there.

"Bettine is not to be trifled with."

"You're a god, what do you care what Bettine does?"

"I care very much what Bettine does. She can't harm me directly, but she could still interfere with my plans." Dušan looked strangely uncomfortable.

"Do you actually care about what happens to Jo, to Ivanka and her sisters?" Vesna looked out the front window. Goran was watering the plants in front of his storefront, but he stopped to look at the teahouse. She knew he couldn't see them sitting there in the gloom, but she sensed he knew they were there. She and Jo had managed to gather a whole troupe of people around them, people who might all be in Bettine's sights.

"I am not as hollow-hearted as you would like to believe."

"Jo is not going to come running back into your arms now that Leo is dead, if that's what you're thinking." She'd be surprised if Jo ever let herself feel anything again. Did Dušan still love her? Who could know the mind of a god?

"To answer your real questions, I will always care for Jo, in my way. And what makes you think a god always knows his own mind?" He turned around to look out the window, following Vesna's line of sight. "Goran has done well with the sisters."

"He has. Though Ana ..."

"Ana has found her own."

Vesna stood. "I'm going back upstairs." There wasn't any more quiet to be had in the teahouse than there was in the flat with Igor and the cats.

"Bettine is going to want to know where you stand."

"You know how I feel about the Board, and you know how I feel about what my family has done."

"I told you what I want." He stood and collected their dishes and walked them back to the kitchen.

He had told her what he wanted, a re-enchanted world, but he hadn't been clear about what he was willing to do to get there.

———

Jo woke again. It was fully daylight. The curtains did little to keep the sun out, and she squinted at the light. A figure sat on the edge of the bed opposite, but Jo couldn't make out its face in the silhouetted darkness against the sunlit window.

"Go away." Jo put her pillow over her head only to have it snatched away.

"I'm not going anywhere."

The strange Victorian Southern accent gave her visitor away. Jo sat up and leaned against the wall. "How did you get here?"

"Does it really matter?" Rebecca stood up and opened

the curtains. She handed Jo a robe, the blue one patterned with origami cranes. "Take a shower. You're about to have a visitor."

"You're already here." Jo balled the robe up in her lap. "Why though?"

"We can't have you barking about without a guide. I've found someone I think will do the job nicely, but they're preoccupied, so you're stuck with me for a bit."

"Do I ever get a say in this? Maybe I don't want another guide?" As problematic as her relationship with Helena had been, Jo had trusted her. And in the end Helena had tried to save Leo by tumbling with Berta into oblivion. Jo hoped she had found her way to the Next, though the possibility that she had been thrown back to Dušan's realm by going through someone else's door worried her. That would be two souls she was at least partially responsible for sending there.

"Technically, no. You don't get much of a say. Shower."

"Do spirits really care if I stink?"

"Not particularly, but did I say your guest was a spirit?"

"Who then?"

"Shower. We'll talk when you're less disheveled."

Jo dragged herself to the bathroom and peeled off the clothes she'd been wearing for days. She let the warm water run over her crown and down her body while she stared at a leaf caught in the drain. It had to be from when she'd come home and showered at Vesna's insistence. Vesna had stood there in the bathroom, as dirty and wet as she was, and waited while Jo cleaned up.

From the phone call in Leo's car to standing in the shower again was mostly a blur, with a few stark images like still frames from a low-res video shivved into her memory. She remembered Leo's heart pumping in Berta's hand and the cold of his body next to hers. She remembered the warmth of Vesna cradling her in the forest and the rain. Men had come with a stretcher to collect Leo. She had stumbled out of the forest with Leo's saint medal clutched in her hand, and Dr. Struna had shown up at Jo's flat after she'd seen to Ana at her clinic. Vesna had come by since then, maybe multiple times. Milo. Otherwise there was just darkness and sleep and dreams she would be happy to forget.

At the center of it was her hollowed-out husk. She had let Leo love her, had found she loved him in return, and had been gutted by it. She felt nothing and everything to the point of nothing.

She turned the water off and ran a towel over her skin and through her hair. Rebecca was futzing in the kitchen, humming a song Jo knew but couldn't name.

"I made you some tea and something to eat."

A plate with a single piece of toast, spread thickly with butter and marmalade, and a cup with a trace of steam rising sat on the table at one place setting. Rebecca sat opposite with her own steaming cup and gestured for Jo to join her.

"I'm not really hungry." Jo started to push the plate away, but Rebecca stopped her.

"I know you aren't, but you still need to eat. If nothing else, it will remind you that you have a body."

Jo sighed and took a bite of toast. It tasted of nothing. She washed it down with tea that only registered as hot.

"You have every right to be depressed and angry." Rebecca watched Jo eat, as if to make sure she didn't dump it all into a non-existent potted plant.

"Thank you for your permission, but I'm not angry or depressed. I don't feel anything." Leo had once said to her that she shouldn't wish to feel nothing. Leo had also whispered he loved her after he had failed to fight for his own life to be with her. Maybe she was a little angry.

"It will come." Rebecca turned sideways in her chair with her elbow on the table. The expensive buff-colored linen of her suit rustled as she crossed her legs and looked at the front door of Jo's flat.

As if on cue, there was a tentative knock followed by a more-assured one.

"That will be your guest." Rebecca stood up and crossed the room to answer the door.

Jo pushed her half-eaten toast and tea away and pulled the bow at the waist of her robe tight. She didn't know who she had been expecting, but it definitely hadn't been Dušan. She found it hard to believe he hadn't had a hand in everything that had happened. There was a spark of anger toward him, but it was starved of emotional oxygen as quickly as it ignited.

"Hello. Am I interrupting your snack?" He looked to Rebecca, then Jo.

Rebecca shrugged. "I tried to get her to eat, but … I'll leave you two to discuss."

Jo stood up. "If you're my guide for now, what's the song?"

"The song? Oh, yes, I hadn't thought of that." Rebecca looked at Dušan like he might suggest something. He didn't. "Tom Waits. Do you know that song 'Time'? Let's use that." Rebecca left, humming the chorus to the verse she'd been humming to herself in the kitchen.

Dušan turned his gaze on Jo. "You should get dressed."

"Fuck that. I'm not going anywhere." Jo plopped on the couch. "Whatever you need to say to me you can say right here, and then you can leave."

"You can be as angry at me as you wish, but there's nothing I could have done about Leo." Dušan sat at an angle on the edge of the futon and gave her a look of pity.

"I really wish I could tell when you're lying to manipulate me versus just lying in general." She moved away from him and put her back against the wall, knees pulled up under her chin.

"It's true. I could have told you that Leo would die. Ivanka warned him, but I couldn't stop it."

"I don't believe you. You're the fucking god of the dead and you couldn't do something about Berta's lingering spirit? You couldn't banish her to your realm of the lost?" Jo wanted to scream at him, but Rebecca had opened all the windows. Spitting her words at him would have to suffice.

"If Berta hadn't taken him, something else would have. A heart attack in his sleep, an errant driver. Mortals all have their time, Jo." Dušan looked at his hands folded together in his lap. "But I am sorry for your loss."

"If I am now Jo the Deathless, then I should get used to it, right? I'm going to get to watch …" The thought of burying all her friends pierced the numbness for a moment and made it hard to get the last few words out. "Watch everyone I care about die?"

Dušan put his hand over one of her feet. The warmth would have been soothing if she could have been soothed. "There is no getting used to it. Every death is a loss."

"Did you know I would become this thing?"

Dušan looked down a long moment before meeting her gaze again. "Yes."

"And you didn't think you should disclose that? I asked you if you had anything I should be worried about." Conferred immortality had not been on her list of possible sexually transmitted diseases. Would she need to disclose that to any future partners? Ha.

"It was a selfish act on my part, but I was a man in love." He looked at her as if he were apologizing for eating the last apple without asking her if she wanted it.

Jo pushed his hand off and swung her legs back to the floor. "You are not 'a man' and I don't believe you about the other thing."

"I told you before that I loved you in my way."

"I told you before that I think you're full of shit, Črnobog."

"That may be so, but that isn't why I came to talk to you."

"Why am I not surprised?" Jo rolled her eyes.

"This won't last, this emptiness. But perhaps it serves a purpose for now."

Jo imagined her feelings bricked away and plastered over, safe from her ever getting back to them. If she couldn't die and her temporary guide wasn't going to let her dry-rot in her bed, they were all going to have to accept that all they would be getting was her husk.

"Bettine will be here tomorrow, and she will want to speak with you. Gustaf thinks you should leave town again, but I would advise against it."

"Do you trust him?" The urge to leave came over her. The thought of being far away from Dušan and everyone was appealing, but it would also mean she was leaving Faron and the others to deal with all this crap by themselves.

"I don't trust the Board, but I think Gustaf has seen the error of their ways." Dušan leaned back into the futon and looked at her. "Get dressed. You need to get some air."

Jo stood up. "Can you still hear my thoughts?" Faron had told her that Dušan couldn't get in his head any more, maybe she'd been gifted that same reprieve with her changed mortality status.

"No. I cannot, but I still know you."

"I have to wonder if you ever really did. How could you think I would want any of this?"

"It wasn't about what anyone else wanted. It was about what was necessary." He stood then, close enough to her that her instinct was to step back. She didn't.

She brushed by him toward the bedroom. The contact crackled along her arm, differently than when he had touched her earlier.

"Where are you going?" He turned on his heel and followed her into her room.

"I'm getting dressed." She dropped the robe and rummaged through the wardrobe tucked into the corner for underwear and something to pull on.

Dušan leaned on the doorjamb and watched her. He didn't leer, but his interest was keen. "You have more tattoos."

"I thought you saw them at the river."

"I was gone by the time you'd re-emerged." He caught her arm, stopping her before she pulled her T-shirt on. "Why an eclipse?" He reached out and traced the line of one of the coronal flames to the center of the dark moon with his free hand.

Jo blessed her numbed emotional state. Her body didn't betray her by reacting to his touch in any way. "It was to cover the scar from Achelous. If I had known I would develop miraculous healing powers, I wouldn't have shelled out so much money for it." It was a shame those miraculous healing powers didn't apply to her emotional wounds.

"It is very good work. Better even than this." He ran his thumb over the head of the snake at her clavicle.

"It's the same artist. He only has private clients now." She pulled her T-shirt on and smoothed the hem over the top of her skirt. Sašo had done all of her tattoos. She'd forgiven him his connection to Dušan because of his talent, and though he was expensive, he never charged her full price.

Dušan's expression changed. There was a longing or wistfulness that surprised her.

"I wish you would just tell me what you want from me." Jo ran her fingers through her hair. It was still damp at the ends, but she'd managed to get most of the tangles out.

"Do you remember when I said all of this wasn't for my entertainment, it was a war?"

"Yes. The mess with Avgusta." The memory of Avgusta's spell casting her into an imaginary fire had woven its way into her dreams the last few days when she wasn't drowning. She doubted she could ever forget that.

"Avgusta was a skirmish."

"It's Bettine you are at war with." The truth of it blazed like a spotlight into all of the boarded-up corners of her mind.

"The Board, yes."

Jo slapped more plaster over any emotions that might be leaking out of her mental fortress. "They are as responsible for this mess as you are. All the fucking secrets. If I help you, know it isn't for you."

A smile tugged at the corners of his mouth, but it didn't reach his eyes.

CHAPTER 25

Jo rummaged through the pantry shelves for something to add to the day's batch of scones. Vesna had decided they should reopen, just for the day. The teahouse would be a public place to meet with Bettine. None of them relished inviting her into their private spaces, and she couldn't exactly have them kidnapped and hauled off in a shop full of witnesses.

A forgotten bag of dried cranberries, a gift from Aunt Jackie in her care packages, had been hiding behind a bag of spelt flour. Those would work. Jo turned around to add them to the other ingredients she'd laid out on the work bench.

Rebecca was standing in the kitchen door.

"Aren't you supposed to give me some warning now?"

The speakers attached to her iPod on the tea service counter crackled, and Tom Waits's gravelly voice spilled out into the shop. Rebecca didn't even crack a smile.

Jo had been happy to have something to do, something that let her brain check out while she worked to keep all those thoughts and feelings safely behind the messy walls she'd built. Rebecca's presence indicated that grace period was more than likely over.

"Are you going to offer me something?" Rebecca looked back over her shoulder to the tea station.

"I'm off my hospitality game." Jo set the cranberries on the counter and walked by Rebecca to the tea station. "What would you like?"

"I'm not much of a tea drinker. What's the most coffee-like thing you have?"

The bells on the front door rang against the wood. Vesna walked in with her head down, flipping through a stack of mail in her hand. Fred followed, reporting for work even though Jo had told him he didn't have to come in.

"Fred, this is my grandmother, Rebecca. Rebecca, Fred."

Fred shook Rebecca's offered hand. "Grandmother?" He shook his head. "Perhaps I would rather not know."

"I think Rebecca could use a cup of your special."

Fred nodded, and he and Rebecca chatted while he made tea. Jo stepped back to her *mise* for the scones and stared at the ingredients on the counter like they would measure and assemble themselves. Her thoughts moved on from a *Bedknobs and Broomsticks* version of her life where scones got made by magic to whatever supernatural battle royal she'd agreed to soldier up for.

Fred tapped her on the shoulder and handed her a cup of tea. "Why don't you drink this, and I'll get the scones started."

"Thank you." She took a sip, knowing it would be syrupy and strong enough to stand a spoon in. It didn't disappoint.

"Are you sure you're ready for this?" He put his hand on her shoulder and turned her slightly toward him so he could see her face.

His kindness came the closest to undoing the bricked-up and spackled-over dam of her emotions. She couldn't answer with more than a nod.

She walked out of the kitchen, cradling her tea in her hands. Rebecca and Vesna were sitting at a table in the middle of the dining area. Vesna stood and offered her seat to Jo.

"I'm going to help Fred get started. Ivanka should be here soon." With that, Vesna disappeared into the kitchen.

Rebecca took Jo's tea and set it on the table in front of her. Jo waited for the tiniest tap against the plaster that would shatter her into dust. Her grandmother put her elbows on the table and laced her hands together.

"I promise you'll have time to collapse and grieve, if we can get through today." Rebecca's eyes bored into her.

"Do I want to grieve or throw things? I don't even know." Jo felt like she was out of sync with everyone and everything. Like if someone looked, they'd see her standing still while everything else moved apace around her.

"You can grieve Leo and rail against the choice he made. You can mourn your mother and hate her at the same time." Jo appreciated her not giving her the pity face Dušan had offered her the day before.

"Okay, so what needs to happen today?"

"We need to satisfy Bettine's curiosity and get her the hell out of here." Rebecca sat back in her chair.

"There has to be more to it than that." All of this discussion and maneuvering couldn't just be an effort to pass inspection.

"I honestly don't know. Dušan is playing his cards close to the vest."

———

Vesna looked up at the clock over the sink in the kitchen. Bettine should have already been there. The teahouse was full of tourists who'd wandered in, regulars who came to support them after being closed for Leo's funeral, and a contingent of their strange little band of supernatural weirdos. Her mother had even showed up and was holding court at a table with Igor and Goran. Dušan, the Dark Lord, was conspicuously absent. That fact needled her more than she would have liked.

Gustaf poked his head into the kitchen. Vesna had never seen the usually calm Observer so worked up. She'd let him pace in the service area even though he was in the way.

"Maybe her train is late." He looked at his watch and then up at the clock and then at Vesna like she would be able to offer anything to soothe his nerves.

"She'll get here when she gets here." Vesna brushed by him with another plate of scones and tea sandwiches. She peered into the office as she went by.

Jo was sitting on the edge the desk listening while Faron told her about an old woman recognizing Dušan and him in the street. She'd have to ask about that later.

"You okay in there?" Vesna smiled weakly at them both.

Jo shrugged.

"It'll be over soon." Faron leaned against the desk next to his mom and put his arm around her shoulders. It struck Vesna for the first time that they had each saved the other, and now they would both live on long after she was dust. There was never going to be an over for them.

She sat the plate of food on the right table and looked up as the bells rang. Gustaf rushed by her, having spotted their visitor through the front window before she had gotten to the door.

Vesna joined him as Bettine came inside, followed by two men with presences that far exceeded their slight builds.

Gustaf seemed to be struck dumb, and Vesna had to concede Bettine was nothing like she had expected. Goran had indicated Bettine would be a woman in her eighties. Either she had a portrait rotting in her attic or Bettine was not merely human. She looked to be in her forties, and well-preserved forties at that. Which meant she hadn't aged a day since she'd left Ljubljana with Goran's mother, Breda, in tow forty years ago.

"You have not changed." Gustaf rushed the words out in a breathlessness Vesna couldn't name as shock or admiration. Ah. There had been a relationship, or an inkling of one, there. Gustaf's heart wasn't as gray and emotionless as his exterior; it had been broken all those years ago. And the wound had just been ripped back open.

Bettine looked around the shop, her gaze hesitating at the tables filled with those who lived beyond the Veil. When she looked at Vesna again, their eyes met. "I am sorry for your loss. I did not agree with Brother Kos's approach to his position, but I believe he was a good man."

Vesna thanked her with a sad smile. For Bettine to acknowledge her uncle's death in such a way meant she had no understanding of him. He was a good man in part because he refused to continue the Kos family's reign of terror.

"I'd like to conduct this meeting in a more private location. Perhaps we should go to my rooms at the hotel." It was an imperative not a question.

Gustaf nodded, still slightly agog at the untransformed Bettine. Vesna snuck a sidelong glance at his aura. It was in turmoil, roiling between the usual calm blue-gray that clung to him like an envelope and lightning flashes of orange and red. Vesna turned then and did a sweep of the room. Jo and Faron had stayed in the office, which Gustaf had decided was best.

Mrs. Kos caught Vesna's eye and nodded. It was a small gesture and Vesna still marveled at her mother's abrupt change of heart, but it wasn't so strange when she thought of how fiercely protective her mother was of her people. Because of Vesna's connection to them, everyone pretending to sit quietly and drink their tea had become her mother's people. No amount of belief in the devils of witchery would overbalance her protectiveness. Vesna was grateful for that and felt that same protectiveness course through her.

Bettine turned and led her guards—that's what they had to be—and Gustaf and Vesna out of the teahouse into the courtyard. The unchanged woman had not offered a hand in greeting, and she didn't offer any words as they walked along the river toward Prešeren Square other than to marvel at how changed the city was from her last visit.

As they neared the square, Vesna caught a glimpse of

Dušan heading toward the teahouse. No one else seemed to notice him. He met her gaze but didn't signal that he had seen her. She lost sight of him in the crowd of tourists taking their photos with Prešeren and his muse, and their little band walked on toward the Lisica Hotel.

CHAPTER 26

Jo jumped at the bells on the teahouse door. They were great for letting them know they had a customer when they were holed up in the kitchen working, but now they just rankled the frayed end of her nerves.

Faron went out to the tea station to see who it was.

She didn't like that Vesna and Gustaf had left with Bettine. Meeting with them was the purpose of her visit, but she'd hoped it could be there at the teahouse where she and the others could keep an eye on Bettine. Maybe they would have stayed if so many people hadn't shown up.

Faron returned to the office with Dušan in tow.

Dušan didn't pause a beat. "It's time for you to go."

Jo raised an eyebrow at him. "I thought you said I had to stay?"

Dušan smiled in a way that made Jo's stomach drop. "Not you, love. Him. She's seen that we didn't empty the city ahead of her arrival."

"Where am I supposed to go?" Faron didn't look surprised, but he didn't look happy about it either.

Dušan rummaged in his jacket pocket, produced an envelope of train tickets, and handed them to Faron.

Faron looked through the tickets. "You want me to take Ivanka and Ana with me? What about Veronika? Isn't Olga going to have something to say about disappearing with her nieces?"

"I have already spoken with Olga and she understands the necessity of getting Ana, especially, out of Ljubljana. Veronika has a job to do here." Dušan rummaged in the other pocket. This time he produced a single folded sheet of paper. "A car will meet you at the train station in Zagreb."

"Where are they supposed to go from there?" Jo wasn't sure she liked Dušan playing cruise director with her son.

"It's better that you not know, *Miška*."

She pursed her lips at his pet name for her, the little mouse. He knew she hated it, and he insisted on using it when he was at his most patronizing.

"Do you trust whoever is meeting them?" It was a stupid question. She didn't know if Dušan trusted anyone, but she felt the need to extract some additional bit of information from him. She shifted her position on the desk and waited for him to answer.

"Yes."

So much for gleaning any additional information.

The odd situation of the three of them, a dysfunctional family to the point of farce, standing together in the office of the teahouse—the business she had built with her friends who'd become her family—would have struck her as amusing if she hadn't been so concerned about Faron's safety.

Faron sat back down on the edge of the desk and put his arm around her shoulders again. "I'll be fine, and Ivanka and I will take good care of Ana." The silver-flecked eyes that looked back at her were ageless. It was her Faron's face, but the mind behind those eyes was irrevocably changed. He'd known this was coming, or he wasn't surprised by it.

She nodded.

"You should get going. Ana's bags are packed, and she is waiting at Olga's for you to collect her. You and Ivanka should take what you need for an extended trip. Take a taxi. You don't have time to walk."

Faron nodded and stood up from the desk. He pulled Jo into a rib-crushing hug and kissed her on the cheek before he disappeared through the office door.

"I know you aren't going to tell me where you're sending them—"

"No, I am not. But they will be taken care of until this situation is resolved."

"And what is this situation, really?" She'd sifted through the pieces she'd collected from her various conversations, but she still didn't really understand why Bettine's visit to Ljubljana was so dire. There was a possibility she would replace Gustaf with a new Observer, if she thought he wasn't doing his job. That did worry Jo.

"I will explain in a moment." He turned on his heel and left her sitting on the desk with her mouth slightly open.

She stood up and followed him out as far as the tea station.

Dušan sat at the table with Vesna's mother, Igor, and a gray-faced Goran. After a few words, Goran and Mrs. Kos left. There were a few more words with Igor, then he, too, left the teahouse. Fred joined her from the kitchen.

"I called Reka. She's on her way. She and I can close. Go do whatever it is you need to do." Fred tucked his hand towel into the back of his apron.

"I don't know what it is I need to do."

Fred nodded his head at Dušan as he approached. "I think you're about to get your marching orders."

———

Though Bettine's suite at the Lisica was spacious, it felt crowded and uncomfortably close to Vesna as she perched on the edge of a cream-colored loveseat. Bettine had offered the two of them water, but neither had taken any.

Bettine's guards stood near the door, an unsubtle barrier between Vesna and Gustaf and the outside. Their presence contributed to Vesna's rising claustrophobia. After moving in and out of the main sitting area and the bedroom, Bettine finally settled into the chair opposite and crossed her legs. She was unaffected by the tension in the room, or she was enjoying it. That possibility hadn't been lost on Vesna. Bettine's aura wasn't overly bright, a sign the woman knew how to rein it in, but what Vesna could see was clear and calm, almost happy.

"See. This is much quieter." Bettine took a sip of water and set her glass back down soundlessly on the side table.

Gustaf coughed into his hand but didn't speak.

Vesna had tired of the pretend niceties. "Are you an Immortal or a Long-Lived?"

Gustaf sputtered next to her on the loveseat. He wasn't going to ask, and Vesna wanted to know what she was up against. Bettine just smiled in her leonine way, enjoying her quarry's discomfort.

"It is so hard to tell, but I do believe I am mortal. Life has left me with a few scars." She smiled a sad little smile at Gustaf, as if there were some imperceptible mar their near-romance had left on her heart. It was a distraction, and Vesna's stomach turned watching Bettine play him so easily.

"It was my understanding that Immortals and the Long-Lived were barred by the Board from holding positions of power in human institutions." Vesna delivered her line as calmly as possible. Bettine was not going to rattle her completely, or at least not visibly. Vesna could keep her aura in check, too.

"You assume the Board is a human institution."

Gustaf stiffened next to her on the couch. Vesna didn't risk looking at him. There was empathy; he had been duped by the organization he had devoted his life to. There was anger too. He was a smart man and was letting either his guilt or his lingering fantasy about this woman paralyze him.

Bettine gave him a look of pity thinly veneered with concern.

"It was begun as such, of course. Charlemagne in his wisdom." She laughed and absentmindedly waved her slender hand in the air. Vesna got the distinct impression that Bettine may have known Charlemagne. "And it is ostensibly still an institution of humans, the Observers especially. But a few of us with grander designs have taken places on the Board." She plucked an imaginary bit of fluff from the arm of the chair and waved it away.

Gustaf was still mute by Vesna's side. Had his circuits simply overloaded at all this new information, or was he in awe of Bettine and what she truly was?

"And what are these grand designs?" Vesna leaned back against the couch. She couldn't match Bettine's disregard for the frisson in the room, but she could mimic it. "Surely, it's been noticed that Long-Lived have joined the Board?"

"That's for later. What I want to ask you is if you intend to proceed with your uncle's plan of diluting the role of the Witchfinder to party host or if your leanings are perhaps more in line with your father and grandfather?"

"Based on your tone, I think you will be disappointed by my answer." Vesna stopped there and waited for Bettine. She'd watched Gregor negotiate business deals often enough to have learned that you never gave more than you had to, and it was always best to let the other person talk themselves into a corner.

"I suspected as much. You have too many liaisons with witches and Voices for me to expect anything more of you."

Bettine's tone was dismissive, but the words struck Vesna very differently. She didn't have liaisons with witches; she was a witch. She was the daughter of a weather witch who had hidden herself in the house of the enemy. If Bettine didn't know that, Vesna had her at an advantage, however slight.

"It's a shame to have the Kos name squandered, but given your uncle's proclivities, I am not surprised. I can see you will be of little help. But I think you might still be useful."

Bettine turned her gaze on Gustaf. "You, however, are a disappointment."

She waved her guards toward the couch. Their auras became visible as they approached. A black cloud clung about the two men like monks' robes. They were human but possessed by darkness and enthralled to Bettine.

The slightly larger one approached Gustaf and pulled him up to a standing position. The slighter one yanked Vesna off the settee as his partner snapped Gustaf's neck. The little gray Austrian crumpled back onto to the loveseat, his head lolling against his chest.

Vesna fought against her captor, but there was no winning against his supernatural strength. She was restrained and locked into the bedroom of the suite. She sat on the bed, struggling against the binding on her wrists. It was more than tape or cord. When she squinted, the telltale markings of magic suffused the binding with a blue glow. At least they hadn't bound her arms behind her.

She gave in to her emotions for a moment and cried for Gustaf. He had finally seen the danger in what the Board asked of him, if far too late. He had cared for Jo and tried to warn and protect the rest of them as best he knew how. His death at the hands of Bettine's minion was undeserved. Vesna was grateful it had been swift. She said a quick prayer to whatever gods might be listening that his soul would find peace in the Next.

There wasn't time to wallow in that grief and anger for long. Bettine was more dangerous than Vesna had imagined, even given her own deep dislike of the Board and all they stood for. There was nothing in the room Vesna could see that would cut through ordinary bindings, let alone magically enhanced ones. She swore at her mother under her breath for denying who she was; Vesna could've used a spell or incantation to get her out of that mess. She said a more directed prayer to Dušan, in hopes that he wasn't so distracted by his chess game that he wouldn't hear her.

———

Dušan shooed Jo back into the office when he finished his conversation with Igor and the others.

"Where did you send them?" Dread had risen in Jo's throat as she'd watched them disappear into the darkening courtyard. Something had gone horribly wrong. Her stomach was plotting a revolt, and her mouth tasted like the gunk trapped in the dishwashing sink drain with some evil thrown in.

Rebecca appeared in the doorway and joined them, closing the door behind her.

"I've sent a message to your friend Gregor and his partner not to return to Ljubljana. Matjaž is also away on business and will remain so. The customers are leaving, and Frédérick and Reka have been told. They both leave within the hour. Veronika is on her way here."

Jo looked at Rebecca and Dušan, her gaze ping-ponging between their faces, waiting for someone to tell her what the hell was going on.

"Thank you. Efficient as always." Dušan turned then to Jo. "Bettine has come to put things in order."

"Gustaf not snitching every sneeze and fart to Bettine hardly seems like rebellion." Jo sat down heavily on the edge of the desk.

A light knock on the door distracted them all.

Fred poked his head in to say that everyone had gone. He opened the door the rest of the way and joined them in the cramped office. Rebecca and Dušan were visibly displeased, but he ignored them and went straight to Jo.

He took both her hands in his. "When this is over, I will be back. I know you don't put much stock in prayers, but I will pray for your safety and that of the others."

"We will take whatever prayers you have to offer. I'm so sorry you're caught up in this mess."

He smiled at her. "I made my life with witches, one must expect things will not always be easy."

"What about Reka?" Their dishwasher had few resources and couldn't just pick up sticks and leave the city.

"She will begin her journey with me."

"I know. It's best not to tell me."

"Or anyone." He smiled again. "I will be back. I promise." He touched the little brown bird tattoo on the inside of her wrist. "I always wondered why you had a sparrow there. We sparrows gather together, and it is very hard to get rid of us."

Jo nodded, and he left. Her eyes burned, but she imagined another layer of spackle over another reason to weep. When this was over, if this had an over, she would give her portion of the teahouse to Fred and Reka. Fred had put so much energy into building the business, and Reka had been the first dishwasher who had stayed longer than a couple of months, solidly ignoring the weirdness that had gone on around her.

"Are you sending me away, too, with Veronika?" Jo looked up at Dušan, her eyes still burning.

"No. We are going up to your apartment for you to change, and I'll explain from there."

CHAPTER 27

Jo shifted out of her work clothes into ones that would travel better, black pants and a long-sleeved black T-shirt. She pulled her hair into a ponytail and rejoined Dušan and Rebecca in her tiny living area.

"Do I need to pack?" She patted her pockets and went to retrieve her wallet and keys off the bed.

"Not yet." Dušan gestured for Rebecca and Jo to lead the way out of the flat. He closed the door behind them. "You'll have time for that after we rescue Vesna."

Jo dropped her keys and wheeled around on Dušan. "From what? What about Gustaf?"

Rebecca and Dušan looked at each other like parents deciding how much to share with a child.

"What happened?"

Rebecca took Jo's hand, her fingers as cold as Jo's. "Gustaf is dead. We have time to save Vesna though. She isn't who Bettine wants."

Jo waited for the landing to crack open underneath her and drop her into the center of the Earth. She stared, mouth agape, at Rebecca.

"I know." Rebecca took a deep breath. "Stay with me through this."

Dušan hadn't said a word and started down the stairs. Jo went after him, the sound of Rebecca locking the door echoing in the stairwell around them.

Jo didn't catch him until they got to the bottom of the stairs and were standing on the cobbles of the courtyard. It was fully night, and the teahouse and the other businesses around them were dark. Veronika was waiting for them, standing in the pale light that spilled out of the stairwell into the unlit courtyard.

Jo grabbed Dušan's arm and thought of the years of pain he'd caused her and Faron and all the unsaid accusations and curses she had wanted to lay at his feet, or better yet, smack him over the head with. He had completely fucked up her life, her son's life, and now he'd endangered Vesna too.

Veronika gasped and stepped away from them into the shadow.

"Good. You are coming into your own." Dušan freed himself from her grasp and smiled at her.

Jo snapped back into the moment and looked for Veronika in the dark. The girl stepped tentatively back into the light.

"What the fuck was that?" Veronika was several shades paler than she had been.

"What was what?" Jo looked from Gustaf to Veronika and back.

"Your eyes. They went all black, but they glowed. What

are you?" Veronika stepped in closer like she would find the answer written on Jo's skin.

Rebecca stepped off the last step in the courtyard. "Queen of the Witches." She slid Jo's keys into the pocket of her pants.

Dušan showed no surprise and didn't even have the grace to look like he cared.

Rebecca walked closer to him, ignoring Jo and Veronika, until she got right up in his face. "That was your plan from the beginning, wasn't it? Find a Portal, knock her up. But she had a son instead, and you had a change of plans. Were you just tired of doing the extra work?"

Dušan didn't back away from Rebecca or her accusation.

"We don't have time for this." His calm in the face of Death's anger wasn't unexpected, but it still bothered her.

Jo found her voice again. "Not now, but when Vesna is safe, you have a fuckton of explaining to do, Črnobog." Jo brushed by him and headed for the door to the courtyard. She pulled the heavy doors open and found Igor and Mrs. Kos standing in the street.

"You two need to get the fuck out of here." Jo brushed by them and turned toward the river.

Igor caught her arm and spun Jo around to face him.

"Look. I'm not kidding. You need to leave. Bettine murdered Gustaf."

"I know. And she has Vesna. How could you possibly ask me to leave?" Igor's voice was heavy with emotion but restrained. He wasn't a man who slid easily into histrionics.

Jo had only been thinking of herself and of getting to Vesna as quickly as possible. As much as she wanted to throw Dušan into the river, he had written the playbook he expected them all to work from, and that included the two other people standing there who loved Vesna as much as she did.

"You're right." She put her hand over Igor's. "Okay, Črnobog, what's the plan?"

Mrs. Kos gasped and crossed herself.

"He's a complete asshole, but, despite the bedtime stories, I don't think he's actually evil." Jo locked eyes with Dušan. "You do have a plan, don't you?"

"The immediate plan is to retrieve Vesna and get Bettine and her guards out of Ljubljana."

Igor looked at the women's faces and back to Dušan. "Good plan. But how?"

Rebecca stepped into the conversation. "Bettine is a Long-Lived—"

"How do you know she's not an Immortal?" Jo had no idea how to win a fight against someone who couldn't die. An image of birds of prey locked in a death spiral crashed through her thoughts.

The corner of Rebecca's mouth twitched into a half smile. "Death knows. Bettine isn't impervious, but she is smart. We have a slight advantage, though, in that she has no idea who most of us are."

Dušan nodded in agreement. "Mrs. Kos, you're our final backup. If Bettine gets out of the hotel with Vesna, you'll need to conjure up a hell of storm to slow them down."

Angry sparks darted through Mrs. Kos's aura. Jo was sure

Vesna's mother could whip up a hurricane, if needed. She was less sure about standing next to a potential human electrical fire and not getting struck by lightning. Vesna's revelation about her mother's long-hidden abilities had been a surprise and another piece of the puzzle sliding into place.

Dušan continued with his marching orders. "Jo, Rebecca, and I will confront Bettine. Veronika will stay in the hall in case anyone gets past us."

Igor piped in. "And me?"

"You will wait in the lobby. And as soon as we go up, you should call Gustaf's contact with the police, Inspector Klančnik, I believe. She'll have her hands full, but we will need to leave unimpeded."

Jo looked over the faces in their circle in front of the open doors. A sense of loss settled into her bones. Rebecca caught Jo's gaze. Death knew they weren't all going to make it back.

CHAPTER 28

Vesna sat quietly on the edge of the bed with her eyes closed. Bettine was on the phone with someone in the other room of the suite. Vesna could tell by the cadence of her voice, but the heavy hotel doors muffled the words themselves.

With concentration bordering on strain, she'd managed to loosen the tie on her wrists, but she couldn't pull her wrists apart. That had to be the magic. Neither Bettine nor her henchmen had done anything that looked like a spell. Vesna guessed they'd brought a bewitched tie with them, which meant they had this planned from the beginning. It may have also meant that none of them could do magic themselves.

What had Jo told her about Rok? He didn't have powers, but he had developed psychoscopy over his long life. Is that why Bettine had not offered to shake hands? Had she suspected Gustaf or her of being capable of something similar? Bettine's aura had been too locked down to detect if she was a magic user. Vesna had gotten used to what those looked like with Goran and Veronika. Retroactively, she'd realized that's why Helena's aura had always bothered her. Hell, she'd missed it with her own mother. There would be time enough to pick through all of this later. The more pressing concern was to see if Bettine had any other tricks tucked into her drawers.

Vesna sat up from the bed, listening carefully for her captor's continued conversation in the main room. She pulled open the small drawer in the night table next to the bed with the tips of her fingers, grateful for the solidly built and well-maintained furniture of an expensive suite. The drawer was empty save a linen-colored pad of paper printed with the Hotel Lisica logo.

She stepped across the carpet to the dresser and pulled open the top drawer only to find underwear and a scarf. The next drawer held clothes, and underneath the neatly folded stack of tops—Bettine planned to be there for some time given the amount of packing she'd done—Vesna uncovered a soft black bag. Inside were more ties like the one around her wrists and a small vial of gray liquid that looked as if were shifting rapidly from vapor to liquid and back again. It was an awkward maneuver, but she tucked a couple ties and the vial into the damn-near-useless pockets of her pants, closed the drawer, and sat back on the edge of the bed.

The door lock clicked, and she tried to look as bereft as possible. Bettine came in, the shorter guard on her heels like a kicked puppy.

"You'll be more comfortable on the couch." Bettine didn't look like she cared about her comfort in any way, but perhaps the woman had thought better of leaving Vesna alone for too long.

Vesna stood up and pretended to stretch as if she had been in that position since the door had been closed on her. The guard herded her back to the settee. Gustaf's body hadn't been moved, but she didn't shy away from sitting next to it. She hoped his spirit had gone to Jo. If her prayers hadn't reached the local god, maybe Gustaf's shade could reach the local Voice.

Bettine stood in front of her, waiting. Vesna had no intention of asking questions. She'd gotten the distinct impression that Bettine wanted to see her squirm and that she took pleasure in the discomfort of others. Vesna wouldn't give her that. Her denial to play along rattled the woman, but she hid it well, for the most part.

"I can't quite decide what to do with you. Should I ransom you for your friend Jolene Wiley, the last Portal, or should I just have Jean dispatch you and be done with it?"

Vesna shrugged.

"You would let your friend give her life for yours?" Bettine was trying to find a pressure point that didn't exist.

Vesna smiled coolly back at her. "Jo does what she wants."

The cracks were showing in Bettine's façade. She'd expected an easily cowed, reluctant Witchfinder. Vesna laughed softly. There were a lot of things Bettine didn't know. Vesna might still die, but she wasn't going to go down without a fight.

Bettine plopped into one of the chairs opposite the settee and stared at Vesna. She didn't even acknowledge Gustaf's corpse. The guards flanked the back of her chair now that they didn't need to bar the door for two unrestrained guests.

"I guess we'll wait. I assume your friend who 'does whatever she wants' will come looking for you before too long." Bettine picked up her empty water glass and tried to take a sip before setting it back down, further irritated.

"She will." Vesna leaned back, Gustaf's face in the periphery of her vision. Someone had closed his eyes. Either Bettine wasn't as evil and uncaring as she wanted to appear, or his unseeing stare had made her feel guilty. A gray smudge of mist rose from Gustaf's body and made its way toward the door. Vesna tried not to follow it with her eyes. Bettine couldn't see it or hadn't noticed, and Vesna didn't want to tip her off in case she had something in her bag of tricks to restrain a spirit.

———

Jo stood at the end of the hall listening to Dušan give Veronika a crash course in a difficult shielding spell.

"Should I try it now?" Veronika looked uncertain. She was powerful, but after almost killing her younger sister and actually killing Jo, she was wary of wielding witchcraft without some guardrails.

"No. You'll blow us out of the hallway. Just know that if the time comes, you'll be able to do it." Rebecca put her hand on Veronika's shoulder to reassure her. Jo noticed how different the gesture was than the patronizing smile Dušan gave the girl. She still wanted to throttle him for dragging them all into this. It was his war to fight, but he'd had no compunction about conscripting a unit of traumatized, battered people who hadn't recovered from the last round.

"You can hate me later." Dušan whispered it into her thoughts. Good to know he could still do that, but she hoped he couldn't hear her thoughts unless she wanted him to.

Out loud he added, "I don't need to read your mind when

your feelings are displayed on your face, *Miška.*" He turned and walked toward Bettine's suite.

"Wait." Jo felt then saw Gustaf's shade. "Gustaf is here." He walked toward her, trying to keep his head straight though it lolled to one side then the other.

Veronika looked around, but Rebecca and Dušan could see him.

He was grayer than he had been in life. "Vesna is alive but bound with more than cord."

"I'm sorry." Jo wanted to reach out to comfort him, but thought better of it. He hadn't been an affectionate man. Still, his connection to her and the others had cost him his life.

"There is no need for apologies. I chose to serve the Board."

That he was resigned made it worse. "Are there any others with Bettine?" Jo didn't know what else to say to him.

"No, only the guards you saw. I don't know what her plan is, but she wants you, Jolene Wiley." His face fell further. Jo hadn't believed that possible. "I'm sorry I didn't understand sooner."

"You did what you could, and you've warned us now." Jo took his ice-cold hand. "I can open your door." He had tried to comfort her that first day he'd spoken to her outside her shop when she'd been shaken by the dead clamoring to speak with her.

"Gustaf Lichtenberg." She said his name slowly and clearly, trying to give some dignity to passing into the Next in a hotel hallway.

Nothing happened.

Rebecca reached out to the door closest to them and turned the handle. Blue light made its way up the doorframe and suffused the door itself, transforming it from a blank hotel room door with a peephole to one out of a cottage in German fairy tale. Gustaf gave them all a slight bow and disappeared through his door. The light collapsed to a point and disappeared through the peephole.

"Why couldn't I open his door?" Had all her back and forth from Dušan's underworld and the In-Between broken her ability to do the one fucking job she had as a Voice?

"I'll explain later, or he will." Rebecca gave Dušan an arched-eyebrow side eye as he walked down the hall away from them and knocked at Bettine's rooms.

A second later one of the guards opened the door for them.

"May we join you?" Dušan turned on an oily, diplomatic charm.

The guard pulled the door wide and let the three of them in. He stuck his head out to check the hallway, but Veronika had retreated to the stairwell to wait until the door closed.

Bettine stood up. "I see you brought friends." She locked eyes with Jo. "Afraid to meet with me alone?"

"Not in the least, but I'm not running this show." Jo tilted her head at Dušan.

"Dušan Črnigad, alchemist and necromancer extraordinaire, I've heard so many tales about you. Are you really a sad, old god or do you just like to use that story to lure gullible Americans to your bed?" She gave Jo a pointed look.

Bettine's words bounced off Jo without hitting whatever mark they had been lobbed at. Bettine didn't know the half of her beef with Dušan. Dušan reacted very differently. He ascended to his full height, his street clothes disappearing as his black robes billowed out around him. The temperature in the room plummeted, and snow began to fall from the pristine ceiling. Črnobog had arrived.

He held out his blackened arms, a belt of bones clattering at his waist, and placed his palms facing Bettine's two guards. With a flick of his hands, he summoned the dark clouds that surrounded them to him. Two mists made of wing beats and eyes like the thing that had taken her father, but weaker and smaller, twisted out of the human shells they'd inhabited. They tried to resist but quickly disappeared into Črnobog's robes. The two men who had been possessed by the B-grade demons fell to the ground.

No shades rose from them, but Jo knew they were dead.

Bettine's eyes widened ever so slightly. She backed up and yanked Vesna up from the couch by her bound wrists.

"I guess they weren't just rumors then." A slight smile played over her lips. She slid her hand into the pocket of her pants and pulled out a glass vial filled with a shimmering liquid that shifted from red to gold as it moved.

Bettine had managed to find dress pants with functional pockets. That was dark magic right there.

"I can leave with Vesna and dispose of her once I'm out of here, or I can leave with Jolene Wiley." Bettine pulled Vesna farther forward, almost pulling her off her feet.

Vesna looked uncomfortable, but she didn't look like she

was afraid. Either Vesna had a plan or she was in shock. Jo bet on her having a plan.

"Take me. I'll happily go with you. I'm assuming you know how Portals work, and I have to be honest with you, you aren't my type at all." She had no idea how or why a Long-Lived would have need of a Portal. Unless they were near death. Maybe they could use her as a shade would and fuck their way back into the world. They'd be mortal though, right?

Bettine laughed. "I have no interest in using you as a Portal. I only want to make sure no one else can use you to bring back more like his bastard son. The days of the gods are over."

Jo walked closer to Bettine. Rebecca reached out to hold her back, but Črnobog gestured for Death to stand back.

"I think you might be wrong there. Release Vesna's binding and let her go to Rebecca." Jo took another step.

"I'm sure the Dark Lord here can set her free." Bettine pushed Vesna toward Črnobog, who caught her as she stumbled.

Bettine grabbed Jo's arm and pulled her to her side. She held up the vial in her other hand and tipped it, sloshing the color-shifting contents back and forth. "We are leaving now. If you try to stop me, I'll shatter this."

Rebecca moved away, and Bettine led Jo toward the open door.

No one else had asked, so Jo took it upon herself to find out what advantage Bettine thought she had. "What's in the vial?"

"Enough magic to knock every mortal in this hotel on their

ass. Some of them might survive." Bettine moved closer to the door but kept looking at Rebecca and Črnobog, reluctant to turn her back on them.

"You are mortal." Rebecca's tone made it both a reminder and a portent.

"I'm protected." She pulled Jo through the door and dragged her down the hallway to the stairwell.

Veronika met them at the top of the stairs as the fire door closed behind them. Jo breathed a little easier, hopeful the doors could contain a magical conflagration as well.

Bettine showed Veronika the vial. "Move or I'll use this."

Veronika looked from the vial to Jo's face for instructions. "I'll be fine. Go to Rebecca and Dušan."

"Is Vesna …" Veronika paled.

"She's fine. Go." Jo gestured toward the door with her chin.

Veronika moved aside, and Bettine and Jo made their way awkwardly in tandem down the stairs. Bettine's nails dug into the tender flesh inside Jo's wrist. Now that she had her prize, she wouldn't be separated even to keep them from tumbling down the stairs.

Bettine opened the fire door on the ground floor enough to see there was no one near. She dragged Jo out into the sparkling, white marble lobby. It was empty. No one was checking in, no one was bustling to or from the restaurant. Even the desk staff and concierge had left their posts. The piped-in music muffled the echo of their walk across the floor to the main doors. Igor had disappeared along with the doorman.

There was only Mrs. Kos standing on the cobblestones in the deserted street in front of the hotel. At the far end of the wide pedestrian lane where *Miklošičeva* met Preseren Square, blue lights flashed against the buildings. Igor's phone call had managed to evacuate the hotel and the street in less than half an hour.

Bettine started to walk past Mrs. Kos, but an errant gust of wind pushed her back toward the hotel doors.

Bettine gave Mrs. Kos a look that would have melted a lesser woman into a puddle, but Mrs. Kos stood her ground. Her dyed-black hair swirled out around her with tiny sparks of energy glittering at the ends. "Where do you think you're going?"

"Look, old woman, you do not want to trifle with me." Bettine brandished the vial at her. Mrs. Kos only smiled as the breeze picked up again and became a steady wind. "I am not afraid of you, traitor."

Another gust buffeted Bettine, with Jo in her grip, back again.

As Bettine raised her hand to dash the vial to the cobblestones, a man's voice yelled, "Now!" from the darkness between the buildings down the street.

A shockwave of glittering red and gold smashed against a solid shimmering wall of air encircling the three of them. The wind trapped inside the column rushed upward, taking the last wisps of gold with it into the flat, starless sky.

Mrs. Kos collapsed. Bettine had released her grip on Jo's wrist with the concussive wave of magic. Jo knelt to tend to Mrs. Kos, but there was nothing to do except cradle the woman's head off the rough cobblestones. A trickle of blood ran out of her ear.

"Tell Vesna I am sorry. Do not forget to tell her, Jolene Wiley." Even on the edge of death, Mrs. Kos could be counted on to mother anyone near her in the sternest way possible.

Jo nodded. Tears welled behind her eyes, but she couldn't let go, not while Bettine lived and breathed. Rage made a better medium than numbness to keep patching the wall that kept the flood at bay.

Mrs. Kos took her last breath, and Jo let her head down onto the street and closed her eyes. She turned on Bettine, who was still trapped inside Veronika's impressive shield with her and didn't appear to have any more vials in her miraculous pockets.

Bettine backed into the shield, bouncing off it, when she saw Jo's face. "What are you?"

Jo couldn't find words to answer. She imagined the earth opening up underneath Bettine and dropping her, body and soul, into the place of the lost dead Dušan had dragged Jo to, where her father languished, and where Helena probably lingered as well. She'd go herself now and stay if she could take Bettine with her.

The ground began to shake, loosening some masonry around them and destabilizing the shielding column. It wavered, then it shattered into a cascade of glittering shards of blue light that disappeared into the cracks between the cobblestones.

After a moment of frozen surprise, Bettine turned and ran down the street. Dušan, Rebecca, Igor, and Veronika appeared from the shadows to block her way. Bettine stopped and looked back over her shoulder at Jo. The expression on her face shifted rapidly through fear, indecision, and then resignation.

Bettine did have one trick left. She pulled another vial from her pants pocket and smashed it over her head, self-immolating in a flash of blue flame.

Jo watched as Bettine fell to her knees, her flesh blackening and falling away in the intense heat of the magical fire. Jo knew what it was to have flames licking up your body. Bettine must have had an enormous secret to keep if she was willing to die so horrifically.

Vesna ran up the street, past the spectacle of Bettine and straight to her mother's body. Jo knelt beside her friend, her arm around Vesna as she cradled her mother's head in her lap. Vesna's shoulders shook as she sobbed. Her friend's pain and sorrow pierced through every cell in Jo's body, but she couldn't cry with her friend. If she started, it would never stop.

Mrs. Kos's spirit rose up from her body and stood in front of them, giving Jo the original mom-face that Vesna had inherited and used on Jo and everyone they knew at some point.

"She wanted me to tell you that she was sorry." It seemed such an insignificant thing, an apology at the end, when no amends could really be made. But Jo had not received the same from her mother before she had walked through that screen door into the Next. There was no way for Jo to know if it would have made a difference.

Vesna cried harder, rocking back and forth.

"Tell her I'm here." Mrs. Kos knelt on the other side of her body and put her hands on either side of Vesna's face.

Vesna looked up and laid her hand over her mother's on her cheek. She couldn't see her, her eyes weren't focused on Mrs. Kos's face, but Jo was glad she could feel her.

"She's still here, Vesna."

"I know. What is she saying? There's a mist or an aura of her, but I can't hear her."

"Tell her she is the Witchfinder now. Tell her to find them and protect them from people like Bettine. That is what Leo wanted. It's what I want."

Jo nodded and relayed the message. Leo's name was hard to say, but she pushed through, another imaginary layer of plaster over a dam ready to burst.

Vesna nodded, tears still streaming down her face. "I will."

Mrs. Kos's door opened behind her. Jo hadn't done it. Mrs. Kos had conveyed this last message to Vesna, completing her work on this plane.

The expression on Mrs. Kos's face was impossible to parse, but Jo saw the love in it as she stood, looking at her daughter. There was pride and sorrow, a sense of shame, too, but Jo went with love. "She loves you."

Vesna nodded again. "I know."

Mrs. Kos turned and opened her door. It looked exactly like the front door of her home, down to the chalk marks on the lintel that had puzzled Jo when she had first visited. Mrs. Kos stepped into the Next without looking back and closed the door behind her. The others rushed up the street and stood in a half-circle in front of them, only Igor joined Vesna and Jo on the ground.

"Inspector Klančnik will need to speak with both of you briefly." Dušan offered his hand to Jo. She didn't want to leave Vesna, but Igor was there for her, and Jo didn't want to make her face Marta Klančnik any sooner than she had to.

Was Marta safe from whoever else was going to come for them? She had been almost as involved with all this business behind the Veil as Gustaf. And Dr. Struna? Was anyone who knew anything about any of them safe?

Jo's vision blurred, and her thoughts were crammed with images. Dr. Struna, packing up her supplies and sending Robert, her assistant, away on a long vacation. Dr. Struna climbing into her disguised ambulance and driving out of town. Marta, too, had purchased a ticket. Her vacation would be delayed a day, but then she would hand off the paperwork to someone else.

Rebecca caught her eye. "I told you, even the gods don't want to know everything."

Jo's vision cleared, but her head felt like an overfilled bike tire. She knew it was but a trickle of what Rebecca or Dušan must experience. How did they function with that much going on in their heads? She turned to Dušan. "You knew how this would end. You knew people would die, and you led us all into this without telling us?"

"There were thousands of ways this day could have ended, each decision each of us made changing the outcome a fraction. I knew someone could die. But there were endings where everyone lived, including Gustaf." Jo hadn't been prepared for Dušan's sincerity. When she looked at him, really saw him, she saw that he, too, was weary.

Igor stayed with Vesna while Jo and Dušan went to talk to Marta. Rebecca had the luxury of slipping away and taking Veronika with her. Jo suspected Veronika would be deposited at the train station with a ticket to Zagreb to catch up with Faron and her sisters.

"What did you have Igor tell Marta was going on?" Jo had no desire to sit through one of Marta's interviews, but she at least wanted to be fully briefed before going in. Marta already thought Jo was trouble, and this whole thing was not going to help their relationship one bit.

"He told her enough of the truth. We had to tell her Gustaf was dead and that the Board was involved. Goran may have also called in a bomb threat from a burner phone from parts unknown about the same time." Dušan stopped and looked at her. "Your earthquake was a small enough tremor that we didn't need to explain anything to the police. Though you may have sent every geologist in Eastern Europe scrambling to their computer screens. It was enough to break Veronika's concentration."

"I did that?" She had been steady while everything else shook.

"Of course you did." He gave her that same patronizing smile he'd given Veronika in the hallway before they'd confronted Bettine.

She would try to wrap her head around that later; she had other reasons to be angry with Dušan. So many fucking reasons. "You told everyone else Gustaf was dead before you told me?"

"You know why."

She was an emotional time bomb, that plaster wasn't going to hold indefinitely, but she didn't need to be lied to. Not about her friends. So many were dead. She pushed that thought back behind the wall and replaced it for the moment with the satisfying sense of irony that Bettine's death would be explained away as a failed suicide bombing. The woman was a terrorist, from an organization of terrorists who used the fear of imprisonment or murder to keep everyone behind the Veil on their best behavior.

Well, that was going to end.

"I'm just glad your tremor didn't bring the whole city down on our heads." Dušan put his hand in the small of her back and directed her toward the flashing blue lights at the other end of the street.

CHAPTER 29

Vesna stood next to her brother at the edge of a hole in the ground that held a box filled with her mother's remains. Gustaf's burial had been the day before at Žale in Ljubljana, and only she and Jo had attended—plus a put-upon cemetery employee. Jo stood at her side again and Igor behind.

A larger circle of her mother's friends and distant relatives enclosed what was left of her family in a bubble of concern. Their care had been appreciated over the past few days. Dušan had relented on making them leave immediately after filling in Marta. Jo had argued that the Board was going to need a minute to regroup. Vesna didn't care what Dušan said. She would see her mother properly buried and prayed over by the parish priest who had taken her confession. Generations of her family had denied a proper burial to witches and to those who were simply unwanted and accused. She would not visit that last indignity upon her own mother, who had gone so willingly to her death to save others.

The care of those family friends who lived outside the Veil was for her grief and her brother's. They didn't know that she and Igor and Miha and his fiancée would have to leave after the funeral. Those she loved and held the closest were being forced to scatter to the winds.

The old ladies in black dresses, which they wore more and more frequently as their friends died, smiled at her reassuringly. She could survive grief.

Grief didn't concern her anymore. She would carry it with her always, for Leo, for Gustaf, her mother, and her friend who couldn't die but whose heart would probably never heal in all her long days. Her grief was finite. It would die with her. Jo's was forever. Her mother had opened her door and walked unafraid into the Next. That's what Jo had said. Her mother had faith in her god. Vesna believed in gods too. The church could crumble into dust, happily so, but gods were real, and they hurt as much as they healed.

She would take comfort from her mother's faith in her as the new Witchfinder and from her charge to protect the witches.

The priest said his last words followed by a soft chorus of "amens" from the mourners. There was a pause before a cluster of people walked away toward the gates. No one wanted to be the first to leave the family at the graveside.

"I need to go by Mother's house and finish closing up. Then we can go." She looked up at Igor.

Miha kissed her on the cheek. "Is there anything else we can do?"

Dušan had made arrangements for him and Inesa to leave that afternoon. Vesna didn't know where he was going and had no idea what he had told his fiancée. If she was going to marry into the Kos family, she would find out sooner or later what she was in for. Maybe it was good that it was sooner.

Miha had not believed Vesna when she had called him to tell him their mother was dead. He hadn't believed it until she told him what she'd done, which meant she'd had to reveal the secret her mother had kept from them both. He had waited until he'd joined her in Ribnica to carry out their mother's last wishes to share his own secret. Her brother was also a witch. Like their mother, he could control the weather. He'd spent his life believing he'd been cursed by God, for what was unclear, but there had been an allusion to masturbation in his explanation. She hoped he took the time away with Inesa to tell her the whole story and get over his hangups.

"Go on. Jo and Igor are going to help." She kissed him back, and they parted ways at the cemetery gates.

Vesna walked with Igor and Jo to the rental car and drove the short way back to the center of town to the house she'd grown up in. After the viewing—her mother's will had been clear about a home funeral—Jo and Igor had boxed up the things left out and stored them in a closet. The house now looked ready for a shoot for a very boring decor magazine. They were going to cover everything with sheets, none of them knew when they would be back to clean out the house for good. Neither she nor Miha wanted to live in the village, in the shadow of the Kos legacy, and they agreed they would sell it when they could return.

Dušan was waiting for them on the street in front of the house when they arrived.

Jo opened her mouth to speak, then closed it. Dušan wouldn't tell them if he'd heard anything.

He gave his condolences again. "Your mother's name was

Stefka."

Vesna nodded. "I almost forgot myself. She was always Mother or Mrs. Kos. It suited her though. She who has the crown, or wears the crown. Something like that."

"My grandmother always talked about earning stars for your crown in heaven. Your mother's must be ablaze right now." Jo took Vesna's hand and waited for Dušan to tell them whatever he had come to tell them.

"I took the liberty of closing the house for you. Your bags are inside the door. I'll take Jo back to Ljubljana." Dušan handed Vesna the keys to the front door.

She looked in her purse and looked at Igor who checked his pockets. "How did you—"

"Does it matter?"

Vesna shook her head. Igor collected their bags, including a heavy one with more of her father's records and papers for her to sort through.

She hugged Jo, said goodbye to Dušan, and got back into the car with Igor before she let herself take a full breath.

"You okay there?" Igor squeezed her knee as he navigated out of the village.

"I don't think I have much choice in the matter now." She pulled the paper Dušan had given her out of his pocket. They were going to Vienna to meet with an unnamed party and would get further instructions from there.

CHAPTER 30

Dušan dropped Jo at the French Revolution monument with an excuse for not walking with her to the apartment and a promise to be back before she left. She watched as he made the circle in the roundabout and headed back toward the highway. The sky was perfectly blue and cloudless, and the tourists and locals swirled around in high summer colors as she made her way along the river to *Zajčeva* and turned into the deserted courtyard of her empty building.

Even Vesna's cats were gone; Dušan had arranged for a long-term foster service to take them. Vesna had cried as the woman left with Antony and Cleopatra mewing loudly in their carriers. After the cats were gone, Jo had hugged her friend and gone back to her own apartment, crawled into bed fully dressed, and slept until they'd had to get ready for Gustaf's funeral.

Jo looked up to the railing on the top floor where Gustaf's flat was. Dušan had taken care of that too. He didn't want the Board to have access to Gustaf's papers and computer, so a removal company had come and packed everything up and taken it to storage Dušan had arranged.

He'd arranged everything so carefully, after. After everyone had been taken or scattered. She had no idea where her friends had been sent or when, or if, she would ever see them again. Dušan had sent Jackie a message but told Jo not to contact her in case the Board went after her and Michael.

Jo had already packed. All of her personal belongs, aside from her household goods, fit into a backpack and a suitcase. Life was simpler that way, and Turner leaving her high and dry had at least proven to her that she didn't need stuff to survive.

Someone walked into the courtyard behind her. Jo turned, surprised to find Mary standing in the archway, her holy nimbus glowing even in the bright daylight.

Jo let out a long breath. "Is Dušan sending you off somewhere too?"

Mary laughed. "There are advantages to being part of several thriving traditions."

Jo cocked her head. "Several?"

Mary shrugged. "I belong to many others besides the Roman Catholic Church. The Board has no power over me."

"I do probably need some help, but I wasn't ready to ask yet."

Mary ran her hand through the dark hair at her crown. "Dušan thinks he knows what he's doing, but he isn't going to be able to fix this on his own."

"He managed to get himself into this and drag all of us with him." Jo continued to do as Dušan asked, only because he appeared to have a plan and she had no fucking clue what to do next, or even what they were really up against.

"That he did." Mary took a few more steps into the courtyard. "And he's shifted the course of things more than he knows, but there's no letting this go now. He hasn't just endangered those who live behind the Veil here."

Jo stared at Mary as the truth of her words sank in. "That's why he's sending us all away? As emissaries for whatever the next stage of the plan is?"

"Funnily enough, I don't know for certain. I can't read his mind, and it is only one of thousands of possible futures."

"This is why Rebecca said even the gods don't want to know everything." Rebecca had been surprisingly absent since the night at the hotel. Jo chalked it up to either getting on with her day job or taking care of errands for Dušan. Given how cozy she seemed to be with Ol' Črnobog, Jo was glad she'd disappeared for a bit.

"Omniscience isn't quite what mortals imagine." Mary gave her a half smile. "Rok is in your apartment waiting for you. Dušan has given him instructions on where to take you. You can trust him, he's a good man, but he is also loyal to Dušan." Mary walked right up to her and pulled Jo's necklace out of her shirt. Jo had added Leo's St. Mary medal to the bull's head medallion for Achelous. "Rok gave you this because he wears another now. Dušan sent him to you in Chattanooga. Whether Rok has told you or not, Dušan sent him to you that day in the park, too, when your son fell and Rok came to help you."

Jo stepped back from Mary and clutched the medallions in her hand, holding them to her chest. "It's been fake this whole time? Rok's been Dušan's spy?"

Mary put her hand up. "No. It started that way, I have no

doubt. He cares for you, more than he is willing to admit to himself. I don't know what he would do if he had to choose."

"Choose between me and Dušan?"

"Rok believes he can really only serve one god at a time."

"I'm not a god." Rebecca's words about being Queen of the Witches rang inside Jo's head.

"Technically, neither am I." Mary turned and walked back through the archway and disappeared into the street.

Jo didn't try to stop her. The woman—the goddess?—had come to say what she had to say. That's how it worked. Jo didn't like it, but she'd gotten used to it. Mary's words had made her blood boil a bit though. Dušan had abandoned her and Faron, and yet he'd sent his spies to keep an eye on her.

She climbed the steps up to her flat and stood outside her door for a moment before she went inside. Did she act surprised? Did she tell Rok what she knew, what Mary had said? She unlocked the front door and kicked her shoes off in the space inside, then opened the inner door.

Rok was sitting on her futon leafing through one of the sketchbooks she'd set on top of her bag. He was right where Milo had been sitting before.

Milo. Fuck.

"I can't leave yet."

"Why?" Rok set the sketchbook down open to a page she'd drawn when she'd been holed up in the mountains. He didn't have any bags with him, though hers both sat on the floor next to his feet.

"Milo. He said he wasn't ready to leave until I was okay.

I have to open his door for him. Though I'm not sure I can even do that." She looked around the apartment as if she would find him there, hiding under the table or sitting in the sink.

Rok got up and stopped her, turning her to face him with a hand on each shoulder. "*Are* you okay?"

"No. I mean yes. For now, I guess." She plopped down on one of the dining chairs and looked up at him. "I don't know." Would he carry everything she said back to Dušan?

"Milo can wait. You need to leave as planned. Dušan said—"

"Fuck Dušan right now. And you can tell him I said that when you report back what I had for breakfast and who I've had sex with lately or whatever it is he expects from you." She crossed her legs and leaned back, making her feel like Rebecca, as if she could have that much cool. "And are you even sure he has your best interest in mind? I mean let's look at the statistics here. People I fuck die." She thumbed the edge of the placemat on the table. "Or sometimes they're already dead or apparently gods of the dead. Aren't you the least bit worried Dušan thinks you might be expendable?" This was not how she'd planned for this conversation to go.

"A lot's happened. I know you're upset."

"Upset? You have no idea." The walls she'd been slathering over with plaster were cracking.

"You aren't the only person who's lost someone."

"That makes it worse. Dušan wasn't happy just fucking up my life and Faron's, he had to drag all these other people into it too." She tried to take a breath to calm herself, but there was no stopping. She stood up, face to face with Rok.

"You have no idea what you're talking about." He said it quietly, but it landed like a dismissal of everything that she'd been through, everyone and everything that had been taken from her and Vesna and Gustaf and …

Words left her. An anger she couldn't hold back any longer surged all the way to the ends of her fingertips. Her body swelled with it, like her skin would rip open and fall away, leaving a molten core of rage.

Rok watched her.

The room around them began to shake. The glasses rattled in the cupboards, and the photo of Rok and Faron on top of Triglav fell off the wall and shattered on the painted floor.

Rok grabbed her and wrapped his arms around her torso, tucking his chin over her shoulder. Why was he touching her? Another wave of rage rushed over her, and she tried to push him away.

A cabinet door popped open and the stack of mail she'd ignored fell off the top of the fridge. Rok clung to her, wrapping his arms tighter, until she screamed, the sound echoing in her own head like thunder.

The floor opened up underneath them and they dropped into nothingness. The black abyss she'd fallen through with Dušan and again the night she'd died and jumped through Helena's waiting door, had opened in her flat without a door, without Dušan.

Rok kept his head buried in her neck and his arms tight around her as they fell. Her anger ebbed and flowed until finally she was left hollow again, floating or falling. The only sound was her blood pulsing in her ears.

She'd wished for this. She'd wished for Death to take her more than once, most recently while curled up next to Leo's cold body on the forest floor.

She might not be able to save her father or Helena, but at least they'd all be down here together until Dušan, Asshole Lord of Darkness, deigned to come get them. Had she killed Rok too?

The landing wasn't gentle this time. They hit hard enough to bounce, and she took the brunt of it with Rok on top of her. He scrambled off and away and sat in the dust a few feet from her, staring.

Dušan's underworld realm of the lost—he'd made sure she'd understood they weren't damned—hadn't changed a bit since her last visit. It was still bleak and gray with burnt-looking trees, the branches scratching at the sky like skeletal hands. Like the last time, there were no throngs of the dead. It was just the two of them sitting in the dust.

Rok looked like he was in shock.

She sat up and took a deep breath. This had definitely not gone to plan. Or at least not to hers.

"It worked." He looked down at his hands like he was making sure they were still there and then looked back up at her. "Oh, why do you have sketches of Hemingway in your notebook?"

"What?" It was her turn to stare at him. Clearly he was in shock. "That's what you're going to ask me now?"

"It just surprised me." He looked around at the barren landscape that changed with only an increasing density of dead trees closer to the horizon.

"What did you mean by 'it worked?'"

"I was supposed to make you angry. I hadn't expected you to show up already pissed off." He crossed his legs in front of him. He was adjusting quickly to what had just happened. Faster than she was.

"Why were you supposed to make me angry?" She got on her knees and sat back on her heels.

"Dušan said it was the only way you'd be able to bring us here."

Her anger flared inside again, a little blue flame at the ready, but fear stopped her. There could be some worse place they could fall through to if she didn't keep her shit together.

She took a breath. "Dušan said it was the only way to bring us here, why?"

"Because it was the only way you could get to the Nav until you accept the key."

"The Nav?"

"The Nav. Where we are now, you know, like Hades or Helheim. The underworld where the dead go."

She stared at him. "All the dead?"

"No. It's a bit complicated." He ran his hand down his beard, which was growing in wilder again—like it had been before his brief hipster turn. This wasn't the conversation he thought he was going to be having either.

"Why would I accept the keys to the Nav?"

"Because Dušan, um, Črnobog has been keeping them for

you."

"For me?" All of the freaking gods, this was like pulling teeth. "Why would Dušan be keeping the keys to the underworld for me?"

He pulled the weighted part of his chain out of his shirt and showed her two medallions, one a Slavic solar wheel and the other a crescent moon on its side like a bowl. "Because you're back, and this place belongs to you, Jo. To Morana. To the Goddess of Life and of the Dead. To the Queen of the Witches."

LOOKING FOR MORE FROM VICTORIA?

The complete *Voices of the Dead* series is available now from 1000 Volt Press.

Who by Water - Voices of the Dead: Book One

Our Lady of the Various Sorrows - Voices of the Dead: Book Two

Strange as Angels - Voices of the Dead: Book Four

Sign up for the Notes from the Dead Letter Office at victoriaraschke.com for information about upcoming book releases, author events, and an exclusive *Voices of the Dead* short.

THE ZOMBIE CHURCH IS REAL

The Trans-Universal Zombie Church of the Blissful Ringing is a real organization and registered religious group in Slovenia. The church supports the rights of refugees and regularly works to combat the rising tide of white supremacist nationalism in Europe. They also run a pro bono clinic in Nova Gorica, Slovenia, that mostly serves patients with chronic illnesses like diabetes and high blood pressure who can't afford ongoing treatment but aren't deemed ill enough to receive free emergency services.

You can support their work at the clinic by sending donations by mail to:
Hiša dobrot
Vipavska cesta 104
5000 Nova Gorica
Slovenia

Or by international transfer to:
SWIFT: BAKOSI2X
SI56101000053803567
Refrerence: CHAR
Banka Intesa Sanpaolo d. d.
Pristaniška ulica 14
6502 Koper
Slovenia

To learn more about the church go to their public, English language group page on Facebook.

ABOUT THE AUTHOR

Victoria Raschke writes books that start with questions like "what if you didn't find out you were the chosen one until you were in your forties?" When she isn't holed up in her favorite coffee house to write, she can be found at the nearest farmers' market checking out the weird vegetables or at her home where she lives with a changing number of cats and her family who supports both her writing and her culinary experimentation — for the most part. Her first book, *Who by Water*, was published in 2017.